God is a[l]
~Roman[s]

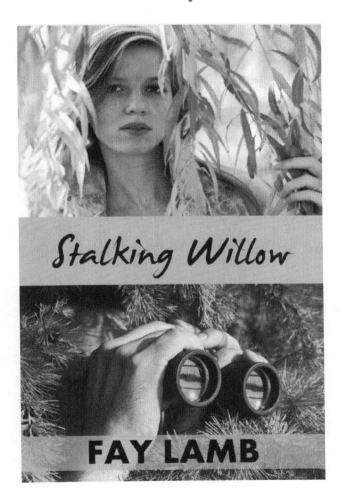

Stalking Willow

FAY LAMB

[handwritten inscription, illegible]

Stalking Willow

© 2013 Fay Lamb

ISBN-13: 978-1-938092-36-7
ISBN-10: 1938092368

This book is a work of fiction. Names, characters, places, and incidents are either products of the author's imagination or used fictitiously. Any similarity to actual people and/or events is purely coincidental.

Published by Write Integrity Press, 130 Prominence Point Pkwy. #130-330, Canton, GA 30114.

www.WriteIntegrity.com

Printed in the United States of America.

This story is dedicated with much love
to all of my many cousins,
the descendants of Victor David and Pauline Ethel New
and the descendants of Herbert Sherrill
and Elizabeth Fay Thompson.
God blessed me abundantly by placing me in your midst.

CHAPTER ONE

In the growing darkness a maniac waited for Willow Thomas.

Outside the high-rise office the dusky blue sky gave way to the night. With a shudder, Willow turned away from the window and started her computer.

Tap-tap-tap. Her pencil eraser hit the oak desktop. Dare she risk going home?

The monitor cast a bright glow into the semi-darkened outer office. The desks there, all lined up in neat little rows, represented the rungs on the ladder she'd climbed to become a junior executive for Peterman and Bruin Advertising. Today she'd hooked a lucrative account with Anglers' Fishing Lures, Inc. Another step up.

What did she have to show for ten years in New York? A college degree, a growing career, and now, peril. Not one friend she could call, no one to walk her home, not a single somebody to watch her back.

Tap-tap-tap. She'd rather risk running into the madman with a camera than open up to anyone. She shook her head. Never again.

Somewhere on the vast floor of offices, a vacuum hummed. A hint of ammonia filled the confined air. The cleaning crew had arrived. At least she wasn't alone. Dropping the pencil, Willow clicked on the e-mail icon.

She needed to concentrate. Had anyone in a crowd of strangers looked familiar to her? Did she recall someone looking at her through a camera lens?

She sat back in her seat. As she suspected, the mysterious e-mails waited in her inbox, the font of each subject line printed in bold.

Watching You!

Watching You!

Watching You!

Only three. Since lunch. After she'd changed her address. How could he get her new e-mail so fast? She'd notified only her father, the office, and the bank.

She clicked on the first one and opened the attachment. He'd caught her walking down Fifth Avenue. The image captured a side view of her face. Of course, she wasn't looking straight ahead.

She'd been alert, constantly scanning the crowd.

Something to the left of her path must have drawn her gaze.

And she'd missed seeing him.

"Come on, Willow, think." She picked up the pencil, slammed it down on her desk, and looked to the ceiling above, studying the rectangular patterns on the fluorescent light covers.

"Who can it be?"

"Talking to yourself?"

Willow jumped. "Jeffrey, you frightened me."

Jeffrey Peterman crooked a finger under his dark blue tie to loosen it and unbuttoned his white dress shirt. He leaned his medium-sized frame against the door.

"Anglers' Fishing Lures liked the artwork, signed the contract. I'm relishing the victory. You should be happy I'm working, boss." Not exactly a lie. She was working to discover the identity of a maniac.

"I heard. When you showed me the drawings, I knew they'd take the bait."

"Ha." She smirked at his pun.

"Go to dinner. Celebrate with friends, but don't stay here."

"In a few. Night, Jeffrey."

"I'm cleaning up my desk. Be gone before me." He snapped his fingers and pointed at her before moving out of sight.

"Yes, sir." She saluted.

What a show. As if he really cared. Jeffery was good at acting the part of the concerned boss, but he never put his words into action. She closed her eyes. A friend right now would sure be nice.

Willow's cell phone rang. She frowned when she saw the caller's name. "Hi, Scott."

Her father cleared his throat.

She hadn't given him the respect he wanted. Willow would never call him Dad. A man who stayed with a woman like Suzanne Scott—what kind of father was he?

"Checking in," he said.

"I'm fine." Why had she told him about the e-mails? Now he'd have an excuse to call her every day.

"Have you gotten any more notes from your secret admirer?" His familiar deep timbre and his false jovial demeanor did more to soothe Willow's nerves than she wanted to admit. Maybe he did care—a little.

A smile played at the corner of her lips, but she pushed it away. After all, his famous lifestyle probably made her the target of this stalker. Just as it had done ten years ago. "I think it's more serious than that."

"I'd like to send a bodyguard, kiddo."

"And alert the press? Forget it." That's all she needed. She waved her left wrist back and forth to straighten the simple silver bracelet she always wore—a gift from Granny. Her gaze lingered there. Granny would know what to do.

"Your mother and I would feel safer if you'd let us send someone."

Willow cleared her throat and closed her eyes. "How is Mommy Dearest?"

"Willow …"

Her lips trembled. More than a friend, she longed for a mother's embrace and soft, soothing words telling her she'd be safe. She missed Granny and Quentin—her real mother and her only friend.

Willow picked up the pencil and the ever-present sketchpad from her desk. Her hand flew across the page, the lead rasping against the paper with each stroke—drawing the scene she'd been trying to recreate for years.

"I've seen this type of thing happen with your mother. Sometimes it's nothing. Other times, kiddo, the person is berserk."

Willow closed her eyes. If she could call the police without the press hearing about it, what would she tell them? So far, the stalker had merely sent photos of her by e-mail. They came through at an alarming rate, but taking pictures wasn't against the law, especially if your parents were celebrities.

Her father rambled on as Willow continued to draw.

"Willow, are you listening to me?"

She hadn't heard a word. "Sure."

"Then go. Get away from the office. Don't you miss the lake? You haven't been home since Granny died."

She bit hard into her lip. Scott did care about her. She'd spare him any further sarcasm today.

"Got a question for you. Would you have given up one minute of your life in Amazing Grace to live in Hollywood?"

Maybe her silence was harder for him to take than her unloading the dump truck full of bitterness upon him. "You never gave me that choice." Her hands continued to fly across the paper, making the memory concrete. "Scott, it's late."

"Go home. To North Carolina."

"I'll think about it." Not. "'Night."

"'Night, kiddo. I lo—"

Willow hung up and gave her full attention to the drawing. Long minutes passed before she finished. She held up the picture: seventeen-year-old Quentin McPheron sitting against the post of her Granny's dock with a fishing pole in his hand. Not quite as good as the original, wherever it had gone.

She placed the sketchpad on the desk and stared at his handsome face. No matter how Quentin had treated her, Willow would always care for him.

"Come on, Willow. Walk out with me." Jeffrey called as he stepped out of his own office.

Willow held up her hand. "Give me a minute, Jeffrey. Can I trouble you for a lift?" She closed out the open e-mail.

A new e-mail landed in her inbox, taunting her.

Surprise.

The subject lines never varied—until now. Her hand shook as she clicked on the attachment. The picture sprang onto the screen.

With a gasp she turned in her chair, stood, and backed away.

"What's wrong?" Jeffrey rushed to stand behind her, resting his hands on her shoulder.

Willow turned in his arms. Jeffrey wrapped her in the embrace. Would he let her stay here, safe and warm?

"What is that? Who sent that to you?" The tender touch of his hand against her head, cradling her, sent shivers down her spine. How long had she craved a caress, someone who truly cared?

But the cost was too high, more than her momentarily ransomed soul wanted to pay. Willow pulled from his hold and ran the back of her hand over her eyes. "That's my place. Someone trashed my apartment. Jeffrey, I need to get home."

Willow paused as they walked the hall leading from the elevators and around the corner to her apartment. Jeffrey ran into her and mumbled an apology.

"My door's open," she whispered.

Noise came from inside the apartment, and her heart hammered. Had her stalker expected her to arrive home alone? Didn't he think she'd call the police?

Jeffrey edged down the corridor, his footfall soft against the beige carpeting. He peered inside. "Excuse me," he spoke to someone.

"Who are you?" a male voice demanded.

"You're in a home that doesn't belong to you. Maybe you should tell me who you are." Jeffrey held up his hand, a silent command for Willow to wait.

"Detective Bob Hominski." A man in an unremarkable blue suit and a too-skinny red and blue striped tie peered out and down the hall at Willow. "Ms. Thomas?"

Willow stepped forward. "Yes, sir."

"We found the door opened and the place a mess."

Willow nodded and stepped inside. She shook hands with the detective.

"Jim's my partner." He motioned toward a tall lanky fellow in a similar unremarkable suit and tie.

"So I take it this isn't your usual state of disarray," Hominski raised his brows.

Willow covered her mouth with her hand and shot him a narrowed-eyed glare. How dare he joke when everything she owned appeared to be in ruin.

Pictures she'd drawn lay in ripped pieces throughout the living room. Broken glass and frames covered her wood floor. The shards would never come out of her oriental rug. Her curtains hung in tatters. The drawers in her kitchen alcove had been dumped. Silverware littered the floor. At least the creep hadn't topped the whole mess off with food from her refrigerator.

She stepped out of the large area and down the short hall to her bedroom. Hominski followed. The space was a complete disaster. She opened her mouth to cry, but no sound came.

"Sorry, ma'am. I probably should have warned you."

Willow lowered her head and made her way back out into the living room. She bent down and grabbed the insides of her favorite throw pillow. The cottony smoothness in her hands did little to soothe her nerves.

Tears filled her eyes, but rage pushed them away. She paced back and forth across the small living room until the crunching beneath her feet frayed her last nerve.

"Do you have a boyfriend?"

"How about an ex-husband?"

"Have you made any enemies?"

Like corn in hot oil, the detectives popped, popped, popped the questions.

"I have no boyfriend. I've never been married. I don't have many friends, and I certainly don't go out of my way to make enemies."

She'd had enemies once, but she doubted her cousin, Laurel, and that hideous Tabitha Cowart had anything to do with this. She hadn't seen them in over ten years, and surely they'd grown out of the high-school bullying stage by now, even if Willow hadn't healed from the taunts they'd unceasingly thrown her way.

Willow tugged out her laptop, booted up Outlook, and showed them the pictures she'd received from the beginning— one month earlier to the last one of her destroyed apartment. This time a picture wasn't worth a thousand words, just one— *enemy.* "Whoever is responsible for all of this isn't a part of my world."

A crash sounded in the powder room. Detective Jim bolted back into the living room. "Just being thorough."

How much longer would the detectives stay, walking over and destroying what was left of her personal property?

"Willow, why don't you come home with me?" Jeffrey touched her arm.

She'd forgotten he was here. He'd stayed. Maybe she'd been wrong about him all this time.

The softness in his mocha eyes beckoned her to take refuge.

She turned away from him. "I can't do that."

He tugged on her sleeve. "C'mon. Grab something to wear, and let's go. You'll be safe at my place."

Safe from the stalker but not from the press who, if they found out, would love to report that Suzanne Scott's daughter was in a tawdry affair with her boss. She needed to protect Jeffrey from the bad publicity. "No thank you, but I appreciate it. People would talk."

"Let them. I've been trying to get the nerve to ask you out for a long while. I can think of worse rumors to fly around the office."

Did he think her so easy that a date meant she'd stay overnight with him? Her granny brought her up to know right from wrong, and, well, that was wrong on so many levels.

"Willow, I have the extra room. You'll be safe from your stalker and from me."

She shook her head. "Thank you, Jeffrey, but I can't."

He frowned. "Now that you know how I feel, I'll definitely ask you out when you return. If you won't stay at my house, I suggest you get out of town. Do you have a place to go? Somewhere outside the city? Parents' home, anything, where you'll be safe? If not, I have a house in the country. It's yours for as long as you need it."

Scott and Suzanne had a chalet in Switzerland, beach houses at Martha's Vineyard and Malibu. They probably had a home in Tahiti. Right now, Tahiti would be a nice change of pace.

Jeffrey's fingers pressed lightly on hers. "Willow?"

"I have a place." She stepped away from him. The lake house Granny left her would do, back in her hometown of Amazing Grace, but she never intended to return there the same way she'd departed—on the run from a stalker.

The two detectives shared a look, the meaning lost on her.

"You've earned a vacation." Jeffery closed the distance and placed his hands on her shoulders. "Take it. Just let me know where you are and how you're doing? Work remotely on the Anglers' account. Make it your priority. You did a great job reeling them in."

She would smile at his lame attempt at humor if the detectives weren't still stomping all over what little the stalker left for her to recover. "Thank you, Jeffrey. For everything."

He kissed her forehead. "I mean it, Willow. When you get back here, you save a date for dinner. I'll call you tomorrow to check in." He strode out the door.

Detective Jim followed him.

Detective Hominski studied his notes and walked around the place once more before stopping in front of her. "I know these questions seem tedious, but I'm hoping to jog your memory. Is there someone you crossed?"

"Detective, I haven't crossed anyone. I don't like conflict, avoid it like the plague." True. She avoided it. Somehow, though, it always found a way to seep into her life. Still, she didn't believe Aunt Agatha would leave North Carolina to do something like this. No, Aggie was a vindictive prude, but she wouldn't hurt her—not this way.

"So, you have absolutely no idea who would want to do this to you?"

Detective Jim returned. "We have a problem, Bob." He stepped inside.

"What?" Hominski looked over his shoulder.

"We got dirt chasers outside. They're asking about Ms. Thomas."

Detective Hominski cocked his head to the side and raised his eyebrows.

Willow cringed. He probably wasn't the type to take lightly the lack of information from a victim. She wished she'd gone with Jeffrey.

But if she had, the tabloid reporters would have been all over them, and Jeffrey would have learned her secret. Surprise. Your life just got as complicated as Willow Thomas's— daughter of Scott Thomas, and his lovely, but aging wife, actress Suzanne Scott.

"Ms. Thomas, why would the paparazzi have an interest in you?" Hominski scrutinized her too closely.

More importantly, how had the vultures circled her carcass so quickly? She'd been able to live in relative peace, keeping to herself. One call to the police station and they were crawling all over her like this?

Could that be the stalker's plan? Draw her out in the open? Make her vulnerable? If so, that person knew too much about her already.

Willow pinched the bridge of her nose. "My father is Scott Thomas." She prayed they'd recognize the name so she wouldn't have to admit her relationship to Suzanne. She couldn't stomach putting that truth into words.

"Scott Thomas." Hominski tapped his index finger against his temple as if evoking a memory. "Screenwriter. Director."

He'd forgotten to add producer, but Willow wouldn't remind him.

Detective Jim gave her his full attention. "The last I knew, those devils aren't interested in kids of directors and writers, not unless the kids make spectacles of themselves." He leaned in, peering at her like an eagle swooping down on its prey. "Have you given them any reason to take interest in you?"

Hominski shook his finger at her. "You're Suzanne Scott's kid. The one they did all the reporting on several years back. Pretty sly of your mother using her husband's first name as her stage name." He cleared his throat. "Oh, sorry. Must be a touchy subject with you, her never wanting to see you at all."

Willow shook her head. Touchy, no. Heart wrenchingly painful, yes.

So, Detective Hominski had an ear for Hollywood gossip. Maybe she could work with him. Willow motioned him away from Detective Jim.

In the kitchen, silverware clinked as she pushed it aside with the toe of her shoe. "I've worked hard to put the past behind me. You can see why."

"If I were a betting man, I'd say a Suzanne Scott fan is looking to gain her attention."

"It's important to shut this down quickly. They think I'm the door to a sensational story about Suzanne. Their interference is making it easier for the stalker."

The detective scratched his chin.

Willow waited, her breath caught somewhere between inhale and exhale.

"You say you got a place to go?" Hominski asked.

She had only the lake. Would the stalker know about Amazing Grace? Not many people knew the small town existed—at least until the truth broke ten years earlier.

She'd have to take the chance. "I think so."

"What about your father hiring a bodyguard?"

"He's suggested that, but that brings attention."

"It also brings safety, young lady." He motioned around the room. "Does this look like you're safe?"

"Not an option. I just want to get out of town. Can you help me?"

Hominski stared at her for a long moment. A heavy sigh lifted his broad chest. He shook his head.

Willow fingered Granny's bracelet.

Hominski's eyes were drawn to it. "Mean something to you?" The detective obviously didn't miss much.

"A gift from my grandmother."

He continued to stare at it.

"Well, what do you say?" Willow leaned in. "Can I count on NYPD to help me flee the city?"

Detective Hominski scratched his temple with his pen. He pressed his lips together, and took another look around the ruins of her apartment.

The odds didn't look promising.

His arms fell to his side, and his pale blue eyes met hers. "Jim, disperse the maggots. Arrest them if they don't disband." He shook his finger at her a second time. "Wherever you go, I expect you to take precautions."

"Scout's honor."

"You ever been a scout?" Hominski smiled.

"No, but I'll hold to the creed."

"I can arrange to get you out, but that's it. They're going to be able to get the facts as soon as our report is complete. I'll try to bury it for awhile. Leave me a contact number."

Willow looked around her living room and kitchen. A stranger had invaded her sanctum. Jeffrey, her father, and the detective were correct. She had to leave.

"Get your stuff. You'll have to clean up this mess some other time. Before you go, I'd like to show you a trick to keep you one step ahead of this nut job."

Willow didn't argue. Instead of a bodyguard, Scott could send a cleaning crew. She moved down the hallway toward her bedroom and stood looking at the devastation. Her sheets, her mattress, her pillows were ripped to shreds. The table lamp was broken and laying on the floor beside the broken shards of her dresser's mirror.

She climbed over the clothes the intruder had strewn across the path to her closet and pulled out the shirts, slacks, and skirts he'd been kind enough to leave in one piece.

Since her dresser and chest drawers were turned upside down and some of the clothes under them shredded as well, she had to dig through to find jeans and other incidentals. She piled them on a corner of her mattress and reached under her bed for the musty suitcase that had remained there since she'd moved to the apartment many years before. After stuffing her clothing inside, she zipped the suitcase and leaned on it for a second.

Who knew she'd feel a loss at leaving the four walls she'd despised when she'd first arrived in New York—alone, angry, and afraid? She shrugged off the emotion, lifted the suitcase, and trudged down the hall and back into her living room.

"Jim's dispersing the crowd," Hominski took the suitcase from her.

Willow nodded. Cut and run. She'd done this before. She always thought she'd return to Amazing Grace a much different person, but no, she was still alone, angry, and very much afraid.

CHAPTER TWO

Funny how you remember the little things.

Willow stood between the wooden door and the old homemade screen doors of the house. The latter squeaked as she pushed it open. She reached back and pulled the heavier house door closed, keeping her hand on the screen, preventing it from banging. While Granny lived, the one thing she never abided was a slamming door.

Stretching her arms upwards and sideways, Willow eased the tension in her tired, aching muscles. She pushed the baseball cap down over her dark hair and stepped off the cement steps of her grandmother's porch—her porch now.

The path leading down to the lake was worn but not overgrown as she'd expected. Only a few small patches of yellowish-orange Carolina clay showed amongst the lush green grass. Granny's roses, rhododendron, and hemlocks were trimmed and the soil around them weeded. Scott must have hired someone to maintain the grounds.

Turning to look at the two houses sitting side by side, Willow stepped backward down the path. She expected Quentin's dad, Dave, to peer out the large picture window of the red brick home next door and wave. Thoughts of the elder McPherons so near offered her comfort, but not knowing Quentin's whereabouts tugged at her heart.

With a deep breath, she looked back to her home. "Oh." She held her hand to her heart. Green shutters sat on each side of the home's windows, a willow tree carved into each one of them.

Willow would give him credit; Scott was trying to make up for lost time.

She fought back the tears and headed down toward the lake without pausing before crossing the one-lane dirt road that ended at the McPheron driveway. The only other home on the lake was a small rustic cabin built by Willow's great-grandfather. That home, where Granny lived as a child, sat in the woods behind her house, a part of her property.

Willow stepped onto the long wooden dock jutting out over the water. New boards stood out here and there along the expanse, replacements for the old worn ones. Again, Scott deserved credit for trying to reach out. Maybe he deserved a phone call from her.

No. Why call when an e-mail could do the job?

Reaching the end of the dock, Willow gazed into the murky green waters of Lake Gethsemane, Amazing Grace's tribute to its Biblical namesake. Soon the lake would lose its muddy surface, and the sun would sparkle against the water's brilliance.

With spring's arrival, every shade of green surrounded her from the valley to the top of the mountains encompassing the lake. Wisps of gray clouds dipped down over the mountains, and a thin mist drifted up from the water. White dogwoods in bloom laced the woods, and pink hydrangea completed the colorful palette of the Creator—as Granny used to call the shifting shades and scenery of the Carolina Mountains.

Willow pressed her shoulders downward. Pain zinged across her back as she fought to ease the tension in her muscles. She rolled her neck and winced before sitting on the dock's piling.

Her gaze went to the spot opposite her, and the memory of the day she'd drawn the picture of Quentin lifted the corners of her lips. Those muscles ached as well. How long had it been since she'd smiled—or laughed?

When she thought of him, it was always in that pose. He was sitting with his back against the piling, a fishing pole in his hand, right leg bent, left leg stretched toward the post where she sat. When Willow had seen him here that day, she couldn't resist the temptation to capture his every emotion. They were carved deep in her heart. He hadn't seen her hiding near the willow at the edge of the water.

An hour must have passed before she'd finished sketching out the lines of his slender, well-built frame, dark hair pushed back from his tall forehead, and the smile—that sweet, tender smile, as if he knew a secret he wouldn't dare share.

The memory of his image and that long ago day pushed air from her lungs. How she wished she hadn't lost the portrait. In her embarrassment, Willow left it where Quentin first laid eyes upon it—the county art festival.

She stood, pressing her hand against the aching in her chest. "Quentin?" she whispered his name, letting the plea fall into the morning air. Her desires were as useless as her love for him had been. His reaction to her drawing had devastated her.

A slight breeze tugged at her smock and took her away from the reverie. She lifted her hand to the baseball cap, ready to release her long dark locks but stopped. Her hair would be a dead-giveaway—with the emphasis on dead.

The birds chirped from tree to tree, and a breeze picked up, whispering through the leaves of the old willow.

A heavy footfall on the pier made her skid to a stop. She closed her eyes as fear shivered through her. She was alone here. And vulnerable.

Stupid.

Stupid.

Stupid.

She tensed, awaiting the assault.

"Caught you."

She jumped, turning around at the man's booming voice so close behind her, and lost her balance. She teetered backward, arms flailing.

"Whoa. Willow. Whoa." He ran at her.

She struggled not only to keep from falling into the water, but also to stay out of his reach.

"Willow, stop fighting or we're both going to take a bath."

The sound of her name on his lips and the grasp of his arm around her waist brought with them a sigh, whether of relief or exasperation, she couldn't tell.

"Quentin." She found her equilibrium and pulled from his grasp.

He lifted his hands in surrender and stepped back. "You could have called. I'd have opened the place for you."

Had he lived on another planet ten years ago? "I didn't want—I made a last minute decision, took an extended vacation."

"I'd have taken the covers off the furniture, cleaned the place up a bit."

"I did that last night." She pulled at her top, straightening it, then made sure the baseball cap was firmly affixed to the top of her head.

"I saw you come in."

"You still live in your parents' house?" She hadn't meant for the condescending tone to escape, but her heart spoke, not her brain.

"I bought it from them. They moved to Florida like all senior citizens do eventually."

That subtle humor—how she'd missed it. Even now, against her will, she laughed. He could easily have taken a return shot at her rather than at the self-exiling older generation who were leaving in droves to find a warmer climate in a flat landscape.

He reached for the bill of the worn Amazing Grace High School baseball cap, the one she'd stolen from him so long ago—the one she'd found on her bed stand. "Cute," he said.

She ducked away from him. "I don't want anyone to know I'm here." And he'd never get his hat back either.

He waved her off. "Anyone here would know you."

"And that's why you sounded so shocked when I turned around?"

"That it was you wasn't what shocked me." He started away from her.

"What was it then?" She left her challenge out in the open like a baited hook.

He stopped and turned his green-eyed gaze upon her. "From the look on your face, I thought you would faint from fear and fall into the water." His voice softened with each word. "Are you okay?"

She had nothing to say to him, and at the same time, she wanted to tell him everything.

"Really, Willow. Are you okay?"

"I'll be fine in a few days. I just need to find my bearings."

"You know where I am if you need me."

She thought he'd moved away. Not wanting anyone to know how much she cared, she'd never asked Scott about him. "You're where you've always been." She barely spoke the words.

He tucked his hands in his pockets. "Right next door." He kept his voice low, then smiled and stepped off the deck. "But in case you need me during the daytime, you can call for Coach McPheron at the high school. It's good to see you again even if you look like a beaten old rug."

"Gee. Thanks." Same old Hoot. Just says what he means—or what he knows will rile you. All the same, she probably did look like a mat tromped over for years. His feet had treaded there as well.

As he walked toward his home, she allowed her gaze to flit across the woods behind and beside their homes. She straightened at the flash of light, the sun reflecting off something metal through the early morning fog. A sparkle and then it was gone. A chill crawled down her spine. Only someone who didn't belong would wander around in those woods.

"Hoot?" She forced the whisper from her heart and into the air, but he did not hear. "Hoot?" Had any other name sounded as sweet to her ears? She'd not spoken her nickname for him since eleventh grade.

When he heard and stopped, she lowered her head before he could see the emotion play upon her face. She sank to the piling once again.

"You're not okay?" He returned to her side with his quick and easy stride. "Willow, tell me. I'll take care of it."

His words opened a world of invitation to her—a world of lost opportunity gone by. What did she know of the life he now led?

"You're trembling."

She looked up into his eyes, the color of the evergreens surrounding her home. "Are you married?"

A smile played at the corner of his lips. "Someone once told me she couldn't stand me enough to marry me. Nothing's changed. I'm still the same old unlovable boy you refused to marry when we were kids."

"Divorced, huh?"

He laughed again. "No, I'm waiting to annoy the right girl."

She pushed herself up, careful not to release a telling sigh of relief.

They walked side by side toward the dirt road, stopping at the foot of her worn path. "What do you have planned for your first day back?" he asked.

"I thought I'd take a ride into town and spend the day. I need a few things for the house."

He looked at the watch on his arm, the leather was worn, but she recognized it.

She'd given it to him on his fifteenth birthday.

He offered her a sympathetic smile. "I wish I could join you for coffee at Manna from Heaven, but I don't have time before school starts."

The bakery. Good suggestion. "Henry Appleton still owns the Tree of Knowledge?"

"Yeah. Mr. Henry and Ms. Annie would love to see you. They ask about you all the time."

"And what do you tell them?"

"Whatever news I get from your—from Mr. Thomas."

So, he asked about her. Yet, she and Quentin hadn't spoken often even before the tabloids broke the story. Funny, Scott never mentioned Quentin's curiosity, though, she doubted it would have made a difference.

"Well, have a good day at work." She stepped past him, hurrying up the path and into her house. She couldn't stay alone on the lake, and she didn't want him to smell her fear.

Checking all the doors, she threw her laptop bag over her shoulder. She reached for the clear roll of tape she'd found in Granny's "catch-all" drawer and placed on the counter last night. Then, as Detective Hominski had shown her, she tore a few strips from the roll and placed them first against the inside of the back door where they couldn't be seen. Outside the front door, she bent and placed one strip near the bottom. After double checking the lock, she ran to her car. Quentin was pulling out, and she meant to follow him toward town.

Her cell phone rang as she reached her car. She plopped in her seat and fumbled for it within her purse. The number was a New York cell phone exchange. Jeffrey said he'd check on her. "Hello." She threw the car in reverse and began to back out of the drive. "Hello."

No answer.

"Jeffrey, if this is you, I'm not getting good reception where I am. E-mail me, okay?" She threw the phone back into her purse. At the end of the drive, she put the car in first gear and raced to catch up with Quentin, her eyes scanning the mountainside. The lack of reception on her cell phone was a good thing. No one wanted to be on a cell phone when they made the death-defying curve aptly named Widow's Peak. The tight turn at the top of the mountain never lessened its terrorizing hold over her.

As she passed the dirt entrance, Willow glanced up toward the old cabin. A truck with North Carolina plates was parked in front. She breathed a sigh of relief. A local. Maybe Scott had rented out the old place. Quentin would know. She'd ask him later.

Quentin studied Willow in his rearview mirror as she followed him up the lake's winding mountain road. She followed him close enough that he could see her hands clutching the steering wheel long before their vehicles reached Widow's Peak. She'd always hated the turn leading them down the other side to the highway.

In town, Willow waved at him when she pulled beside his Jeep. She wrinkled her perfect little nose at him then turned her flawless lips into a smirk. He'd missed seeing emotion play across her beautiful face. He could read her better than anyone, and right now, despite her attempts to keep it from him, she was scared to death.

Her trailing him down the mountain was no coincidence. The fear flashing in her eyes—the color of Dutch chocolate so rich he'd develop a craving after one look into them if he wasn't careful—and the tenseness of her posture when he'd reached to keep her from falling into the water, spoke volumes.

But she looked good in his old baseball cap. He'd put it on her head after he led the Amazing Grace Archangels to a state championship in their sophomore year. She never gave it back. That might have been the last time he saw her smile—until today. He was glad he'd left the hat where he found it on the stand by her bed. Her wearing it told him more than she'd ever say.

He winked and turned left when the light changed. A glance at his watch told him he barely had enough time to grab a cup of coffee in the teachers' lounge before running to the gym for his first period class. Willow had given him the watch, and he'd never been able to part with it.

As children he and Willow were inseparable, always together, always in tune with each other. In high school their interests had pulled them into different circles. By senior year, they'd hardly spoken to one another. Willow had grown sullen toward him.

No wonder, with the lies she'd harbored. They would have pricked any soul.

He gripped the steering wheel tight, his fingers clenching the worn leather. When the tabloids spilled the truth, and Granny died, Willow fled the spotlight. Instead of running to California, to her parents—the ones she'd always said were her aunt and uncle—she'd moved to New York without telling him good-bye.

Quentin wanted to push the anger aside, but how?

He looked out the window and pictured her in his baseball cap again.

A smile turned his lips.

Willow was home.

She called him *Hoot.*

The road up to the high school was a steep one, leveling out at the edge of the parking lot. Quentin turned right toward the ancient brick building and his reserved spot.

An unusually large crowd of students filled the school's courtyard. Had he missed a prayer meeting around the flagpole with his Christian students? Willow's presence could rattle him enough that he'd forget his name if he allowed it.

Chants rose and fell on their lips. No prayer meeting. Quentin climbed out of the vehicle and reached for his backpack.

"Dent, Dent, Dent." The mob's mantra filled the air.

A fight.

"Denton Goodyear!" Quentin threw his bag back inside the Jeep and ran toward the fray.

"Troy, Troy, Troy." An opposing pack rallied for a victor as Quentin pushed inside the circling crowd.

Quentin's buddy, Darrell Jacobs, squeezed through the kids, coming from the opposite direction. "Get back." Darrell tugged his way inside the space where two boys wallowed on the grass, throwing errant punches. "Scoot."

"Scatter!" Quentin roared. "Now." He made eye contact with as many of the spectators as possible.

The horde gave way.

Quentin nodded to Darrell before reaching down and grabbing Denton Goodyear's forearms. He pulled back with enough force to tell Denton he was serious then he shifted Denton's weight off of Troy Groverton.

Quentin plastered his lanky quarterback to the ground.

"Aughhh …" Denton struggled for freedom, but Quentin held him tighter. "You're hurting me, Coach."

Quentin twisted to see if Darrell had everything under control with Troy. The other boy was standing without restraint, rubbing a sore fist. Darrell was bent, spitting blood on the ground. Figured. Darrell was a mathematician not a fighter. He'd probably walked right into a wayward jab.

"You okay?" Quentin tossed the question.

Darrell nodded.

"Troy, what's this all about?" He looked to his wide receiver.

"Coach." Denton struggled within Quentin's grasp.

"You stay there and eat dirt." Quentin tightened his hold. He turned his gaze on the students who dared defy his order, many of them members of his football team. "I told you to scram. Move it now, or I'll have every one of you scrubbing the locker room tomorrow. That how you want to spend your Saturday?"

The crowd fell away.

"I don't know, Coach." Troy wiped dirt from his face. "I guess Dent got mad at me because I talked to Tina. He jumped me. I had no choice."

"You always have a choice." Darrell pulled out a handkerchief and wiped his mouth. He stared down at the red stain and shook his head.

Troy pointed at Dent. "Not with him you don't."

"Mr. Jacobs, would you mind walking Mr. Groverton to the office? Mr. Goodyear and I will be right behind you. Stop squirming," he warned the boy on the ground.

Only when Darrell had ushered Troy into the school did Quentin allow Dent to stand, never taking his grip off the boy's arms, still pressing them against his back. "Troy telling the truth? Did you jump him?"

"Yeah, but—"

Quentin pursed his lips and shook his head.

"But—"

"Son, you don't jump someone from behind. You let them know you're coming. On the field, do you face the defense?"

"Yeah, but—"

"On the field, Troy's facing the same direction as you. He has the same goal in mind."

"Well, right now, he's got my girlfriend in mind."

"Someone tell you this?"

"I saw 'em. He was talking with Tina last night."

"And Tina isn't allowed to talk with other people?"

"Not with Troy."

Quentin released the boy's arms and gripped his shoulders, staring hard into his face. "Dent, your books, your truck, your bicycle, your jock strap, those are your possessions. You don't own that girl. She's either with you or she's not."

"She's not." Denton ran his hand through his unruly blond hair.

The truth. That's all he wanted, but he hadn't wanted to see the haunted look in the kid's blue eyes. "Well, you can't go around fighting every boy who talks to her."

This young man was not much different than his father. Something about the acorn falling close to the tree niggled at the corner of Quentin's mind. How could he get through to the kid?

Dent wiped his eyes with the back of his hand.

"Are you an Amazing Grace Archangel? Do you want to lead the team?"

Denton stared at him. "You know I do."

"Well leadership doesn't just happen on the field. You lead off the field as well. What you did to Troy—getting both of you Saturday detentions for the last two weeks of school, and causing you both to sit the bench for the first game of next season—that's not the way to guide the team to victory."

Dent stared at the ground.

"Is it?" Quentin demanded.

"No, sir," Denton answered with the call of a Marine.

"I expect you to do the right thing when we walk into Principal Jones's office. You understand?"

"Yes, sir."

"Let's go." He walked in silence beside Dent, opening the school door for him, and followed him into the principal's office.

"I have to get my backpack." After forty-five minutes, Quentin stepped out of the principal's office and pushed open the front door of the school.

"What did you say to make those kids understand?" Darrell followed behind him. "A Goodyear actually apologized for something."

"Denton is not his father. Cooper Goodyear would never utter an apology, heartfelt or otherwise." Quentin needed to remember that, too, and he needed to get to his first period class. His assistant coach couldn't handle that class of freshmen alone. Quentin walked with Darrell toward the parking lot.

"Yeah, and just to prove it, here he comes," Darrell said.

"What?" Quentin looked to his friend.

"McPheron, I swear I'll …"

A fist slammed against the left side of Quentin's face, near his eye. He spun with the impact. Someone jumped on his back.

With a fluid motion learned in high school wrestling, Quentin tossed his attacker over his shoulder and onto the ground.

"Ommph." Air rushed from deep within Cooper Goodyear's gut. The overweight man looked like a gasping fish as he struggled to re-inflate his lungs. Quentin touched his throbbing eye with his hand and stumbled backward, catching his breath.

What would make a man with eleven years on Quentin think he could go toe-to-toe with him—even in an ambush?

Quentin straightened, a red haze fogging his vision. It was time to end what should have been finished years before. "Don't get up, Cooper. Have the good sense to stand down and not give me the excuse I need to take you apart."

"I don't think you should …" Darrell pulled out his cell phone, punching in numbers.

Quentin cast Darrell a warning look.

His friend lowered his phone.

Cooper stood, staggering at first. Then he planted his feet into a solid stance.

Quentin waited. *Dear God, all I want to do is knock his head off. Make him pay for all the misery he's cost.*

Yeah, God said revenge was His, but Quentin wanted one chance to gain retribution—for his friend, Laurel, and for Tabitha. Cooper had helped ruin one girl's reputation and caused the death of the other.

The stench of Cooper's alcoholic sweat made Quentin sick. His eye throbbed, and he wanted Cooper to walk away before it swelled shut.

Cooper dropped his fist and straightened. "You can't come after me, so you go after my boy." He wiped perspiration from his brow with the back of his hand. "Did you ever consider that your friend Laurel wanted what I had? She knew more than most seventeen-year-olds. What she didn't know, I taught her. You're just jealous you had nothing to teach her."

The man sure wanted a fight—tearing scabs off emotional wounds that would never really heal. Quentin moved forward, but Darrell stepped in front of him, bringing his face close to Goodyear. "If you ever disparage Laurel Thomas again, you'll answer to me. Do you understand?" The geek roared like a Roman soldier rather than a Greek philosopher.

Cooper stood in silence until Darrell turned to leave. Then Cooper went after Quentin's friend.

"Nope." Quentin stepped in front of him, his fist tightened. Cooper slammed into him, but Quentin stood his ground. He'd give anything to lay the guy flat, land one punch to the soft belly of a man who could never put his high school glory days behind, who spent too much time chasing young women and drinking beer. Both of his vices had hurt friends Quentin loved.

Cooper backed away, raising his hands. He turned and started toward the parking lot.

"Why'd he back away?" Darrell asked. "Not like him at all."

Quentin pointed to the woman standing in the main entrance of the school, and they made their way toward her.

The gnawing feeling he hadn't practiced what he'd preached to Cooper's son began to eat at Quentin. Yeah, he hadn't stooped to Cooper's level, but he'd wanted to. And even without throwing a punch, his and Darrell's jobs could be in jeopardy.

"Mr. McPheron. Mr. Cooper." Principal Jones stood with her back holding the door open, hands on her hips, lips pressed into a thin line.

They stared at the school's fearless leader. Quentin couldn't think of an excuse, and the evidence of the crime was written all over his face.

"Well done, gentlemen." The principal's fierce glare eased a bit. "Well done."

CHAPTER THREE

Willow peered into the window of Manna from Heaven Bakery. Nothing much had changed since she'd left. The dark wood paneling still lined the walls and made the place look cozy even from outside. Walnut framed glass cases housed the goodies the owner, Mr. Walters, produced. Customers formed a line from the counter to the entrance.

A blonde backed toward the door, talking with someone inside. Willow's cousin, Laurel. Willow pulled the door open for her.

Laurel stepped out. "Thank you." Her cousin nodded without looking in Willow's direction.

"You're welcome." Willow cringed. She'd almost managed to sneak by. Granny's insistence on manners caused her faux pas.

Laurel turned and pushed back her long blonde hair from her face. "Willow, you're home?"

Friendly and with a smile. Very unlike Laurel. Willow released the tension in her shoulders and straightened for a challenge. "Yeah, I'm home."

Laurel nodded and started down the street, turning once. Her hand raised in good-bye was an unanticipated gesture.

"Go figure." Willow shrugged and stepped inside.

She drank in the aroma of fresh brewed coffee and warm bread. In front of her, all kinds of baked delicacies awaited. She ran her tongue over her lips. Even in New York, she'd been unable to find a better éclair than the ones Mr. Walters made.

Behind the counter three women adorned in black pants and white shirts, their hair tucked under hairnets, waited on customers. In the back, bakers continued to produce more of the sweet stuff that made her mornings worthwhile. Seating was limited in the bakery, but Willow kept her eye on a table nestled in the back.

A sign on the wall read *Wi-Fi*. Had Mr. Walters progressed into the modern age? Good. She'd be able to check in with Jeffrey.

The door opened and other customers entered. Willow rearranged the weight of the laptop case on her shoulder and stepped in line. She tugged down the bill of her baseball cap. While Quentin and Laurel would recognize her anywhere, only a few others could identify her.

"Willow, why are you here?" The worst of them all had found her out.

Willow inhaled, counting backward from a hundred. By the time she reached zero, her aunt might leave her alone. She fingered the bracelet on her left wrist and looked to the woman.

Aunt Agatha's gaze fell upon the bracelet. In the past, Agatha had been very vocal about Granny's decision to leave Willow the heirloom, as well as her home. Would her aunt make a scene now?

"I asked you a question," Agatha demanded.

Willow planted a smile on her face. "Aunt Aggie, good to see you."

Agatha patted her football-helmet shaped hairdo. Her hair dye matched the pigskin and her girth was that of a linebacker. "We don't want you back here. Your uncle nearly had a breakdown when your parents aired their family secrets."

And that was her fault how?

"Why did you come back?" Aggie fixed stern gray eyes upon her.

"I have a home here, and please lower your voice. I'm trying to keep my arrival out of the press."

"Like that will happen. Where you are, trouble is bound to follow. You're just like your mother."

Ouch. Had Agatha always been this cruel?

Willow again shifted the weight of her laptop to ease the strain on her shoulder. If only she could shift the pain in her heart as easily. "I don't believe I can be anything like a woman I've never actually met." She narrowed her gaze upon Agatha. "I don't believe you've met her either?"

"Oh, your mother and I have quite a history. One I'd like to forget. All you have to do is watch her on one of those horrible movies she makes. There's a little bit of her in all of them."

And Willow knew which part of the multi-dimensional characters showed Suzanne Scott's true self, but Agatha was wrong. Suzanne did know how to act—unless you asked her to portray a mother. "Well, excuse me. I'd like to get my coffee and sit down."

"Not in here, missy."

"Excuse me. Public place."

"Excuse me." Agatha placed her hands on her round hips and lifted one side than the other. "My place. Bought it when Mr. Walters retired."

"And started bringing the quality down ever since." An older lady slipped into line behind Willow.

Willow turned, biting her cheek to keep from laughing aloud. Despite her efforts, her lips slid upward into a smile. She had an ally. "Mrs. Appleton." Willow hugged her high school English teacher, careful to keep the laptop against her, not allowing it to fall into the frail octogenarian's frame.

"You're a little too old to still be so formal. Annie will do."

"It's good to see you," Willow said.

Annie lifted her head, and a look of defiance fell across her features. Willow had witnessed that look often in high school when some punk kid thought he could intimidate her. "I only come here because Henry loves those French cream thingies." Annie scrunched up her nose and set her stare upon Agatha. "You haven't ruined those yet."

"Annie Appleton, I ought to kick you out along with her," Agatha huffed.

Annie stepped out of line, and with aged and trembling hands, she pulled Willow with her. "Let's go, sweet thing. We know when we've been offered a gift. You'll get better coffee down at the bookstore."

Willow laughed as she helped Annie out the door. "How's Mr. Appleton?"

"Well, he's not going to be too happy that I got kicked out of Manna. He does love those twisty cream things, but seeing you will bring a twinkle to his eye."

"I was planning to hang out at the bookstore today if that's okay."

"I'd love it." She patted Willow's hand. "I was thinking on your grandma the other day. I sure miss her."

"I miss her, too."

"Well, that's because she left a lot of good memories, don't you believe?"

"Yes, ma'am," Willow agreed.

"How's that rascal of a dad?"

Did she mean Scott or her Uncle Ted? After all, until the tabloid story broke, everyone including Willow thought her father's oldest brother was her father. Willow never met Ted, and she wished she'd never met Scott. "Doing well. We spoke yesterday."

"I never figured him for Hollywood, but I remember his writing. He did have an amazing imagination."

So Annie read the tabloids. Of course she would. Her husband ran the town's only bookstore. "My father used to write—stories, I mean? I know he's a screenwriter, but did he write novels?"

"Oh, sweet thing, he could spin a yarn and have you believing just about anything. With his screenwriting, he's just bringing his work to the movies. Are you still drawing?"

"I've been working too hard to do any serious projects other than a doodle here and there." Did it matter that nine times out of ten, the doodling brought about the same picture?

"Well, you're home now. Use the talent God's given you."

A smile lit Willow's face. Annie was always her biggest fan. She'd been the one to cast a net into the pool of Willow's imagination, giving her the desire to bring life to canvas with paints and pencils—doing with one frame what her father did on hundreds of frames of film. Maybe she and Scott had more in common than she'd realized.

Annie tapped on the glass door of the Tree of Knowledge Book Store.

Mr. Appleton tottered toward them. "That old man needs a walker, but he won't listen to me." Annie pulled her grasp from Willow as he pushed open the door. "Henry, look who came home."

"Willow Thomas. Sure good to see you." Henry kissed Willow's cheek. "Come on in. We've remodeled since we last saw you. If you've got your computer in the bag, the best place is that table right over there." He pointed to an area a little more in the open than Willow preferred.

Granny had taught Willow good manners, and she wouldn't be rude to Henry for the world.

"They say there shouldn't be a difference, but I find I can surf the net faster from there," Henry continued.

So Henry also kept up with trends. "Thank you. I'll make myself at home, and you two don't worry over me." Willow moved toward the table Henry had indicated.

"Annie, where's my breakfast?" Henry asked.

"You'll have to eat my treats today. Agatha tossed me out—again." Annie winked at Willow.

"Oh, well. I'll survive. Willow, I'll bring you coffee when we get the place open. Annie, dear, would you mind making sure Stanley pulled all the older magazines when he delivered this month's publications? His old eyes are failing him as badly as mine."

Willow settled into the area Henry suggested. Though nestled amongst shelves, she could see out the window, and others could see her, but safety wrapped around her like a warm blanket on a cold day. She was safe in the presence of the Appletons.

Unlike the dark alcove of the bakery, the bookstore was bright with sunlight and florescent lighting. For those who didn't want to hide away, there were booths lining the front windows to the left of the store, beside the sandwich and tea shop the Appletons also ran.

The dear couple had grown gracefully old together. During Willow's high school years, Henry never failed to daily leave a flower on Annie's desk.

Annie meandered to the magazine rack as Henry had asked. When she reached it, she lifted a long stemmed rose from the shelf and turned to smile at her husband.

Why did Henry's sweet action cause the dart of pain in Willow's soul, and why did a vision of Quentin pass through her memory? She and Quentin never dated. They had played games that children play—hide-and-seek and blind man's bluff. Why then did she grieve the loss of something she never possessed?

When her teenage hormones raged and her body tuned

into him, he'd already left her behind, partying with Laurel and her friend, that awful Tabitha Cowart. An occasional lunch with Darrell Jacobs spared her the humility of having no friends. She never understood the attraction Quentin held for girls like her cousin and Tabitha, or why he had not invited her along for the ride. Even Darrell joined them occasionally.

"You look so sad." Annie touched her shoulder.

"I'm fine." Willow pushed a smile into place. "Seeing you with the flower reminded me of high school."

"Henry's always been the sentimental type. You need to find yourself one of those, but a lot of them aren't stable, you know. Even Henry has a loose screw."

"I heard that Annie Appleton. Only a man with a loose screw would tangle with you," Henry bantered.

"I know, dear." Annie again winked at Willow.

Henry waved Annie toward him. "Come. Leave Willow alone. Stand with me at this counter. I can't bear to be away from you very long."

The Appletons fit so well together that Willow could never imagine them apart. She moved her gaze from them and stared at a row of books on a nearby shelf. All those years ago when she and Hoot played along the banks and inside the cool waters of the lake, when they would catch fireflies at night and put them in jars, and when they'd sit on the dock and talk about their futures, Willow could never imagine Hoot separated from her for more than a few days. They knew each other's thoughts, completed each other's sentences, laughed at the same parts in a movie even when no one else seemed to have gotten the joke. Then came high school, and everything changed.

The door opened, and a young man and woman entered pushing a baby in a stroller. The man leaned over the child, making sure the blanket was covering the little one. Willow ached for what she'd once considered the inevitable but had come to accept as improbable.

She shook off the melancholy and unzipped her laptop case. Jeffrey would be sending her an e-mail, and she wasn't really on vacation. She pulled the computer from her bag, opened it up, and turned it on.

As she waited for her computer to boot, a familiar unease crawled up her spine. Was it the anticipation of opening her e-mail?

That was crazy. No one would expect her to come home. Her stalker wouldn't have a clue where she'd gone. Still, she pulled a notebook from her pack and fanned the pages of paper.

Her virus protection began to scan. Clicking on her e-mail would produce fruitless results. The computer did things its way, and when it scanned for viruses, it refused to multitask.

With each passing moment, the warmth and safety vanished as if someone had pulled the covers from her on a cold, windy day.

Enough. She'd left that feeling behind in New York City. If anyone stalked her here in Amazing Grace, she'd soon see him.

Finally. The virus scan offered an efficient little report telling her so many files were scanned resulting in zero viruses. Then it ran through its system check, and she clicked on her e-mail icon. *Checking. Authorizing. Receiving Mail.* The bold lines fell across the pane. Junk mail, then "Scott Thomas. Subject: Checking In."

Willow clicked on her father's name and read his brief note. "Worried about you. Can you tell me what's going on once in a while? Are you okay? Did you go to Amazing Grace? Any more problems?"

Willow hit reply, and her fingers flew across the keyboard. "Fine, Dad. My boss drove me home night before last after someone trashed my apartment. I'm in Amazing Grace now. Don't tell anyone. Thanks for keeping up the place. You didn't need to, but it was nice of you. Those shutters on the house are beautiful. Annie Appleton asked after you. Is it true you used to write?" Sending the message into cyberspace brought her back to the inbox and numerous e-mails.

Several messages contained the same subject line. A different one this time.

Willow's shoulders began to creep toward her ears. She pushed them down, and pretending to rub tired muscles, looked around her.

I See You.

I See You.

I See You.

I See You.

I See You.

I See You.

You Can't Run from Me.

The messages were dated and timed moments earlier.

A new one came across.

I Still See You.

Willow lifted a shaky finger to the keyboard and opened the first e-mail. She bounced her leg up and down under the table, fighting to hold back any other show of emotion, and waited for the picture to load. Her breath stopped as the picture came into full view—Willow and Annie walking out of Manna, Annie holding to her arm. Each subsequent picture followed them down the block and into the bookstore.

The last shot showed her inside the Tree of Knowledge, sitting at the table, rubbing her neck.

Scott Thomas excelled at multitasking, and when he saw the e-mail from his daughter, he leaned forward and clicked it. If not for the creak of his leather chair, the action would have gone unnoticed by the crazed co-producer sitting in front of him. Willow's e-mailed reply opened. "Fine, Dad ..."

He smiled and lifted his gaze to his current business partner.

"You need to do something with that wife of yours," Curt said.

Scott's smile disappeared. "Curt, you've worked with Suzanne before. She's temperamental, but when the cameras turn to her, she makes all of this worth it."

Curtis Newport rubbed his balding head then leaned forward, elbows on knees, hands clasped, and chin perched upon them. "Suzanne's star is fading. She's no longer twenty-five. Her temper tantrums are going to take her right out of this business. Then what will she have?"

Suzanne would have Scott, and when he retired, they'd have each other. "Give her a break. She's never played a supporting role to a second-rate actress, but she's hanging in there."

"With claws out. If Vicki walks, Suzanne is history."

Scott didn't blink. He wouldn't give Curt the satisfaction. "I'll ask her to play fair."

"Honestly, Scott, what are you going to do? She had a good run. If she behaves, she can last another ten years in supporting roles, maybe even win another Golden Globe or Oscar. If she continues to sabotage herself, your only option will be to buy or keep screen rights, produce, and direct your wife. That spells disaster. Couples younger than you have failed in those ventures."

Didn't he know that? "Don't worry about Suzanne."

The door to his office opened, and Suzanne stormed inside. Dressed in a blazer and skirt, she looked every part of the career mother she was portraying in the movie.

"I can't bear one more moment with that little bimbo." She raised her hands in the air, looking to heaven before dropping her gaze to the ground and shaking her head with theatrical panache. "I just can't take this."

"Enter center stage." Curt stood.

"What's that supposed to mean?" She spun toward Curt. "Listen to me, buster. If she doesn't show me some respect, I'm going to teach her a lesson or two."

"Suzanne," Scott said. "Calm down." He stood and moved around his desk.

With grace born of years on the stage, Suzanne turned toward him without a word. He didn't often speak to her in such a dry tone, so when he did, she listened.

She avoided him and sat in the chair he vacated, brushing her auburn hair from her face. He'd suggested she cut it, but she'd insisted shorter hair would make her appear old. For the first time, he noticed the longer style elongated her thin face and brought out the lines around her eyes, making her appear aged beyond her forty-eight years.

He shook the thought from his mind. He'd visited Willow not too long ago. His daughter reminded him of a younger Suzanne. His wife looked fine—beautiful, in fact.

Curt closed the door on his way out, and Suzanne turned fiery eyes toward Scott. "I don't like him. Never have." Her attention went to his computer screen, and her wry smile reminded him of a small child who'd sneaked a treat. Maybe Suzanne longed for a relationship with Willow after all.

But he needed to discuss something else with her now. "Funny, I think Curt likes you very much. He met with me in an attempt to save your career."

Suzanne leaned back and studied her painted fingernails. "Save my career? He needs to look after his own."

"That's exactly what he's doing. Can't you see that your behavior causes trouble for everyone? You need to change your tune and get this movie made within budget."

"I just want people to treat me with respect."

"Vicki has indicated to you often how pleased she is to work with you. In return, you call her names and carry on over every scene."

"I can't teach her, you know. I'm not her mother. I'm her co-star." Suzanne raised her hands and dropped them heavily back to her lap.

"No, you're her supporting actress. This is Vicki's movie as we've discussed numerous times."

"I'm not old enough to be that woman's mother."

"Suzanne." He pointed to the computer screen. "Vicki is the same age as our daughter."

She glared at him before waving her hand as if dismissing any notion of Willow being her child. So much for the theory of his wife wanting to play a real-life mother. Suzanne turned her back to him.

"This is your chance to play the role of a lifetime. The publicity over Willow left a bad taste in the critics' minds where you're concerned. Portraying Vicki's mother could do more than win you an Oscar."

Suzanne ran her fingers over his Golden Globe award for Best Director sitting on his bookshelf. She'd won Best Actress for another movie that same year. Would his wife ever come to terms with the fact that those days were behind her? His screenplays were a hot item in Hollywood. He was still a sought-after director, producer, and writer, but her glory days as a leading actress were fading.

He moved beside her, brushing her chin with the back of his fingers. "More importantly, it could win back the hearts of those who condemned you for your choice of career over motherhood."

Yes, her choice.

He pulled his hand away.

He'd wanted to keep his daughter, but Suzanne had agreed she would bear his child and not terminate the pregnancy on one condition: she never wanted to recognize Willow as her own.

Scott shook away his anguish and slipped his arms around his wife's trim hips. "Suzanne, honey, do this for me."

She sighed. "How can I refuse my sweet boy?" She touched his hair, brushing her fingers against his temple.

He was nineteen again, and he had won her love—rescuing her from his older brother's sudden disinterest. Why had Ted allowed Suzanne to get away from him?

"I'll behave. I'll act the doting mother, and I will win that Oscar." She kissed his cheek. "All for you."

She'd do him this favor in the make-believe world of Hollywood, but she'd never consider easing Willow's pain—even for him. At least this agreement would get Curt off his back. "Thank you." He nuzzled her lithe neck.

She pulled away. "Never a better time than the present."

And away she went, leaving him alone and desirous of her time, yet exhausted by her antics. He sat back in his chair, his attention drawn back to his daughter's e-mail.

"Fine, Dad." His daughter likely wrote those words without thought. One day, he'd hear her say them in the natural way that would mean she forgave him.

So, she'd made it to Amazing Grace. The place was a safe haven he'd sought often since the death of his mother. Willow would find safety there, too.

"Is it true you used to write?"

Was his daughter that clueless about her legacy? He would leave her the continuing royalties and rights to screenplays he'd written, and the movies he'd directed and produced. The royalties alone would take care of her children and grandchildren. He'd made sure of that. His love for Suzanne had taken his daughter from him, but Suzanne would never take from Willow what he intended to leave for her.

Interesting. Willow thought he'd kept the old house up. That McPheron boy contacted him frequently. He always requested permission to do this or that, and he would never accept pay for his work. Quentin McPheron had crafted those shutters with his own hands—not Scott.

Quentin had hankered after his daughter since she'd left Amazing Grace. Maybe he could get her to stay where she belonged.

The door slammed open and Curtis stomped in. "Scott, you'd better get to Stage One. Your wife is doing something truly bizarre."

Scott scrambled to the door. "What now?"

"She just pulled off a performance that left the crew speechless." Curt slapped Scott on the back. "Let's go coo over her and make her feel like the star of the show. I don't know how you've done it all these years, but you make her dance to your tune."

No. Scott danced. Not Suzanne. She held the strings, and he moved at her bidding. Willow's life proved that. Still, he loved his wife. Their marriage was strong and nothing short of her outright betrayal would end it.

CHAPTER FOUR

Quentin opened the filing cabinet, threw his planner inside, and slammed the cabinet shut. Frustration would take him off his game if he allowed it. Raking his hand through his hair, he paced beyond his office door to where dingy gray lockers lined the walls. Dust played in the filtered sunlight of the small glazed windows running high along the north and south walls.

Towels spilled from the hamper, and Quentin bent and tossed them inside. Mildew and the pervading odor of sweat and dirty gym socks made his nose twitch. He rubbed it to ward off a sneeze. Every day, he told the boys to make sure they put the towels in the hamper and not on the floor. What was he, their butler? Straightening, he felt the throb behind his eye once again.

He went back into his office, but not before kicking the large trash can by the door.

"Coach?"

Quentin stopped short, closed his eyes, and took a deep breath without turning. "Yeah, Dent, what is it?"

"Coach, I'm sorry. I know my dad gave you that shiner. If I hadn't jumped Troy, this wouldn't have happened."

The boy definitely did not take after his father.

Cooper wouldn't have had the chance to pummel Quentin if he'd seen him coming. And Darrell could have warned him a second or two earlier.

"I know you're mad as—"

Quentin raised his hand. He banned cursing from his locker room. If he hadn't uttered a wanton syllable in the last few hours, no one else would.

"Sorry." Dent bowed his head and stared at his feet.

Quentin swallowed a pint of pride and wrapped one arm around the kid's shoulder. "You owned up to your wrongdoing. Yeah, one thing leads to another, but your dad did have his own choices to make. I don't hold you responsible for this." He meant to point at the black eye but misjudging the swelling, he jabbed his bruised cheek.

Denton chuckled.

"Don't laugh. Your dad's got a strong punch."

"A sucker punch."

Quentin held his tongue. He'd rather the boy list his father's faults. Instead, Quentin would focus on building up the good character in Cooper's son. "Sorta like you ambushing Troy this morning, huh?"

Dent nodded. "Junior Preston says my dad's a coward." The boy looked Quentin in the eye. "Coach, I was a coward."

Thank you, Lord, for showing me a bit of why I've suffered at Cooper Goodyear's hands. If only to teach the man's son, I'd do it again. And I understand the lesson you had for me. I won't raise a hand to Denton's father. Cooper's decisions have cost his kid so much.

Quentin looked up and grasped the teen's shoulder. "Just so long as you know whether you punch from behind or you throw the first punch, both are cowardly. I'm afraid I didn't set any better example for you today than your father. I should have walked away."

Dent nodded and headed to the door.

"Hey," Quentin called.

The kid turned.

"How'd Preston hear about what happened?"

"All the kids are talking about it. They say my dad went after Mr. Jacobs, and you stood your ground between them."

Quentin nodded. He did take a certain satisfaction in putting Cooper in his place, but if Principal Jones hadn't stepped outside, the matter would have escalated. No doubt about it, and Quentin knew in his heart that he'd have given Cooper a fist to eat.

Dent smiled.

Quentin eyed him suspiciously. "You have something to say?"

"What they're really excited about is Mr. Jacobs getting in Dad's face. They don't know what Mr. Jacobs said, but they said he looked intense."

Quentin laughed and shook his head. "Mr. Jacobs isn't the geek you think he is." A little bolster to Darrell's reputation couldn't hurt any.

"Yeah, Coach." Dent opened the door. "He is." It closed behind him.

"Yeah, he is." Quentin started toward the door. He'd need to hurry if he wanted to stuff down a sandwich before next period.

The door swung open. Quentin dodged another black eye by jumping out of the way. "Hey! Open with caution. Read the sign."

Darrell stepped inside. "Cooper called the office. He's demanding our jobs. Can you believe it? The guy's a real—"

Again, Quentin held up his hand to silence a curse, but he doubted his mild-mannered friend planned to utter one. "Principal Jones saw the incident. Don't sweat it."

"Apparently, some of the kids saw it, too. Not something I'm thrilled happened."

"You're the hero from what I just heard." Quentin smirked.

Darrell narrowed his eyes. "Don't joke with me."

"No kidding. The kids saw you get in Goodyear's face."

Darrell's overlarge Adam's apple bobbed as he swallowed. He looked away and back again. "I'd do it again. No one talks about Laurel like that, not in front of me, especially the guy who took advantage of her."

Quentin bit his lip for the second time in less than ten minutes. Laurel did have something to do with what happened to her, but that was ancient history. Though it left a mark on all of them, he'd stopped holding it against her long ago.

"She wanted your attention."

Quentin shot Darrell a warning look. He wasn't to blame for Laurel's lack of judgment.

But Laurel had been naïve and inexperienced. Quentin could have prevented it all if he'd just given her what she craved. But he couldn't give her what he didn't possess. His heart had long belonged to Willow.

Goodyear had been a married man. Even as a teenager, Laurel should have known better.

He wasn't going down the path of second guesses again. He let out a long breath "This isn't my fault. Don't take out your frustrations on me." He pushed past Darrell and headed back into his office. Guess he wasn't getting a sandwich after all.

"Goodyear needs someone to teach him he can't talk about Laurel like that."

"Nothing short of a personal tragedy will get that man's attention." Quentin stared at the calendar on his desk. "Just be thankful Laurel's here, Darrell," Quentin said. "Tabitha's dead." He wouldn't look up. Her loss cut deep for both of them

"Laurel …?"

Quentin waited for his friend to continue, and when Darrell didn't, he lifted his eyes.

Laurel had never visited him here, would never have subjected herself to the stench of male sweat and grime, a constant found in a boys' gym. This was male territory. Laurel was one-hundred percent female. And her gaze was currently fixed on Darrell.

"I saw Cutter and Chelsea in the office," she said. "They told me it'd be safe to come in." She turned to look at Quentin, her eyes widened. "What happened to you?" Her heels clicked on the concrete floor. She touched his eye. He pulled away, wincing from the pain. "It's nothing."

Laurel turned on Darrell. "What happened?"

Quentin wouldn't make his friend explain. "Denton Goodyear got in a fight. We broke it up. The school called Cooper, who came to resolve the issue with a sucker punch." He touched the corner of his lip and gave a nod toward Darrell. His friend studied the ceiling throughout the whole discourse.

"Oh, Darrell." Laurel gave him her full concentration. "Did he hit you, too?" She touched Darrell's swollen lip.

Darrell shook his head. "Took a stray jab trying to break up the battle." With just a bit more swaying, Darrell would look like Gomer Pyle standing before Sergeant Carter. All that was needed was a resounding, "Golly."

Laurel lowered her hand to her side. "I'm so sorry you went through that because of me."

So, Laurel had overheard their conversation.

"No. One of the kids hit me, not Goodyear or Jockstrap here." Darrell cocked one eyebrow up and gave her one of his goofy lopsided grins.

Quentin had given his geeky friend the advantage, and Darrell had tossed it away. He could have milked her sympathy a little more.

"Laurel, why are you here?" Quentin asked.

"Willow's home."

He nodded. "I saw her this morning. Something wrong with that?"

Her blonde bangs bobbed along with her nodding head.

"Willow isn't your enemy."

Laurel scrunched up her nose. "I don't hate her. I don't believe I ever did." She straightened. "She just got in my way back then."

"Then what's the problem."

"I don't hate her, but Momma sure does. Willow walked into a hornet's nest this morning. That's all. I would have warned her, but she had her dander up. I figured she wouldn't listen to me anyway."

"Come again?" He planted his hands firmly on his desk and leaned forward.

"Didn't you tell her Momma owns Manna from Heaven now?" She tucked a strand of hair behind her ear.

Quentin tilted his head and rolled his shoulders to release the sudden tension. He bit back a curse. "Didn't cross my mind when I suggested she go there."

"Well, too late now. Momma's probably gotten her claws into her."

Quentin slammed his fist onto his desk. "Your mother's going to go too far one of these days."

"Quentin." Darrell shook his head. "Not Laurel's fault."

"That's okay." Laurel leaned against the office doorframe. "Momma's a handful, and she blames everyone else for all her perceived troubles."

"I think she has a great life. She has a beautiful daughter, and your dad isn't so hard to live with," Darrell declared.

Quentin stared. Was Laurel blushing at his geeky friend's words?

The third period lunch bell rang. Both men looked at their watch.

"I need to get to class." Darrell reached a clumsy paw out and touched Laurel's shoulder before turning away.

Laurel watched him go. "You know, Quentin, I did want you once upon a time, but for too long now, Darrell's been my

FAY LAMB

knight in shining armor. I just don't have the courage to tell him."

"Beauty and the Geek." As soon as the words left his mouth, he wanted them back. Darrell might not be an athlete, but in the arena where commonsense and brains were needed, he was a good man to have in your corner.

"I'm no beauty. I've learned beauty blooms on the inside. I'm pouring in the water and the fertilizer, but I'm not there yet." She quoted from the pastor's sermon from last Sunday, and it made him smile.

He dialed the front office. "Chelsea, Cutter still there?" What was he thinking? Quentin's assistant coach spent every free moment with his bride.

"He's right here."

"Tell him he needs to cover the last two periods. I've got something to handle."

"You okay, Coach?" Cutter asked over the speakerphone.

"Nothing major. Appreciate it." Quentin shoved his chair under the desk, the momentary reprieve from anger over. "Agatha likes trouble, doesn't she?" He picked up his keys from the desk.

Boys flooded through the door. Quentin rushed Laurel outside. It wouldn't do for the boys to get down to their skivvies before they noticed—like they wouldn't be aware of a gorgeous blonde, no matter the age.

They walked along the outside corridor leading to the front of the school. "You need to tell your mother peoples' nerves are wearing thin with her."

"And give her another indiscretion to throw in my face? No, thank you."

He put his arm around her shoulders and leaned to whisper. "Don't let Agatha make you feel guilty. Seems there are a lot of us holding on to some sort of blame where Tabitha's concerned. Truth is, we all made mistakes that night,

53

but being inebriated and getting behind the wheel of her car was Tabitha's mistake, not yours, not mine, and not Darrell's. We shouldn't have left you two at that party, but you made the right decision to get a cab."

"Momma doesn't agree."

Had Agatha coveted the sympathy generated toward the Cowarts because of Tabitha's death? "I'm glad you didn't get in the car with her."

"I've wished for so long I'd died instead. Then I realized I was never the one in control. God was. And still is."

She'd grown in the last few years. Tragedy combined with God's mercy could do that. "Hey, you want to come with me? Give you a chance to make a new start with your cousin."

"No, I'm on break. Daddy went to lunch, and I promised to get him ready for a hearing this afternoon. I'll save my apologies to Willow for later." Laurel came to a halt. "Quentin, do something for me?"

"If I can." He waited, looking toward his Jeep.

"Be happy with Willow."

Not what he expected, but the thought made him smile.

"You've always cared for her, and well, you didn't get much of a chance in high school."

"No, I didn't, but that was Willow's fault."

"Not all of it," she said.

"What does that mean?"

"Just don't be so hard on her. Remember I caused a lot of your problems."

Not true. If Willow had wanted a closer relationship, she only needed to drop a hint. Instead, she erected a wall of lies and kept him on the outside.

They reached the end of the sidewalk, and Laurel brushed a kiss on his cheek before starting across the parking lot in the opposite direction of his vehicle.

He got into his Jeep and sat there for a few moments before turning the key. If anyone was capable of making Willow flee town, it was Agatha with her sharp tongue and bitter heart.

Funny, he'd never realized how much Agatha and Willow had in common. Maybe he should seek out her uncle Robert for some advice.

But God help Agatha if she did anything to hurt Willow.

The door to Appleton's Tree of Knowledge opened. Willow glanced from her computer screen to the front of the store. Quentin held open the door for a departing customer then looked around the store. When he didn't seem to notice her, she left him to his browsing. It wouldn't do to encourage him by appearing too eager for his company. Yet, she couldn't seem to keep her breath in a calm rhythm.

He caught sight of her, waved, and zigzagged around chairs and bookshelves until he reached her.

"Don't you have class?" She did a double take as he stopped at her side. "What in the world happened to your face?"

"A little run in with the town bully. Nothing to worry about."

"Since when do you get in fights?" If he was going to go around punching people, she wouldn't give him any sympathy.

"I didn't throw a punch. Not that I didn't want to. He was mad because I broke up a fight between his son and another boy."

"Mad? At you? Shouldn't his son's bottom look like your face does now?" She smiled. She couldn't help herself.

"Ba. Ha. Ha." He pulled out the chair beside her without waiting for an invitation. "I heard from Laurel. Apparently, I unwittingly sent you into the lion's den when I suggested you have coffee at Manna."

"No way," Willow laughed. "Has she developed a conscience?"

"That's harsh. You should give her a break. Things have happened in this town since you left." He leaned over and looked at her computer screen.

She turned the screen. "Do you mind?"

"Just curious. You were always doodling or writing. I never learned which you loved more."

"Now, I write little advertisements and create dull little drawings in order to sell things people don't need. When I left here, I put my creativity in my back pocket." She shrugged. Maybe he hadn't recognized the regret in her voice.

"Then the world is missing out on a lot of beauty. Willow, I've never known anyone who can bring a scene to life like you."

"Yeah, I believe you." She scrunched her nose.

He sat back in his chair and studied her for a long moment. Uncomfortable under his scrutiny, she turned to look out the window, watching the people pass by on the sidewalk. Was her stalker lurking outside right now?

"Yeah, that was sarcasm." He nodded. "Tell me you aren't still holding a grudge because of Laurel and the picture. If you are, I'm going to give you a nickname. I have to live with the one you tagged on me. How about Scrappy—like a little dog growling as she chomps down on a bone no one else particularly cares to take from her?"

"Scrappy? You—no. That's okay, Hoot. A little humiliation does wonders for one's dreams. I guess I should be grateful for Laurel and Tabitha's relentless teasing." She closed her document and powered down her computer. "So, you came all the way to town because Aunt Agatha may or may not have been her usual self?"

"Agatha has never been anything but Agatha. I honestly had a vision of her running you out of town."

"I lived in her shadow for eighteen years. What makes you think one run-in would make me leave?" Willow stuffed her laptop back in the carrying case. She had a bigger problem than Auntie Dearest.

No further pictures had arrived, but she'd have to stay on her toes. Keep up her guard. The stalker probably recognized the danger of hanging around too long in a small town. Anonymity was easy to maintain in a large city where hundreds of people passed you daily. In a small, rural community like Amazing Grace you couldn't stay inconspicuous for very long. With each ticking minute she remained inside the tiny bookstore, the blanket of safety wrapped a little more securely around her. But not enough to walk outside.

"So other than being humiliated by your cousin, why did you stop drawing? Your art blew me away."

"Yeah, I saw your response to my picture of you. That kind of blew me away as well." And still, after all the years since his reaction, she wanted to cry.

"You didn't see me, or you wouldn't say that."

"Hoot—no, you're right. I didn't see you standing there, your face all red, a look of shock turning to horror as Tabitha Cowart cackled over and over, 'Willow loves Quentin. Willow loves Quentin.'"

"Yeah, my face turned red." He ran his thumb along the edge of the table. "And yeah, I was shocked. I didn't expect to see my picture as big as life—"

"The picture wasn't that big."

"No, but it was big enough. Me … all sprawled out there on the dock, lost in my own world, drawn by a voyeur hiding behind a willow tree."

Willow straightened. On a smaller scale, she'd done to Quentin what her stalker was now doing to her, but she'd never known he'd seen her. "How did you know I was there?"

"I saw you the entire time."

"Oh." She swallowed hard. That would explain the tantalizing smile.

"And, yes, seeing my picturing hanging there caught me off guard."

"You're probably the one who took it down after it won first prize. The ribbon sure stung Laurel. She went around for weeks looking like she'd swallowed a hornet."

"She looked like that because I learned the dirty trick she played on you. We had a fight about it. Granny's picture should have won the ribbon. I never saw a likeness so real. I can still see Granny sitting in the rocking chair on the porch watching us play when we were kids."

How had he seen Granny's picture? She'd never shown it to anyone. Laurel had stolen it and replaced it with his picture at the art festival. She wasn't about to inquire. He'd know for sure she cared.

He leaned toward her. "I sneaked into the exhibit. I saw Granny's portrait right after they placed it on the divider wall."

"I didn't ask." Willow stood.

"You didn't have to. I can still read you like a book, Scrappy."

She shook her head, but she couldn't shake her smile.

"So did you?" Those piercing green eyes gazed up at her. "Did I what?"

"Love me. Like Tabitha said? Or does my nickname still ring true for you?"

She'd given him the nickname and an explanation for it as a kid to hide her true feelings, but she wasn't about to tell him so. "I thought you could read me like a book." She pushed her chair under the table. "Anyway, let's not go there. I need to get home to ..." She snapped her fingers. "Are you heading home?"

"I should get back to the school before last period. I just wanted to make sure you were okay."

He seemed to be waiting for her to say something. She nodded. She'd gotten herself in a pickle now. All packed up with no place to go.

"Hang work. Why don't we have lunch, go to the grocery store for some snacks, and sit down and watch a movie. I'll even watch a chick flick with you, just to remind you how nice a guy I am."

Maybe he could read her mind. Whatever. Willow wasn't arguing. She started to sling the computer bag over her shoulder, but Quentin stood and took it from her. They walked together to the front desk where Annie had taken charge after sending Henry for lunch. "I'll be back soon," she told Annie.

"I look forward to it, sweet thing." Annie reached for Willow's hand. "Honey, you've already taken my advice."

"I'm sorry?" Willow blinked.

"That boy has always been sentimental over you. I could see it every time he looked at you way back when."

Quentin laughed. "Mrs. Appleton, don't give away all my secrets."

Willow leaned forward. "He's a little unstable, too, don't you think?"

"Hey." Quentin gave her a playful push.

"Quentin, dear, trust me. She just gave you a fine compliment." Annie looked to where Henry had returned through the back door. "A mighty fine compliment if you ask me." She winked at Willow. "You two have a nice afternoon now."

"We will." Quentin held open the door. "What was all that about?"

"Private conversation. Can't tell you." She laughed.

He walked so close to her the heat of his body warmed hers. No one else ever made her tingle this way. She stepped to the side trying to put more space between them, but he reached out and took her hand. "No, Willow. We're not playing this game anymore. You know I'm the man for you."

Her heart pounded. For a brief second she had to decide whether it was from excitement or anger. Decision made, she wrenched from his grasp, stopped, and stared at him. "How do you know I don't have another man in my life?"

That would put Casanova in his place.

He blinked, confusion filling his eyes, much like he reacted as a young boy when something upset him. "I guess I don't." He walked ahead of her. "Where's your car?"

"Hoot, wait. I'm sorry." Despite everything, she still couldn't stand to see dejection on his face. She reached for his hand.

"Great timing with the nickname, Scrappy." He pulled away. "Are you?"

"Am I what?"

"You asked me the same question this morning. Are you involved with someone?"

Just some creepy, demented idiot who liked following her everywhere, taking pictures in her unguarded moments.

She shook her head. "Not that it's any of your business, but who would put up with me and all my insecurities?"

"The boy you once said you didn't give a *hoot* enough about to marry." He laced his fingers with hers.

She'd parked her car in front of Manna from Heaven, and as they approached, Quentin released his hold. "What is Agatha up to now?" He reached for the white envelope left under her windshield. "This is going to stop." Lifting the envelope's flap, he looked at it for a second then turned it toward her.

A piece of clear tape ran across the inside of the flap. Blue ink spelled out, "I know all your tricks" across the tape. The words kicked her in the stomach and her lungs locked up. She bent forward trying to breathe. Quentin's arms wrapped around her. Willow clutched at him for support, pulling him with her to the sidewalk.

She looked around wildly, studying the faces surrounding her. A delivery man wearing shorts stepped down from his big brown truck, a box tucked under his arm. A young woman pushing a baby stroller hurried by, casting a nervous glance at them. Two men in overalls argued outside the hardware store. An older man, his beard wiry and gray … She stopped. Looked back at him. His brown eyes, full of an emotion she could not read, held her transfixed for a long moment. And then he moved, stepping back into the gathering crowd.

LeBlanc sneered. He had Willow right where he wanted her. He leaned down and picked up the object Willow hadn't yet notice she'd lost and moved toward the opposite end of her car where he could hear and not be seen as nosy people stopped to stare. LeBlanc needed to be careful.

The door of the bakery opened, and he sidestepped the heavyset redhead who huffed her way down the two steps and onto the sidewalk.

"Willow …" A stout, balding man called, waving his hand in the air as he crossed the street. He met up with the redhead and caught her arm. "Agatha, honey, leave her alone."

Red gave Baldy an angry look and shook off his hand.

Nothing to do now but see how it played out.

"Uncle Robert." Willow's lukewarm acknowledgement of Baldy made it clear she wasn't interested in the man. She did, however, cut a glare at Red standing beside him. Willow backed up against the big guy—her neighbor—the guy who'd met with her this morning on the dock. The way he wrapped his arms around her now—a boyfriend? Didn't matter, but definitely a deterrent to his plans. LeBlanc needed a new strategy. He'd make sure Boyfriend didn't thwart his plans for the girl.

So far, everything was falling into place. Willow wore her paleness like a white cloak. If Boyfriend didn't have his arm around her waist, she'd go down again. She stared off in the opposite direction as if looking for someone. Good. She'd recognize him if she saw him in the crowd.

"Robert Thomas, don't you dare encourage her." Red stomped her feet. "Not after what they've done to us."

"What they've done?" Boyfriend moved from behind Willow holding out the envelope—the one he'd taken from Willow's windshield. "Aggie, what's this about?"

Red took the envelope. She gave her head a pert shake, raised her eyebrows, and handed it back to Boyfriend. "How do I know?"

"Because you put it there." Boyfriend challenged.

"I did no such thing, and how dare you accuse me—"

"Did you see who left it on Willow's car?" Boyfriend demanded. "Who was hanging around here?"

LeBlanc held his breath. Could Red finger him?

Red scanned the crowd. Was it his imagination or did her gaze look beyond the crowd to linger on him for a moment? She turned back to Boyfriend. "How would I even know what she drives? I don't make it a habit to look after every car parked in front of my store. Best you warn her, though, next time I'll have it towed if it takes up my customer parking for more than two hours."

"Give it a break, Agatha. Do you ever have a kind word for anyone?" Baldy snapped.

Red turned without another word, her hips following after her.

"I'm sorry, Willow. Please call if you need me." Baldy started back across the street from where he'd come, but stopped after a few steps. "Does Scott plan to come home soon? I'd like to see him."

"No. Suzanne has a movie in production. The last I heard, she's being a handful."

Her cover was definitely blown. Why not announce herself to all of Amazing Grace? LeBlanc smiled now. Willow didn't know the half of it. Her mother was a runaway storm on a path of destruction. Suzanne Scott didn't realize that the tempest she'd unleashed planned to double back and pick her up in its fury.

The gawking town folk began to disperse, but LeBlanc couldn't move. Watching Willow had become his favorite pastime. Seeing the fear on her face made it all the more pleasurable. They weren't paying attention to him. He could afford a long look.

Willow wiped her hands on her jeans. "Buying Agatha a bakery, what's Uncle Robert trying to do, turn her into a blimp?"

"Willow." Boyfriend burst into laughter. "You've got more Granny Thomas in you than I remember."

"And what's up with Uncle Robert? Did he have a lobotomy to change his personality?"

"No, I suspect it has everything to do with a right relationship with the Lord. You might try it sometime." Boyfriend opened the car door for her. Willow got in without a word while Boyfriend moved around the car.

LeBlanc turned away. There would be time to catch up with them later and make his presence known.

Stalking Willow

64

CHAPTER FIVE

Wind whistled through the dogwoods and maples, swirling around Quentin like a cat circling his feet. The mist thickened and the air chilled. Lightning flashed overhead, turning the lake water a momentary yellow and confirming the storm's imminent arrival.

Quentin ducked and ran from his house to Willow's carport. He opened and held her car door as she exited. She slung her purse and laptop bag over her shoulder. He stopped alongside her to watch the spectacle in the night sky.

Another boom of thunder hit the air.

Willow jumped.

"You okay?" He chuckled.

She peered up through the rustling leaves of the trees before turning her gaze upon him. "I'd forgotten the power of these mountain storms."

Placing a hand on the small of her back, he led her to the porch.

"Oh, my keys." She rifled through the oversized bag.

Just like a woman to toss keys in her purse instead of holding them in her hand.

"Sorry." She continued to search. A satisfied smile lit her face. "Ta da." She held up the key ring.

He shook his head. "Storm's moving quick."

"Thanks for dinner, Hoot. I'd forgotten how good the food is at Joe's Drive-In."

Instead of lunch, they'd taken a nice drive in the country, stopping to eat before coming home. Good, neutral conversation peppered the meal with just the right amount of civility.

Willow jabbed the house key in the lock, hesitated and then squatted down. She ran her fingers along the bottom of the door but didn't rise.

Quentin leaned down to touch her shoulder. "What is it, Willow? What's wrong?"

She turned and looked up at him, her mahogany eyes wide and full of unease. "Someone's been here."

He took her hand and pulled her to her feet, edging her back from the door. "How do you know?"

"The tape. It's gone." Her face drained of color. Fear replaced the disquiet. "The tape on the envelope, it came from my door."

Stepping in front of Willow, Quentin unlocked the door and pushed it open. "Stay behind me."

"I put tape on the back door, too," she whispered.

Her warm breath fell on his back as she followed close on his heels. They moved in tandem to the end table by the couch where she switched on the lamp.

"Anything out of place?" he asked.

She looked around before shaking her head, clutching the tail of his shirt. Despite his trepidation, Quentin smiled.

"Everything looks the same. Can we check the back door?" She released his shirt and entwined her fingers with his.

They walked through the house, past the dining room, and into the kitchen. Semi-darkness gave way to light when Quentin flipped the switch. Three strips of tape were visible, still affixed at various heights on the door. "All here?"

She pressed against him and nodded.

He faced her, taking hold of her shoulders. "No more games. I want to know what's going on."

Willow pulled from his hold and narrowed her gaze in his direction.

Uh-oh. She'd never responded well to his bossiness.

"What does it matter to you?" She turned her back on him.

Hindsight was a look through the Hubble telescope. He should have said it in a different way.

"I plan to protect you." He moved in front of her.

The old familiar smirk appeared, tugging at the corners of her pouty lips. She tilted her head, chin raised in defiance. Oh, the way those beautiful brown eyes turned almost black. He'd provoked this same response over and over again during their childhood years just to watch the tantalizing metamorphosis, but not this time.

He lifted one eyebrow at her expression. "What was that for? You don't think I care enough to make sure no harm comes to you?"

"I haven't thought much about it."

Quentin closed his eyes and began to count down from twenty then changed his mind. *One hundred, ninety-nine, ninety-eight.*

"What changed, Hoot?"

He opened his eyes. "Nothing's changed."

She shook her head. "You never protected me from Laurel's little games or Tabitha Cowart's wicked tongue. Why now?"

"We're not kids anymore. The fear in your eyes tells me this is more than child's play."

"But traces of childhood always remain with you. And what Laurel did and what Tabitha said were a lot more serious than childish bullying."

He heaved a deep breath and let it out slowly. He'd expect Laurel to hold a grudge this long. After all, she was Agatha's daughter. But Willow had been raised by Granny, a saint who never held anything against anyone. Granny would utter a sarcastic come back then go on with life. Willow might have inherited the older woman's wit, but she sunk her teeth into a grievance like a bulldog did its prey. "Why the tape, Scrappy?"

She frowned. "A little trick a detective in New York taught me. If someone comes through the door while you're gone, you'll find the tape loose or broken. I don't think he came inside, though."

"Who? Is there a crazed ex-boyfriend lurking around frightening you?"

If she said yes, it might kill him.

"It'd be pretty hard for me to have a boyfriend when I've never had a friend."

What was that supposed to mean? He was her friend. Had always been her friend, even when she'd lied to him. Walked away from him. Taken his heart with her to New York City. "It's been a very long day, and I suspect it's going to be even longer. Now, no more stalling. Tell me who has you so frightened."

"I don't know." She unloaded the laptop bag from her shoulder onto the table and opened it. "Give me a second. I'll show you."

Quentin left her in the kitchen while he made a thorough investigation of the house. As he walked back up the basement stairs, another bolt of lightning cut the gloom, the forks visible through the living room windows. The atmospheric light rippled on and on. Seconds later, an earsplitting thunderclap followed. The house shuddered around them.

Willow screeched.

"Hey, hey, hey. You're fine." He rounded the corner and found her sitting before her open computer at the dining table.

A sheepish grin appeared on her face. "Sorry."

She stood, beckoning him to take the chair she vacated. "Here. Look at these."

Her mailbox was filled with a number of e-mails, all entitled *I See You.* He opened one and saw a picture of Willow as she walked along a sidewalk in town. He clicked another one. She was standing in line at the Manna from Heaven. Another one showed her walking down the street with Annie Appleton. He opened the last one: Willow sitting at a table in the bookstore, stark fear lining the features of her face. He rubbed his forehead. "What's this about? Who's taking these?" He looked up.

She shook her head. "I don't know who or why. When I called the police in New York, the paparazzi were alerted almost immediately. This guy—this person—he broke into my apartment." She clicked open another e-mail. "He trashed the place and sent these to me as a surprise. A New York City detective helped me dodge the paparazzi. He showed me the tape trick."

Quentin scrolled through each e-mail, finding picture after picture of Willow. As he searched, a chime sounded announcing new mail. Three more e-mails appeared in her inbox, all with the same subject line. He opened them without asking her permission. "What kind of sick freak is this? Here's one of me walking from my house to yours, another one of us walking from your car to the porch, and one of us at your door." Quentin stood, knocking the chair over in his anger.

Willow flinched.

"We have to call Sheriff Dixon. This guy's out there right now, stalking you." He moved toward her, arms open to pull her into his embrace, but she skirted away from him, hands raised.

He allowed her space.

"Don't you see? I can't call the sheriff. The tabloids will hear about it. A media circus will descend upon this town. I slipped up with the detectives in New York, and the paparazzi came pouring out of the woodwork. That's the only reason why I came here. I thought I could get away from this guy. And the media."

The truth hit him hard. She wouldn't have come home except for a demented stalker threatening her. "I'd rather have a circus than to have you living in fear."

She straightened, and he could almost see her resolve harden. "You haven't lived it like I have." She moved even further away from him.

"The fear or the circus?" he challenged.

She started to speak but clamped her mouth shut.

"The fear or the circus, Willow? What haven't I lived?"

"You don't know what it's like." Her words flowed with her quick outtake of breath.

"Yes, I do. I lived them both," he said.

Her cast-iron stare fell upon him, and the hatred he imagined behind it would have knocked him over if his own anger hadn't already reached the boiling point.

"What?" He drew close to her. "You don't think I feared for you when the lie you kept all those years exploded in your face. Those maggots camped out at the foot of the hill until Sheriff Dixon pushed them back as far as he could. I was there when Granny clutched her chest and fell to the ground. I'm the one who tried to resuscitate her. The one who held you to keep you from going into shock. All I wanted was a chance. One chance."

As badly as he desired to reclaim the words, they released like feathers in the wind. He turned away. Willow didn't need the pieces of his heart handed to her on a silver platter. She needed his protection.

Yet, his words seemed to give her strength. "A chance? For what?" Her height matched his as she straightened. "I gave you every opportunity, and you never took a one. You made me feel unimportant. Out of your league. You found other friends. You left me behind for Laurel and Tabitha and never thought of inviting me along. Even Darrell Jacobs got to be a part of your crowd. But not me." She pushed past him into the living room.

Couldn't she see the truth of their pasts through the jumbled roots of pain, grief, and bitterness? He was talking about the day their lives all changed, and she wanted to discuss high school peer groups. Okay. He'd swim in that direction. Anything was better than having them swim apart. "I left you behind? You let me believe the lies every other person in town believed. I thought I meant more to you than that. You were my best friend. I trusted you with everything, and all the sudden you walked away from me, leaving me standing there like a fool wondering what I'd done. Tell me, Willow. What did I do?"

"Get out of my house, Quentin McPheron. This was a bad idea. Get out."

The waters he was swimming in began to spin like a whirlpool, taking him away instead of toward her. He wasn't going down without a fight. "Not until you call the sheriff. He can put a guard around the house."

"And somehow every miscreant from tabloid world will descend upon me. I have nowhere else to go. Don't you see? Having the press here will make it easier for him to hide."

"This person is dangerous, Willow. You have to get rid of him."

"I asked you to leave."

Should he pick up the phone and dial the sheriff or pull her into his arms?

"Get out!" she yelled.

"I don't want to leave you with that nut job out there."

"And I don't want you here."

He moved toward the door but gave her one last look. "Let me call Robert."

"Uncle Robert wouldn't lift a hand to help me."

"People change, Scrappy, and if you weren't so entangled in your bitterness, you might realize there are people in Amazing Grace who care for you. I can't stay here with you, but Robert can."

She stepped back as if his words had gut punched her in the same way he'd wanted to strike Cooper Goodyear earlier in the day.

She recovered, her smirk finding its way back onto her face and into her posture. "You're right, Hoot. You can't stay here. I'd never let it happen."

"Neither would I."

"Oh." She pressed her lips into a straight line.

He'd hurt her with words meant more for his benefit than hers, but damaging just the same.

"Nothing has changed between us." She opened her front door. "I'll never be good enough for you. Why don't you find Laurel and Tabitha and go have a good time?"

"Laurel isn't like that anymore."

"Then go find Tabitha. I'm sure she'd love to hear I'm home. She never ran out of jokes about me, did she?"

"Yeah, Willow, she did run out of things to say about you—on the night she died eight years ago. Of course, you wouldn't know about it because you never cared enough to call home."

"Home?" she screamed. "You call this home? This place represents nothing but lies. Everything I ever dreamed about my—my father ..." She stopped for a moment, her chin trembling.

He waited for her to gain control.

Willow's knuckles turned white against her hold on the door. "My father was supposed to be Ted, this adventurous guy who set off for parts unknown, grieving for my mother who died giving birth to me. I had a mental picture of her. She was a beautiful princess. And Ted, he was the most handsome man in the world." Her voice softened until it became a light whisper. "And one day he would remember me and come home because he loved me." She stared at him with a face void of tears. "This is not my home. My father wasn't Ted, and my mother—she's no princess."

Before the press had shown up at the door, Willow hadn't known the truth about her parents. They'd both learned on the same day, at the same hour, when they'd returned home that Saturday morning after graduation to find the first of many reporters on her front lawn. He'd been such a fool not to realize.

He reached for her, but she pushed him away with both hands. "Now, are you satisfied? I never told you because I didn't know the truth—not until that endless stream of reporters and cameramen showed up here and took my life away from me. And my father—the one I wanted so badly to love me—he's still sitting in the land of fairytales with the wicked witch who gave birth to me. They're both liars, and I try, Hoot, but I can't love them. I will never love them."

"And me?"

"You left me alone, and when I needed your comfort, you were with Laurel and Tabitha."

Somehow she tied everything back to high school. Why couldn't she see past it to him? He was standing here in front of her. Now. Ready to do anything to take her pain away. He'd even pretend she had nothing to do with their estrangement. "If I could go back and change everything between us ... those last two years, I would. You wanted me as badly as I wanted you." He was a babbling fool, and the confusion on her face told him so.

She cocked her head and the smirk returned. Her mask. "Yeah, that makes sense. Be honest, Hoot. You never wanted me. Not like that."

She shoved him hard, and Quentin found himself standing on the front porch. The door slammed in his face.

"That's right. Kick me out of your life. It's not the first time. But it is the first time you've kicked me out with a psycho somewhere around."

The lights went out.

"Not a smart move. Ever seen *Friday the 13th*? Willow, it's Friday and we live on a lake."

The rain would be here soon. LeBlanc wanted Willow to see him—her boyfriend, too. She'd moved quick, hooking up with the neighbor guy. An old friend, he'd learned from Red's gossip inside her little bakery. Willow was quick, yeah. Easy, no. She'd sure kicked Boyfriend's butt right out of her house. From the sound of her voice, they'd had a whopper of an argument. Good. He didn't need Boyfriend getting in his way.

In all the months LeBlanc had followed her in New York, she'd been pretty much a recluse. Here she seemed at home. Even her yelling at Boyfriend seemed a little more normal to LeBlanc than all those hours she spent in self-imposed solitude.

He felt for her sometimes, wondered what kept her at a distance. Maybe he'd ask her before he killed her.

Now, though, her little circle of friends and family were becoming a nuisance. Not what he expected when he forced her back to the isolation of the lake where he planned to put his plan of terror into action, get the most for his money.

Boyfriend tromped over to his house. Too bad, son. No kiss for you tonight.

The girl didn't like to think of herself as trusting, but this afternoon wasn't the first time LeBlanc managed to get close enough to wrap his arms around her neck and choke the life out of her. He needed help so she'd been safe enough, but if he hadn't required the assistance of another, he might have done what he thought about doing to her so often over the last month. That wasn't his job though. He needed to follow the plan. The pay was good, and he wanted to continue to reap the benefits while delaying the inevitable. Still, if he didn't get Willow to react soon, the pay would cease.

LeBlanc liked her tense, liked seeing the blood drain from her face. Her fear excited him. Soon, it would drive him to do what he did to all the others. He toyed with them all as long as he could. Still like a cat with a mouse, the enticement would eventually overwhelm him, and he'd pounce, snatching the life from his prey. He hated ending the game, but he wouldn't live with the regret for too long. There was always a new mouse waiting for his trap. But first he had to do what he'd been paid to do—get the paparazzi involved. He delayed on purpose, though. Willow thought they were on to her, but not yet. Not until he was ready. He liked this game too much.

A door slammed, and LeBlanc looked up from his hiding place beside the bending willow. He'd laugh if the wind wouldn't carry the sound.

Boyfriend stomped back across the yard carrying a bundle. Maybe Willow hadn't thrown him out. Maybe Boyfriend was smoother than he thought. Maybe Boyfriend went to get his overnight bag.

He peered closer. Boyfriend carried a shotgun. So she told him. Knowing her the way he did, he thought she'd keep it all to herself. Sure, she'd told her old man, but all indications were Willow wasn't too concerned—at least until he trashed her apartment. The plan was genius—up the ante, get her here right where he'd wanted her all along—and she never saw it coming, not the whole thing.

What was Boyfriend doing now? Sleeping on the porch? He gave a brief chuckle but ducked as lightning split the sky. An immediate boom followed.

Boyfriend was a hapless hero. In the end, he would lose her. Permanently.

LeBlanc moved from the shadows to stand by the willow tree. Weeping Willow. Well, she wouldn't weep for long.

LeBlanc looked to the sky, daring the heavens to strike. He opened his cell phone and searched for the right number. Give it a minute, and he'd hit dial and further rock Willow's world.

With a light footfall, Quentin moved back up the porch steps, his rifle in one hand and a pillow and sleeping bag in the other. He might not be able to sleep inside, but he could sure make himself at home on Willow's porch. Sitting against the wall, he bumped the butt of the gun against the floor and prayed he had not frightened her.

Stubborn. Insecure. Bewildering. Maddening. She'd always been those things to him, but he would protect her with his life. He straightened the sleeping bag then placed the pillow behind him against the wall. The shotgun he kept at his side.

He'd been angry when she refused to call Sheriff Dixon. Willow was right, of course. Suzanne Scott's newest movie was in production, and the tabloids would feast on Willow's fear. Just whose attention was Willow's stalker out to get? Was it Willow or her actress mother?

Quentin stared out into the darkness. Shadows danced with the leaves. His muscles tightened. No rain yet, but lightning skidded across the skies above the lake waters. He blinked as another strand illuminated the sky. Was that a shadow near the old willow? Leaning forward, he narrowed his eyes and continued to peer down at the lake. Nothing but the tree limbs moved. The lightning flickering across the sky had played tricks on him.

Still, the pictures Willow's stalker shot of her were at a range to afford deadly accuracy if aiming with a gun and not a camera. And the pictures of him with her. The coward hid in the woods, not brave enough to face them.

His antique ringtone jarred him in the darkness. He yanked the phone from his pocket and flicked it open. "Hello," he whispered.

No answer.

He ended the call and checked his call history. The area code on the top of the list was unfamiliar to him. Probably a wrong number.

The front door opened, and Willow peeked outside.

He looked up at her and offered her a smile. He couldn't help it.

She was adorable wrapped in her old terrycloth robe, her brown hair falling in waves over her shoulders. He was sure if he could see her brown eyes in the dim light they'd be red-rimmed with tears. She never looked more beautiful to him.

She took a deep breath and let it out. "I'm sorry, Hoot."

"Me, too, Scrappy. Stay inside, okay." He didn't trust himself to stand. He'd never be able to protect her. Not only from the stalker, but from his decade old desires.

His phone rang again, and he answered it. "Yeah."

"No matter what you do, you won't be able to protect her. Willow Thomas belongs to me."

"Who is this? Threatening Willow isn't something you want to do with me, buddy."

The caller disconnected.

Lightning again skidded across the sky, giving several long seconds of illumination. Someone stepped from behind the willow, and Quentin would bet he'd just lowered a cell phone.

Quentin jumped to his feet. "Get inside. Lock the door. Don't come out." He tossed her his cell phone and jumped from the porch, rifle in hand.

The figure sprinted up the road. A bolt of lightning shot downward, and the boom was immediate. The person ducked but not Quentin.

He ran forward until he collided with a living, breathing barrier.

"Oomph." The man bounced backward, recovering before falling on his backside.

"Bear." Quentin lifted his rifle. Ignoring the human wall he'd struck, he took aim at the other person running down the road.

"He's out of range, boy." The man put his hand on the gun and pushed the barrel down. "All you'll do is stir up the wildlife."

"You." Willow ran toward them. With rock-solid blows, she pounded against Bear's broad shoulders. "Why are you doing this to me? Who are you? What do you want from me?"

"Willow." Quentin pushed himself between her and the man who had not moved despite the pummeling. Quentin took a few blows himself before he caught her wrists in his hands. "Listen to me. Bear isn't the same person I saw. There's someone else. I know this man. He hasn't been in New York with you. Scott lets him rent the old cabin. Bear maintains it for you."

She leaned forward, her body losing the fierce tension he'd felt in her onslaught of Bear.

He touched his forehead against hers glad the fight had gone from her. "He's a good guy. I promise."

Willow backed away, pulling from his grasp. Her gaze darted between both of them, and Quentin hated the mistrust he saw there. "I don't believe you. I saw him in town after we found the envelope."

"Yes, you did." Bear rubbed his bearded face. "I'm sorry I didn't stick around. If I knew you wanted an introduction, I'd have waited for Quentin to make one. You seemed a little preoccupied at the time, wallowing on the ground and all."

Willow ignored Bear's lighthearted taunt—a side of the man Quentin wasn't used to seeing.

"You look familiar. I know you. We've met."

"No, Willow. You've never met me," Bear insisted.

"What's your name?"

"His name is Bear." Quentin answered for him.

"What's your last name?"

If Willow got that out of him, she'd be doing better than most. No one in town knew his name, and Bear's demeanor never left room for the question.

"Just Bear," the older man said.

"Do you have a cell phone on you?"

"Why?" Quentin asked.

Without hesitation, Bear pulled his phone from his pants pocket. Willow held out her hand, and he placed it there. She fumbled with it for a second then handed it back. She dug into her jeans pocket, pulled out the phone Quentin had thrown to her and pushed some buttons before turning it for both of them to see. "Area code 646."

Quentin took it from her hand. She always was smarter than him. "I don't understand."

"Your friend here is in the clear. He has a local number. The person who called you is New York cellular, Hoot. It's the same area code as my phone. Whoever it is called me this morning. He didn't say anything. I thought it was Jeffrey."

And who was this Jeffrey? He'd have to find out later, but now, he had more important matters at hand. "Willow, how could a stranger get my number?"

Willow's only answer was to retreat to the porch.

"I don't know what's going on." Bear kept his voice low. "But I don't like people on this lake that got no business being here."

"Did you get a good look at him?" Quentin asked. "How'd you know he was here?"

"I don't guess he knew I live in the cabin. I was sitting on my porch enjoying the cool evening. I saw headlights coming along the road just a while after you two passed. The car drove up, did a "Y" at the pass, and drove back down just a bit before turning off his lights. After awhile I could see him make his way down near the house. I wanted to give a wait and see what he had on his mind. I crept through the woods and watched him, making sure you two were out of harm. When you started out after him, I thought I'd head him off at the pass. You were a little too quick, cut into my path, and we collided."

"Sorry, man. I didn't see you."

Large drops of rain began to pelt them.

"Can we meet in the morning to compare more notes?" Quentin asked.

Bear stared back at the house where Willow waited on the porch. "Not the way I expected this meeting to happen." He lumbered off.

The older man was strange, but he was likeable.

"Quentin," Bear turned, "you leave that porch tonight, I'll shoot you myself."

Quentin nodded. "Fair enough."

"It's more than fair. Hoot, huh?"

"'Cause she doesn't give a *hoot* about me." Quentin smirked.

"That gal loves you, boy. Don't think she doesn't." Like Sasquatch sneaking back into the dense forest, Bear disappeared into the woods between Willow's home and his cabin.

CHAPTER SIX

Quentin stretched stiff limbs and pushed to his feet. If he planned to sleep on Willow's porch another night, he needed an air mattress to keep his bones from grinding against the unforgiving wooden floor.

He surveyed the surrounding property, though he hadn't slept soundly at all. He'd even heard Bear's shoes crunching against the rocks on the dirt road.

Quentin shook off his blanket and walked the worn path down to the lake. At least the rain had stopped, leaving a fresh scent in the chilly morning air. "Morning. You could have gotten me up."

"Morning." The older man held up a coffee cup in salute. "I wanted to meet with the Lord before I met with you." Bear tossed the dregs of his coffee into the water and peered out at the mist rising on the lake. His graying hair contrasted with the darkness of his beard, belying the man's age. Quentin didn't think him more than fifty-five.

"Why don't you tell me what you know?" Bear crossed his arms over his chest, coffee cup still in hand

"Funny, I was going to ask you the same." They were marking their territory here, and somehow Quentin didn't think Willow would be happy about it.

"I told you what I knew last night." Bear pointed up the road. "The guy turned his car around, left it up the road like he wanted a clean escape. You don't park your car on a one-lane road if you're expecting someone to travel up it. He knew you two were already here. I betcha he's been here before. Now, tell me what he wants."

Quentin once thought his father the most formidable man
he'd ever known. That was before he stood toe to toe with
Bear's stirring anger.

"This guy is stalking Willow. I don't know who he is or
why he's crawled out from under his rock. Maybe because her
parents are famous. A news story broke a few years back,
shoving Willow into the spotlight for a while."

Bear sucked in a deep breath and exhaled with a low
rumble. He stared back out at the lake, visibly unhappy. "Are
you sure it's related to her parents?"

"I don't know what else it could be."

"The Thomas boys married above themselves, and they
produced some good-looking little girls. She might have
attracted her own type of psycho."

"I don't like you speaking about them like that."

"The Thomas boys or their daughters?"

"You're too old to be looking at Willow or Laurel."

Bear moved toward him, and despite the man's obvious
displeasure, Quentin stayed his ground.

A smile replaced the frown Bear wore. "I appreciate what
you're saying. Believe me, son. I'm not some dirty old man."

"How do you know the Thomas family other than renting
from them?"

Bear glanced out over the waters again before staring back
toward the house. "We have a long history, Quentin. Don't
worry about it. Just know we're in this together."

"After last night, I doubt this guy will come snooping
around again, at least not in such obvious fashion. He wanted
our attention. Now he's got more than he bargained for."

"Be careful. Don't let your guard down."

Quentin nodded. "I'm heading to town in a bit to get some
bolt locks. She needs more security on her house. Will you
keep a look out?"

"Of course."

"Can I ask you something?" Quentin kept one foot on the single step to the dock and another on the dewy ground, keeping space between him and Bear. He'd be ready to dodge Bear if the older man chose to charge him after his question.

"Go ahead."

"Agatha Thomas is a demanding harpy, and Suzanne Scott is a selfish witch. How do you figure the Thomas men married above themselves?"

Bear half-grumbled, half-chuckled. "Both women are pretty smart. They know how to keep their men in line, and in their day, they were the most beautiful women I've ever known."

Quentin laughed. "Agatha? Beautiful?"

"Son, in her day, every man in this town wanted a date with her. You think Suzanne's got the looks? She had nothing on Aggie. Suzanne had a bit more spunk, a lot more audacity, and she did something no one else dared."

"What's that?"

"She took Aggie's dreams away from her. Now, would you want to be the one who did that?"

"Not on your life." Quentin smiled. "You've been around that long, huh?"

"Long enough to know I escaped disaster with both of them. I stepped aside and let the trains collide with Scott and Robert. At least one of them Thomas boys has forgiven me. The other one—he hasn't figured out what a wreck of a life he's living."

Quentin took in Bear's words, letting them draw a picture in his brain. His eyes widened. "You're not Ted?"

Bear snapped his gaze toward him. "I'm not anyone, boy. Do you understand?"

Quentin stomped away then turned. "If you'd heard what Willow said about Ted last night, and if you are him, you'd tell her. She spent her life thinking he was her father. Scott hasn't been much of a dad to her."

"She's Scott's girl. She doesn't need anyone else playing Daddy to her."

"Willow doesn't expect that."

"So what does she expect from Ted?"

Quentin raised his arms then let them fall back to his side. "Exactly what she's expected from everyone in her life and has never gotten." He leveled Bear with his most serious gaze. "The truth."

Willow stood in Granny's room. She intended to move some things around and make it her studio. Granny's old desk would serve as her workstation, but it was parked in the middle of the bay windows, a space that begged for an easel. Still, Granny's essence hadn't left her lifelong home. And nowhere else in the house did grief wrap around Willow like one of the old shawls Granny had worn to church each Sunday.

Willow picked up the heart-shaped earring holder from the dresser. She'd given it to her grandmother on their tenth Christmas together. Granny had opened it moments before Uncle Robert and his family had arrived, declaring the simple gift to be one of her most precious ever.

That Christmas, Laurel and her family gifted Granny with a beautifully crafted opal necklace that represented Laurel's birth date. Willow always suspected Granny found it much more precious than the inexpensive dresser adornment she'd given her, but Granny never said so. And Willow never saw Granny wear the opal necklace.

Something rattled inside the glass heart. Willow opened the little door and peered at an elegant diamond ring. Granny didn't wear rings, and Willow hadn't seen this one before.

Might it be her wedding ring from Grandpa Arnie? He'd died long before Willow's birth, but she knew Granny missed him every day.

Lifting the ring, Willow found it attached to the chain of the opal necklace. A scrap of paper lay under the jewelry. Willow removed the paper before placing the heart and its other contents back on the dresser. She opened the note.

A bittersweet ache squeezed her heart when she recognized the beloved handwriting. "Dear Lord," Granny had written, "I pray my granddaughters learn that, like this case and this necklace, they complement each other. Both are the finishing touches on the world you've given to me. One is no more important than the other, because without either, I'd be less than what I am."

"Oh, Granny." Willow sat hard upon Granny's bed, fighting the constriction in her throat. "Why couldn't you just sit us down and tell us?"

A soft knock at the front door had Willow scurrying to cram everything back inside the jewelry box. With caution hedging every step, she tiptoed down the stairs and peeped around the corner. A tiny sigh escaped when she saw the visitor through the glass in the door.

"Granny, you're pushing." She spoke to a memory as she unlocked the door.

"Willow." Laurel held a carrier containing two cups of coffee and a small bag in one hand. In the other she carried a mailing tube. "Peace offering."

Willow motioned Laurel inside, noticing Hoot's sleeping bag and pillow were gone. She hadn't checked on him this morning.

Laurel looked about the room. "Granny still lingers here, doesn't she?"

Willow nodded and led her cousin to the kitchen where she pulled out a chair and sat down. The tube in Laurel's hand intrigued her, but Willow pressed her lips together. She wouldn't give her cousin the satisfaction of asking about it.

Laurel sat also, placing the cylinder on the floor and the coffees and bag on the table. She opened the sack and pulled a napkin from the holder. "I brought you a muffin from Appleton's."

Willow raised her brow. "Afraid your mother would poison me if she knew you were coming here?"

Laurel laughed and held up one cup and put it in front of Willow. "The coffee is from Manna."

"Should I drink it?"

"Momma wasn't there when I poured it." Laurel took a sip of her own.

"I repeat. Should I drink it?"

Laurel didn't laugh. Instead, she placed her own cup carefully on the table in front of her and leaned forward. "Willow, I'll come right on out and say what's needed saying since …" She leaned back. "You know, I don't even know when it all started with us."

"What?" Willow wanted no part in Laurel's schemes, especially since she usually came out on the short end of them.

"The jealousy."

"You and your perfect home? You were jealous of me?" Willow shook her head.

"Okay, you're stretching it there. Perfect home with Agatha Thomas?"

Willow's lips twitched before she gave in to the involuntary smile. She quelled the unexpected humor only by opening the lid on the cup and blowing on the steaming liquid to cool it down. "Okay. I'll give you that one, but I had nothing that could possibly make you jealous."

"You had Granny."

Willow turned her coffee cup so the Manna logo faced her. Five minutes earlier, she'd actually believed Laurel was the one most loved.

"Granny was my safe harbor. But she was your home."

Willow saw Laurel's point and acquiesced with a terse nod, not wanting to give in too much. "Then I guess I owe you an apology as well. You know, I hated it when you stayed over."

"Well, I certainly didn't make it easy on you. Remember at Christmas? Granny always bought us the same thing, only in different colors. If she bought us a nightgown, yours was blue and mine was pink. No matter what color she gave me, I wanted the one you got. I didn't dare say anything to Granny because it would hurt her feelings."

Willow's face burned. "That's funny. I always wanted what you had."

"Well, if we hadn't outgrown them, we could switch now, couldn't we?" Laurel reached across the table and touched Willow's hand.

Willow pulled away. Laurel would have to offer more than a confession to gain her confidence.

"I know you don't trust me, but things have happened since you left. I'm not the same person."

"I'm sorry about Tabitha." The lie pricked her.

"I know she was mean to you, but that was my fault, too. She fed off my feelings, teasing and making fun of you because that's what I did."

"I don't care about Tabitha, Laurel. For goodness sakes, that was high school." The lies racked up, leaving a sour taste in her mouth.

"I can't apologize for my dead friend, but I am truly sorry for what I did to your friendship with Quentin. I'm so sorry the wall I wedged between the two of you kept me out of your life as well. Losing Tabitha and the loneliness that came with it made me realize what I'd done to you."

"Hey, don't sweat it. If Quentin wanted a relationship with me, he would have climbed the wall, don't you think?"

Laurel took another sip of her coffee again. "I lied to Quentin to keep him away from you. I kept him preoccupied with Tabitha and me."

"He still chose to believe you." Willow swallowed a big gulp of her own coffee. The hot liquid burned her throat on the way down. Tears stung her eyes as she fought to keep from choking. How hot would the stuff have been if she drank it in the store? Agatha apparently didn't care about lawsuits, and Uncle Robert was a lawyer.

"You're letting me off way too easy, Willow. You know, there's only one thing I did to you that I'm not ashamed of. If I had to do it all over again, I'd still trade out Granny's picture and put Quentin's in its place at the art fair. But Quentin was not happy with me."

Willow swallowed again and raised her hand requesting her cousin wait.

"Are you okay?" Laurel leaned over and slapped Willow's back.

Willow coughed a few more times and brushed off her cousin's aid. "He told me," she choked the words out.

Laurel leaned down and picked up the tube.

Willow's heart quickened. She coughed one last time to clear her throat and hide her anxiety. Had Laurel kept the picture of Quentin all these years? Was she finally going to see it again? None of her attempts to duplicate the drawing came out as perfect as the original. She'd give anything to hold it in her hands, see the handsome likeness—the one she could never recapture to her satisfaction.

"This doesn't belong to me." Laurel opened the tube and gently shook it. The ends of the scrolled paper slid part way out. With a careful, almost reverent touch, Laurel pulled it from the container and allowed the drawing to unroll.

With the disappointment came guilt. The picture of Granny, the one Laurel had replaced with Quentin's picture. Willow pushed her chair back and rose from her seat.

Granny.

She missed her so much.

Moving to the kitchen window, she watched a chipmunk run along the back deck, jump onto a bird feeder, and dig in the food—morsels of sunflower seed and fennel that she hadn't placed there. Beyond the deck, grass had grown over the area where Granny always planted her garden—tomatoes, beans, cabbage, corn, watermelon, and snow peas. The garden was gone now, a victim of Granny's absence. Unable to stand the memories, Willow turned back to face her cousin and leaned against the counter.

Laurel's hands were shaking, the picture fluttering as though in a breeze. "Whenever I get to missing her too much, I pull out your drawing and see her watching over us like she did when she was alive, sitting on the front porch, her hands never idle, while we romped and played in the yard."

"You took it because you wanted the picture of Granny and not because you wanted to embarrass me in front of Quentin?"

"I wish I could say that was the only reason, but you already know I'm more than capable of carrying out two devious plans at the same time. I wanted to embarrass you, true. But even more than that, I wanted this picture."

Laurel's shoulders slumped and the bottom of the picture touched the hardwood floor. "I loved her so much, and I was beginning to see her slow down. You probably didn't notice because you were around her every day. I justified the theft by telling myself you could make the picture so lifelike because you had her with you. I told myself the picture would allow me to see her whenever I wanted."

Willow pushed away from the counter. When she'd drawn Granny's picture, she'd forgotten Laurel had played alongside Quentin and her. They laughed and sang together as young children, the best of friends. When had the jealousy completely torn them apart?

Willow reached for the portrait, taking in the essence of Granny's nature—a woman larger than life living a small existence in the place where she'd been raised. In the picture, Granny sat on the porch with one of her crocheted afghans over her lap and a large stainless steel bowl sitting on top of the afghan. Beside her was an old cardboard box she'd carted from the local grocery. The irony of the picture was the box had once contained cans of store-bought beans, and as Granny peered over her surroundings, she was shelling her own garden-grown pole beans she'd placed into the box.

With great care, Willow rolled up the drawing. "You came here with a peace offering. Now, I'm offering you mine." She slipped it into the container and pushed it toward her cousin.

Laurel reached to hug Willow, but Willow backed away. After a moment of hesitation, Laurel took the drawing.

"Calling a truce doesn't mean we're best friends, you know."

Laurel straightened. "No, I guess it doesn't, but maybe it's a start."

"And I won't stop watching my back—not for a long, long time. I can't forget that easily."

"Well, I live with someone else whose favor I'm trying to win back. Again, Willow, I'm sorry for everything."

"I'm fine. I don't need your pity, and I don't need your apologies."

"Willow Jade Thomas, you are so much like my momma that if you don't watch out, you're going to wind up with a pinched face and no friends. You're both unforgiving. Too hard. Be careful or the bitter young woman I see will turn into a bitter old maid."

Willow started to speak, but Laurel got into her face. "Besides, I need your friendship."

"What?" Willow edged away from her, still expecting to see the evil, demented plans hidden in her cousin's features. She saw only peace and a gleam in her cousin's eyes.

"I'm not in love with Quentin McPheron anymore. He never got over you. I'm hoping you'll give me lessons on dealing with geeks, since you've always been one."

"What?" Willow shook her head. She was never a nerd. Was she?

"I'm in love with a geek, and I haven't had any luck convincing him of it. I need your help."

Willow covered her face with her hands, unable to stifle the burst of laughter.

"So, will you help me?" Laurel tilted her head to one side.

"Who is this poor unsuspecting fellow?"

"He could do worse." Laurel laughed.

"Oh, no, he couldn't."

Laurel opened the door. "So, will you put aside all the bad blood between us and teach me to speak geek?"

Willow continued to revel in her hilarity. "Yeah, I guess I'll dust off my *Geekionary*."

"Good." Laurel leaned back in and gave Willow a peck on the cheek before she could dodge her again. "Thank you for Granny's picture. It means a lot to me." Laurel ran off to her car.

It meant a lot to Willow, too. Why did its value seem less before she gave it away? Before she saw the happiness it gave her fiercest enemy?

"I still hate you, you know." Willow whispered to the empty yard. She shook her head and closed the door, gingerly touching the place on her cheek where Laurel had given her the peck.

"Okay, Granny. Are you happy now? I met her halfway."

Willow, honey, halfway would be at the top of the hill, not at the bottom of your side of the mountain.

Willow leaned against the door and closed her eyes. How many times during their childhood had she and Laurel sat in timeout—after a good switch or two from a hickory stick—and how often had she heard Granny say those very words?

Perhaps she could climb up her side of the mountain—but only a little ways. Then, when Laurel knocked her back down, maybe the fall wouldn't hurt as much.

CHAPTER SEVEN

Traffic lined Main Street, the light at the corner stopping the cars intermittently. Quentin fought his rising anxiety with each tap of the brake. The only parking space he could find was a block from The Carpenter's Son Hardware and right outside Agatha Thomas's back door. Closing his car door, he glanced behind Manna to see Agatha in a tense conversation with Cooper Goodyear.

Quentin kept an eye on them. Both stopped their argument to glare as he passed on the sidewalk alongside Agatha's bakery.

A crowd comprised mostly of sweaty senior citizens had already gathered at the corner by the time he reached the intersection. Quentin knew most of them. They liked to meet at the bottom of the hill and then hike the circuit around the historic district for their daily exercise. A more committed lot he'd never seen.

Chirp—Chirp—Chirp. The "jaywalk" bird gave its permission for them to cross. Like robots marching in unison, the golden agers started their ascent. Quentin held his position in the back, keeping his gait deliberately slow. He knew even after years of these vigorous daily workouts, many of the walkers struggled up the steep grade. He wouldn't hurt their feelings for the world by zipping by them like a rangy high school kid. Besides, seeing Agatha and Cooper engaged in conversation back there, made his antennae twitch. What were the two long-time enemies fighting about now?

"Get out of my face, Cooper Goodyear. I've had enough of you for a lifetime." Agatha's shrill hatred cut the morning air. "As far as I'm concerned, you haven't lost enough for what you did to my family."

"I've given you more than enough opportunity to back off, Agatha." Goodyear's voice boomed.

The crowd turned. Obviously, he wasn't the only one interested in this meeting of bitter minds.

"It's okay, folks. Just the old rivalry between the two of them." Quentin stood his ground, assuring they'd continue on their merry cardiac-workout way. All Agatha needed was an audience. Venom would shoot from her heart like a provoked cobra. As they continued on, he jogged to the back of Manna.

"With what you did to my family, you'll be lucky if I leave you with anything," Agatha continued.

"I lost my marriage. My son's grown soft as a result of it. Now, you're after my livelihood. One more rumor or lie about my business practices, Agatha, and I promise you—"

Quentin stepped into their sight and fixed Goodyear with a cold stare. "You'll promise what?"

"This doesn't concern you." Agatha jammed her hands on her ample hips.

Quentin blinked at her. Just once, couldn't she say, "I'm glad you're here."

"The battle ax and I are working out our difficulties. That black eye doesn't hurt enough? You want another?" Goodyear asked him.

"You won't throw a punch when someone can see it coming."

"One day, McPheron, I'll—"

"Don't say it Goodyear. You make threats all the time. Why not back down for once. You never follow through on the promises you make. A coward never does." Quentin planted his feet, ready to steel against any blow Goodyear would send his way, even though he believed fully in the man's cowardice.

The backdoor of Manna slammed shut. Quentin stared at the clicking deadbolt then looked back at his nemesis. "Agatha has suffered a lot of hurt in her life, some of it at your hands, and she'll never let you forget it. Why don't you just stay at your business across the street and never walk this way again. You'll make everyone happy."

"Get gone," Cooper demanded.

"If you think I'm going to turn my back on a coward like you, you're out of your mind."

Where did he go from here? Quentin had never stared a man down. Never had a reason. Would they be here for an hour or two, maybe three, before someone interrupted, or they grew hungry, or one of them threw the first punch?

"I've had enough of you." Cooper stomped off to his store.

Or the more cowardly of the two left.

That worked.

With Cooper safely out of sight, Quentin continued on his way. Passing by Manna's window, he waved at Agatha who stood peering out. She frowned and moved away.

How could Bear see beauty in Agatha Thomas? She was always frowning, angry and full of hate. Quentin couldn't remember the last time he'd seen her crack a smile. Heck, not even Michelangelo himself could pull a work of art out that cold stone.

At The Carpenter's Son Hardware, Quentin found the items he needed to protect Willow's home. When he left the store, Annie Appleton waved at him from the door of her shop. He checked the traffic and made his way across the street without the help of the jaywalk bird.

"Willow doing okay today?" She opened the door.

"I haven't seen her this morning. She was sleeping in, I guess."

"Well, Laurel stopped by. She bought some muffins and said she planned to see Willow. I know how those two are." Annie fussed with the papers on the counter with her trembling hands.

Quentin placed his hand over hers, feeling the frailty underneath his touch. "Things will be fine." His gaze lifted to the area where sandwiches and drinks were served and to the teenager behind the counter.

"Hired him this morning," Annie smiled. "He listed you as a reference. Told him that spoke volumes. Henry's been training him."

Denton Goodyear gave all his attention to Henry. Quentin hated to see the older couple get mixed up with Denton—well, not Dent—his father.

He made his way over to the food counter. Taking Willow a sandwich might get him back into her graces. Maybe Laurel had it right. Bribery might be the way to Willow's heart. Food had always worked before. "Hey."

Dent straightened. "Coach …?" He cast a weary glance in Annie's direction.

"Here's the deal. I'm okay with you using me as a reference any time, so long as you don't make me regret it. Understand?"

"Yes, sir."

"And did you explain you have an obligation as a leader of your team to attend football practice when it starts?"

"Yes, sir."

"You're a leader now, Dent." Quentin nodded. "I'm glad to see you working."

Did he imagine the three extra inches on Dent's height? Was the boy in need of that much affirmation? Cooper might blame Agatha's revenge for the loss of his family, but his own actions were the true cause. What little influence Cooper could have had on his son, he'd squandered.

"What can I get you?" Dent asked.

"I'll have two of those ham croissants and four of those chocolate chip brownies." One for Willow. Three for him—unless she gave ground. Then he'd divide them equally.

Dent hadn't moved, and Quentin looked to where the boy stared. Cooper had entered and was sauntering around the bookstore, giving an occasional look toward his son.

Quentin nodded to the boy. "Better do your work."

Dent wrapped and packaged the order into a delivery box. Quentin handed him his debit card and waited to sign the slip.

The teenager laid the debit receipt on the counter and handed Quentin a pen. "He's just angry because he heard Mom's got me going to church."

Sounded like Cooper. Jealous of anything standing in his way. Cooper wanted a strong bully of a son—a chip off the old already chopped block. With God standing in Cooper's way, Quentin prayed it would be impossible for the fool to ruin his son. "Your mom shouldn't get you to church. You should want it yourself." He signed the slip and handed it back.

"I didn't mean it like that. I like going. I did something last Sunday I thought I'd never do."

"Dent, fix your old man one of those *frou-frou* sandwiches." Cooper called from across the room. "One like the sissy in front of you ordered."

"I'm sorry." Dent lowered his head.

"Hey." Quentin got Dent's attention and gave him a smile he didn't feel. The boy wasn't to blame for his father's bullishness. "They are a little sissified, but don't tell Henry." He winked. "I better let you get busy." He stepped away.

"Coach?"

Quentin had made his way to the door when Dent called. Turning, he found the young man's gaze not on him but squarely upon his father.

"Coach," he repeated without looking away from Cooper. "I've been told a good leader is one that makes his followers fear him."

Father and son locked each other in a stare that reminded Quentin of two gunslingers in the dusty street at high noon.

The only other customer in the store—a stranger—tilted his head as if he awaited the answer.

Quentin smiled at the boy. "No, Dent, not the one who should lead your heart. Respect and fear are two different emotions, unless you're talking about your Heavenly Father. That fear is an awesome regard for what He's done for you."

Cooper slammed the book he'd been reviewing back onto the shelf. "Get my food now, son, if you know what's good for you."

Henry took a step away from the bookstore's cash register. Quentin cleared this throat as he leaned against the counter. Henry stopped. Dent served his father, took his money, and Cooper brushed by without incident.

"Have a good day, folks." Quentin waved on his way out the door. As he looked back in the window, the stranger offered him a nod.

LeBlanc pulled a book from the shelf and pretended to read.

Boyfriend wasn't a coward. That was for sure, and he didn't back away from his principles. LeBlanc would love to see the boy's father and Boyfriend go at it. Boyfriend had already been in some sort of scrap, judging by the black eye he sported—just as ugly today as it had been yesterday.

He'd hate to see the other guy. Boyfriend was in shape. Of course, the kid behind the counter called him Coach. He'd bet Boyfriend could run a mile quicker than any teenager. If that old man hadn't collided with Boyfriend last night, LeBlanc never would have outrun him.

Still, the rush of almost being caught remained with LeBlanc. Didn't hurt that Boyfriend was so close to him only moments ago and hadn't realized he'd been the one on the dock last night.

He put the book back on the shelf and moved to another spot. He needed to wait this one out. The old couple had to leave the room at some point. Then he'd talk to the boy.

The plan was a dicey one, but LeBlanc wanted maximum effect. The risk was worth it. He licked his lips. He wished he could see the relief turn to terror when Willow realized how close he'd been to her—closer than she thought he could ever get again. In New York, she'd stared him in the eyes. She'd talked to him. Even trusted him.

He picked up a biography on Ted Bundy and turned it over in his hand. What a guy. Bundy must have felt the same way while planning the crime, getting into the game, moving in for the kill. LeBlanc liked to toy with them more than Bundy, but in the end, they all ended up the same.

LeBlanc picked up the book and headed toward a table near the sandwich counter. Patting the inside pocket of his coat, he smiled. The boy would be a nice touch. Willow would never see it coming.

And LeBlanc gained an added bonus. Boyfriend knew the kid.

Willow had long since tired of arranging furniture only to drag it back. Granny always had a sense for what was right—Granny's Feng Shui—and her room was no exception.

In the end, she moved her belongings into the room and abandoned the idea of making Granny's sanctuary her studio.

She placed her laptop on Granny's desk by the window overlooking the lake. She'd have to find another location for her paints, pencils, and easel.

She opened the desk drawer to put her laptop cord inside. A small strip of paper caught her eyes. Taking a deep breath, she took it in her hands. Knowing Granny's habits, she'd probably find these all over the house.

She sat on the bed and opened the paper. "Lord, for my family, I pray you find them always busy, never idle, and forever looking to you." Willow laughed and shook her head. "So, she's the reason I don't rest unless I've been working hard. Thank you, Granny." She smiled and placed the paper back inside.

As for God, she ceased looking for Him the same day she stopped the search for her father. The reality of Scott was a far cry from her fantasy of the man she now knew was her uncle. The only real things she'd received from Granny were her home and the silver bracelet. Everything else was a lie.

Leaning back against the desk, she let her hand fall on her wrist. Her touch met bare skin, and she looked down. Granny's bracelet was missing. Willow fell to her knees, looking under the bed, beside the desk, anywhere it might have fallen. Not finding it, she jumped to her feet and started to trace her steps from Granny's room to her old room.

Bang Bang Bang.

Willow jumped at the clamor on her front door. "What now?" Her voice rose to an involuntary scream.

"Willow?" Quentin's worried tremor reached her.

"Hold on." She ran down the stairs, jumping from the third step to the ground floor, something she'd always done growing up in the house. She unlocked the door and threw it open.

Quentin held up an Appleton's snack box.

"What?" She raised her arms and let them fall. "Doesn't anyone think I can feed myself?"

"Everyone in town knows you can't cook. Granny could have written a book on your kitchen exploits. I haven't forgotten the chocolate chip cookies made with baking soda rather than baking powder." He scrunched his nose and stepped through the door without even a "how-do-you-do." Just like old times. "Lock the door, and let's eat. Ham sandwiches and chocolate chip brownies made with the appropriate ingredients."

Oh! She hated it when he bossed her around. Always had. But her stomach rumbled just then. Food or hunger. What kind of choice was that? She caved, closed the door, and locked it. Lagging behind him, she looked under the pillows on the couch and searched on the floor around the end tables and the coffee table.

"I bought some bolt locks, window braces, and a few other things to secure the place." Quentin didn't appear to notice her antics.

Not finding the bracelet, she gave up and went to get her purse on the kitchen counter. She pulled out her wallet. "How much do I owe you?"

"Nothing." He put down the food.

"For the lunch and the materials? How much?"

"It's a gift. Get over it."

Maybe he should get over her. Nothing was going to happen—just as he'd said last night, but she didn't remind him of his hurtful words. What good would it do? The stubborn, pigheaded …

She stopped her mental rant. The comparison Laurel drew of Willow's resemblance to Agatha hurt. She choked back her pride. "Thank you."

He turned and gave her his full-press stare.

Good, she'd gotten him off balance.

"Did you sleep okay?" He opened the box and dug inside.

She nodded. "And I felt safe with your friend Bear making himself visible from time to time. He's a little scary looking, but as long as he stays down by the road, I'm okay with it."

Quentin smiled, and knowing him the way she did, there was meaning behind the turn of his lips. She wouldn't give him the satisfaction of asking.

"How has your day been?"

Twenty questions. Okay. She'd play. "Pretty good up until a few minutes ago."

Quentin straightened. "Gee, thanks." He pulled the sandwiches from the bag.

Puzzled by his reaction, she frowned at him. Now what had him so testy? She replayed her words and huffed out a breath. "No. I didn't mean you're arrival. I lost Granny's bracelet." She moved to the cupboard then to the kitchen sink. "I have water, water, or more water. For variety, might I suggest a little ice water?"

"And for all your complaining, what would you do if Laurel and I hadn't decided to feed you?"

How did he know Laurel had visited? She'd ask, but it didn't really matter. "I'd find something." She wrinkled her nose at him.

"Mind if I say grace?" he asked.

"Go right ahead."

When Quentin bowed his head, she kept her eyes on him. Those dark eyelashes still caressed his cheeks when he closed his eyes. She couldn't look away.

"Lord, thank You for this food. Thank You for Willow's return. Father, we pray that You keep us safe, for no other arms are safer than Yours."

But Quentin's arms would be almost as safe. She cleared her throat, pulled out her chair, and sat.

"The Lord provides." Quentin lifted his leg over the short-backed chair and plunked down. "And He answers prayer, too. I've been praying for years for Him to bring your scraggly butt home."

"And He uses a stalker to do it."

Quentin leaned back in his seat, the front legs of the chair lifting then falling back to the floor. He gave a slight shake of his head.

"What now?" she asked.

His green eyes gazed so deep into hers, she thought he must see all the way to the depths of her soul.

Her heart jumped, seeming to fill her throat. Did he know how he affected her?

"I don't care who God used to bring you home. I'm just thankful He did."

Willow took a bite of her sandwich and swallowed hard, forcing it down past the lump in her throat. Eating in silence proved less painful than biting her tongue to keep from saying something she'd regret later. God always had a way of turning her words back around on her. Most often He used Granny, but Willow suspected God had passed the two-edged sword over to Quentin.

Quentin swallowed his sandwich in three bites and again leaned back in his chair watching her eat until she took the last bite and reached for her water.

Her bare wrist haunted her. She searched the tabletop before surveying the floor around her chair. "I don't know how I could lose it," she mumbled mostly to assure herself.

"Do you take it off before you shower or go to bed?" He gathered up the wrappings for the sandwiches and opened up the box. Tilting it toward her, he raised his brows up and down.

She reached inside for the goodies, coming out with two of the brownies. "Thanks." She bit into one.

A smile played at the corner of his lips.

"What's so funny?" she asked. A growing sense of irritation flared as it always did whenever he acted like he hid a secret. And he seemed to have a lot of those today.

"Not a thing." He picked out one of the two remaining brownies. "So, do you remember taking the bracelet off?" He bit into the treat.

"I never take it off."

"Maybe the clasp broke."

She'd accept that but only after she'd searched everywhere. If she couldn't find it, then she'd cry. Other than memories, Granny's bracelet was only one of two things she'd taken with her when she left Amazing Grace: the bracelet and the memory of Quentin's irritatingly wonderful smile.

"Do you remember the last time you had it on?"

Willow let the past few hours, then days, play through her mind. "I had it on in the hotel where I stopped on my way here. I remember looking at it when I arrived the other day because I'd brought it home."

"You were wearing it yesterday at Appletons."

Willow stared at him. Would he never cease to amaze her? "How do you remember?"

"I remember everything about you. Every time I see you."

"Okay, so does your photographic memory recall when it first noticed me without it?"

He narrowed his eyes and leaned closer to her. "You didn't have it on last night when you kicked me out of the house and left me outside with that psycho."

When could the bracelet have slipped from her arm? What had she done that would let it fall loose? Willow looked under Granny's bed for the fifth time then traced her steps back to her childhood room. She had already pulled every bit of clothing from the hangers and searched through pockets and any other possible place the bracelet might have caught. Could the treasure have fallen off when she carried her clothes from one closet to the other?

Agitation swirled inside her. Her skin crawled with the thought of losing something so precious. Granny had given her the bracelet the day before the tabloids broke the truth. Willow always imagined Granny wanted the bracelet to remind her she loved her no matter what.

And Willow lost it.

Without finding it, she trounced back into Granny's room and gave one last look in the closet. Containers on the floor could have hidden the jewelry if it had slipped off her wrist. She bent to her knees and tugged out the three boxes.

The first one held yarn, balls of red, green, yellow—every color imaginable. Willow ran her finger over them. Granny always took a bag with her crochet needles and a ball or two of yarn with her everywhere she went. Her hands were never idle whether in her garden or with her spare time.

Willow snapped the lid back on and pushed it aside with a smile. Her one foray into crocheting resulted in the longest chain stitch in history. She never figured out how to turn and start a new row. Eventually, even Granny gave up trying to teach her. She'd turned her loose instead, letting her run outside to play with Quentin.

Curious about the contents of the other containers, Willow slid the lid of the second one aside. She reached in and brought out a Mason jar full of buttons, holding it up as if she'd discovered a long lost treasure. How many hours had Willow sat alone in her room playing with the hundreds of plastic circles and other shapes Granny stored here? She shook the jar and watched the contents change positions. Those buttons had always fascinated her.

With one more shake, the buttons shifted to reveal a yellowed piece of paper hidden inside. Even before Willow unscrewed the lid, she recalled the familiar smell of musty plastic. Lifting the lid, the scent tickled her nose—one of those aromas from childhood that would always evoke memories of quiet Saturday mornings when she was angry with Quentin or didn't feel like playing outside with him.

She dipped her hand inside. The paper was aged and crisp. With gentle fingers, she peeled it open. "A special prayer for my weeping Willow, dear Lord. She cried herself to sleep tonight. I could hear her in her room, calling for her daddy. Fourteen years old and so alone. There's nothing I can do to fill the void our lies have caused. Only You, Lord, can heal the hurt inside. When she learns the truth, may she also discover that when one button is lost, there is always a newer, better one to replace it. Grant her peace, Father, and the ability to sew the new button into her old life."

At fourteen, she'd long outgrown the button jar. Granny must have savored the times Willow spent with it as much as Willow did.

Finding the buttons was a lot like finding an old friend. She wouldn't hide them away. She placed the paper back inside the jar and put the jar to the side, the prayer lingering on her mind. Granny could turn anything into a metaphor, but Scott and Ted were never buttons sewn to anything she owned. They weren't even buttons in her jar. Scott lived in California with the ice queen, and Ted was dead for all anyone knew. Nope, Granny's metaphor didn't work in this regard.

The last box was filled to the brim with family photographs. Like the buttons, she loved to pull the snapshots out and wade through them. Granny liked pictures. She just didn't enjoy putting them in any order or labeling them for posterity. As a result, Willow would sit at her feet for endless hours holding up the old black and whites or the faded colored ones. "Who's this, Granny? And this one? Is that my dad?"

Willow slammed the lid down on the box and closed the door to that particular memory. Granny had lied—something she told Willow never to do.

With all of the boxes out of the closet, she found only dust in the corners. It would need to be vacuumed before the contents went back in.

A tingling sensation and numbness spread through her legs when Willow pushed to her feet. She bent and retrieved the button jar, placing it on Granny's dresser by the ceramic heart.

As she stretched stiff muscles, a banging noise intruded into her solitude. Willow went into her old room, peeked out the window, and found the culprit. Quentin tinkered away at something in her backyard, whistling all the while. He was intent on his job, and she wondered just what he was doing. She'd just have to find out.

A loud knock startled her as she stepped onto the bottom stair.

A young man shielded his eyes as he peered through the glass in the door. He straightened up when he saw her. "Sorry, ma'am." He held up an envelope. "I have a delivery."

She unlocked and opened the door.

He handed her the package and tipped his ball cap. "Have a nice day."

Willow looked at the letter and then back at the postman. Since when did they hire them so young and handsome? "Thank you."

"You're welcome." He galloped down her porch steps.

Something didn't sit right with this. The postman could have placed an envelope this size in her mailbox—not that anyone knew she was here. Maybe he wanted to make sure someone was living in the home.

Willow gave a mental shrug and then closed and locked the door. She took the brown-clasp envelope to the couch and sat, studying the labels. The return address was familiar—a company she'd placed and received an order from months before. She turned it over in her hand then back again.

Her office didn't have her North Carolina address. They didn't need it. Her paycheck was direct deposited. Her secretary knew to call her cell phone if she was needed, and Jeffrey had her e-mail. Yet the postmark was from New York, and dated two months previous—around the time she'd received her order.

With a deep breath, she ripped open the package and let the contents fall into her lap.

Granny's bracelet.

And a note.

Willow's hands trembled as she unfolded the letter-sized paper. The handwriting appeared intentionally deranged, large flowing script that broke off into print, some letters large, others tiny. A picture was attached, held in place with a paperclip. She read the single line.

I touched you, and you didn't even know it. Watch out, Willow. I'm closer than you think.

She tore her eyes from the writing and pulled the picture free. What she saw sent goose bumps shivering up and down her spine.

This maniac, whoever he was, was violating her without even a touch. But he said he had touched her. When? Where? How had he removed the bracelet from her wrist without her knowing? Did he enter her house while she slept? No, surely he didn't. Not with Quentin outside. But how?

Her mind whirled in panic and confusion as she tried to bring her fear under control. And then it struck her. The package hadn't been mailed to her.

The delivery boy.

She studied the envelope again, the familiarity of the address bothering her. Using her nail to lift one corner of the label, Willow saw another address hidden beneath. She could just make it out. "Ms. Wil—"

Heart racing, Willow jumped to her feet and threw the envelope away. Her scream cut the air.

The back door crashed open, and Quentin ran in through the kitchen. "Willow?"

She held the bracelet toward him, her hand shaking so badly it waved in the air like a flag at a Fourth of July parade. He took it from her. "Where?"

She cast a weary glance at the envelope. "He—he was just here. I didn't realize. I opened the door."

"Who was here?" Quentin picked up the empty packet and the note.

"I opened the door," she repeated. "Hoot, I opened the door to him. He was standing right in front of me. He handed it to me."

Quentin ran to the door and out onto the porch.

"He's long gone." Willow sank to the couch.

Quentin returned. He ran his hands through his hair. Did she imagine it or had his face drained of color.

"Look at the address under the white label." She pointed.

He squinted at the envelope. "New York?"

"Not just New York. My name. My address. I received something else in that envelope—something I ordered two months ago. He got it from there. The man who dropped this off just now, he's letting me know he's the one who trashed my home. I think he's trying to tell me he was in this house, too. He took the bracelet. But I don't know how. Or when."

"What did he look like?" He handed the bracelet back.

"Young. Too young. Sweet, in fact. I'd never be afraid of him." She clenched the bracelet in her fist. She hadn't been afraid of him. She'd opened her door.

Quentin paced away from her and back. "Willow, this guy is playing a dangerous game. He's obviously a psychopath, and his actions will only escalate. We have to rethink getting Sheriff Dixon involved before it's too late."

Willow covered her mouth with her hand still holding the bracelet. Her breath was uneven—shallow one second then drawing in with great gulps the next. The room tilted, and she fought to keep darkness at bay. "He—he had to take it from me while I was sleeping."

"What's this?" Quentin bent to pick up the photo that had drifted to the floor when she'd thrown the papers away from her.

Silence stretched between them while he stared at the scene she'd also taken in—a digital picture in bold colors printed on shiny gloss paper.

"I—I have nowhere else to go." She sat on the couch and bounced back to her feet. "Maybe I should go to Scott."

"No," Quentin said a little too forcefully. "Look at the picture."

She drew close to him, his warmth lifting the cold chill of fear from around her.

"We're standing in front of your car. There's Aggie and your Uncle Robert. Bear's walking away. See him there?" He pointed to the back of her strange neighbor moving away from the gathering crowd. "And look at your wrist."

"My bracelet is missing."

"I'll wager you anything he took it from you between Appleton's and the car. You had it at Appleton's. You didn't have it here later that night. Do you remember anyone walking near us yesterday—a stranger?"

"And why would I let a stranger get close knowing I have some lunatic stalking me?"

He slapped the picture and his palm against his forehead then pointed toward the door. "I don't know. Why don't you tell me the name of the man who delivered the package?"

Good point, but she wasn't admitting it to him. "And how is it you remember I had the bracelet at the bookstore, but I didn't have it at home. We had dinner together last night. Couldn't you have mentioned it then?"

"Something doesn't fit. What was the postman driving?"

Quentin was choosing to ignore her, raising her ire.

"I don't know." She lost all patience with him. "I didn't look. Would it matter? The rural mail carriers use their own vehicles, unless that's changed."

"You're right. Still, if you didn't see him yesterday, he's either a good pickpocket or ..." he stopped.

"Or what?" she asked, her skin prickling at the thoughts she suspected were running through his mind.

"He's someone you think you can trust."

"Not too smooth making yourself the primary suspect."

"Good one and thank you for trusting me." He winked at her.

Not what she'd meant to reveal. The goof irked her even more.

"He apparently took the envelope from your apartment, which requires some forethought." He took the bracelet and placed it on her wrist, closing the clasp. His hand remained atop the jewelry.

Willow leaned against Quentin, fear draining her energy like a sink full of water when the stopper is pulled. "Hoot, he's bold and he's smart. He knows too much—your cell phone, my every move." She tilted her face up to him. "And I just allowed him to walk right into my house." Because Quentin was outside, and she'd felt safe.

She stomped her foot down, letting go of the irritation flanking her on all sides.

"Ow, Willow. That was my foot." Hoot said with a smile, but he held her close.

And she was happy he didn't let go.

CHAPTER EIGHT

Home early in the afternoon—a rare occasion for Scott Thomas.

He stretched out on the lounge. The Malibu surf pounded the sandy shore. The sound annoyed him. The constant barrage of the deafening crash and whoosh could drive a man crazy. Scott preferred the lapping waters of Amazing Grace's Lake Gethsemane to Malibu. Suzanne loved the tumult of the ocean in the same way she craved mayhem wherever she went.

This place was more a house than a home, somewhere he came each night to sleep. Amazing Grace rested in his heart and called to him like a weeping mother for her child—like his mother had called for her two wayward sons. Robert had peace, and he'd remained in their small hometown. Scott could only hope if Ted were alive, he was enjoying life.

He rubbed his hand across his brow. Teddy. What a convenient scapegoat his older brother had been. Gone, the Lord only knew where, and not expected to return. Even if Teddy had returned home, Mom knew her older son better than anyone. She had assured Scott he'd keep their secret. He'd become whatever Willow needed him to be.

Their mother had thought up the lie Willow lived. Said she wanted to protect Scott's daughter from the brutal truth that her mother—and her father—had not wanted her.

Mom had been angry with him, but she'd made it easy for Scott to abandon Willow on her doorstep. Too easy.

The hard part now was trying to win Willow's favor, when he was far from the father his beautiful daughter deserved.

The sliding door opened, and Suzanne waltzed out in her bikini. She still had the firm body of youth, but he always admired her much more in a modest one-piece. His wife, though, wanted more attention than modesty would allow.

"I'm bored." She rattled the ice in her whiskey-filled glass.

And the mind of a young girl as well. "Why don't you go for a swim?"

She stretched her slender arms out in front of her and examined her long, manicured nails. "No, I don't think so. Why don't we go to dinner later? I could start getting ready."

Keeping her occupied with her wardrobe, her face, and her hair tempted him, but not enough to make him give up this time away from the crowd. "Why don't we just stay in for an evening and let everyone go mad wondering what the Thomases are doing?"

"Because Suzanne Scott needs publicity. I'm giving the performance of a lifetime, and I plan to overshadow that little starlet. The people need to see I'm alive and well, young and carefree."

Not since he'd met her, in their youth, had Suzanne ever been free of cares. When you wanted everything, life was one long list of worries. Scott turned his gaze once again to the crashing ocean. Why did life with Suzanne forever pound against him like the waves against the sand? Somehow, if he could just paddle beyond the rolling waters, he'd find peace.

"So where do you want to go?"

He should have known Suzanne wouldn't give up her plans for dinner.

His cell phone rang. Thankful for a chance to avoid a childish tantrum from his wife, he snapped open his mobile. "Scott Thomas."

"Mr. Thomas, Quentin McPheron. Do you have a second?"

"Scott, I want to make reservations." Suzanne grasped her shapely hips with her hands, foot tapping.

He covered the phone with his hand. "Suzanne, I don't care to go out tonight."

"I'm sorry I called at an inconvenient time, but I think this is important."

Scott turned his back to his wife. "I have all the time you need. Go ahead."

If Suzanne would just walk inside, step away, so he could get to the bottom of the call.

"Willow has a stalker, Mr. Thomas. He's in Amazing Grace, and he's gotten way too close. She's in danger, and I think your daughter needs you."

"Scott, why don't we try that quaint little Italian restaurant, the one everyone raves about? We'll probably run into Jack or George there. We don't want to pass up an opportunity."

"Excuse me for a moment," Scott said, and pulled the phone from his ear. "Suzanne, this is an important call. Please give me a minute, and we'll discuss our dinner plans. We have plenty of time." He waited for her retreat.

She gave him a withering glare before stepping to the edge of the balcony, certainly not out of earshot. Shaking his head, he returned to the call. "I'm sorry. Can you be a little clearer about the situation?"

"Willow. Stalker. Here in Amazing Grace. Dangerous. Your daughter needs you. If I have to be any clearer, then I've called the wrong person."

The polite young boy who'd grown up next door to his daughter had suddenly turned into an aggressive love-struck man. Willow was in trouble. Scott didn't doubt it. "The situation is very clear."

The short snort of disgust coming through the phone lines shamed Scott. He cast a weary glance in the direction of his wife. She was too curious, hanging onto his every word. So unlike her when it came to his business. The only part of his life that intrigued Suzanne was the part that furthered her career.

She saw his look and sauntered over to him. "I want to go out, dear, and you know I'll bother you until I get my way."

"Mr. Thomas," Quentin said. "I never realized exactly what made someone a father until this moment. Why don't you go back to your shrill of a wife? I love your daughter, and I'll protect her just fine. Besides, a man who treasures someone cheap over someone invaluable—he's no type of father at all."

The conversation ended just like that. The boy was angry, and Scott was worried.

He put the phone on the patio table and again stared out over the waves. Suzanne had several more pivotal scenes to shoot. They couldn't handle her without him. He had work to do on the production. They had deadlines.

Dead. By the time he took care of all the things that mattered to Suzanne, by the time he allowed Suzanne to take one more of his dreams away, his daughter could die.

"Who was that?" Suzanne sauntered over to him, sitting on the end of the lounge. She rubbed his leg above the knee and gave him that sultry look of hers, the one that could make him forget everything.

"Nothing you want to worry about." The truth of his words cut into his heart and poured out the question he'd always hidden deep inside: how could a mother birth a child and never have an ounce of feeling toward her?

"Sounded to me like you were talking to Willow's friend. What's his name, Quinn?"

"Quentin. Quentin McPheron." He searched her face for any clue as to where this was leading.

"Why is he calling? Is Willow not interested in him, and he needs Daddy's help?" She walked her fingers up his chest like a spider crawling toward the fluttering moth entangled in its web.

Scott grabbed her hand and pulled her to him, forcing her to kiss him. Startled at first, she pulled away then leaned into him. He kissed her again and pulled back. "How much do you know about what's going on in our daughter's life?"

Suzanne stood. "I don't know anything. I've never wanted to even hear her name."

"Yet you spoke it first. Tell me, Suzanne. How did you know Willow was anywhere close to Quentin McPheron?"

She spun away with dramatic flair then turned back to him. "I—I'm so embarrassed."

She even had the audacity to blush, but she'd obviously forgotten he knew the real Suzanne, and what he saw before him was an act.

"Go ahead," he coaxed.

"I read your office e-mail. She wrote to tell you she was there."

"About those plans for dinner …"

"Let's just forget them, baby. Let's stay in, have Martin fix us up a fine Italian meal and enjoy each other's company," she cooed.

Scott stood and took her hand. "That sounds like a great idea. Glad you came up with it." He winked. "And tomorrow I've got a surprise for you."

"Oh, you know how much I love surprises." She opened the door, and he followed her inside. Taking her hand, he led her toward their bedroom. This might be the last night his wife ever allowed him to touch her again.

Willow had a headache, at least that's what she said when she excused herself to her room before Quentin returned outside. She'd actually cried. Willow usually showed her vulnerability through bitter comment and her sarcastic wit. Silence with the tears had taken him by surprise, and Quentin was at a loss as to how to help her. He liked her fighting and sassy. That he could deal with.

Yet, instead of muttering inconsolable words for her to sharpen her wit upon, he'd chosen to lose himself in the task of protecting her. Now, finished with the placement of the motion-sensor lights, the bolt locks on all the doors, and the window fasteners for each window on both floors, he was sweaty, dirty, and in need of a shower.

He climbed the steps of the deck at the back of Willow's home and entered through the kitchen. After shutting and locking the door, he listened for any movement. Willow rustled around upstairs.

"Hey," he called to her.

"Come on up. I'm in Granny's—my room."

He checked his shoes for loose dirt and walked through the house to the stairs. Funny, after Quentin reached a certain age, Granny put a stop to his visits to Willow's room.

"It's just inappropriate, that's all." Granny explained to them. "You two can stay downstairs and study or sit on the porch, but that's the new rule." For a long while, he'd wondered if his hormones had painted a map on his forehead and the directions led straight to his desire for Willow. You could never get anything past Granny.

They'd abided by Granny's rule, and guilt now tinged his joy at Willow's invitation—even if Quentin was determined to keep it an innocent visit.

He turned the corner into Granny's old room and found Willow sitting on the floor, stacks of photos surrounding her.

"Have a seat. Do you have the time?" she asked.

If he'd been a superhero with five seconds to save the world, he'd not give up these precious moments with her. He pushed a pile of photos over and sat down, picking one from the pile. "I remember this motorcycle. Agatha was not happy the day Robert bought it."

Willow leaned over. "I can't remember us ever looking that young."

The photo showed Robert on a motorcycle—no Harley, that one—an old Yamaha. Quentin's dad was looking on alongside three awe-struck children. When Granny took the picture, Quentin had stuck his tongue out, Laurel was posing pretty, and Willow was standing a little behind them.

Quentin touched her little girl image—such a sad look shone from her eyes. Loneliness.

"What's got you so fascinated?" She brushed her dark locks from her face.

"Sometimes the camera lens shows us more than we think possible."

Willow took the picture from him then handed it back. "Uncle Robert was so happy. You can see it on his face. And Laurel, she always had to be the center of attention." Willow continued to peruse the other snapshot. "She should've been Suzanne's daughter."

"Instead," Quentin heaved a deep sigh, still staring at the picture, "Suzanne's daughter is the one who looks alone and distant, as if she's out of place in that scene—when you had the most right to be there."

Willow shrugged. "Ah, well. Who knows? Aunt Aggie was there that day. She probably said something to me."

She had, and his father had whipped him good because Big Dave realized his son wasn't hamming it up for the camera. He was being disrespectful toward Willow's aunt when he'd stuck his tongue out at her.

He said nothing. Willow had enough seeds growing roots of bitterness. Instead, he turned his attention to prom photos she'd pulled out. One photo showed him with Laurel standing in front of Granny's hearth, the other Darrell Jacobs and Willow. "If you'd told me back then Laurel Thomas would be in love with Darrell Jacobs, I'd have laughed you out of the room."

"Darrell? He's Laurel's geek?" Willow leaned back and laughed. "She wants me to help her win Darrell? That's too funny." As quickly as her laughter started, it stopped. "No, it's not."

He waited. What in the world would make her mood change so quickly?

"She compared me to Darrell. She called me a geek."

"You've never been a geek. You're not smart enough."

She punched him in the arm then grew quiet as she chewed on the inside of her cheek for a long moment. Then the smile returned. She gave a terse nod. "I'm in good company being compared to someone like Darrell Jacobs."

"I can't argue with that, but I want you to know I never saw you as a nerd."

She nodded and held the pictures up in front of her. "Granny made our prom dresses. Even in high school I was still challenged with nightgown syndrome."

"What are you talking about?" he choked out, trying not to laugh.

"Just something Laurel and I discussed this morning." She began to straighten out the stacks then she placed them into neat little piles within the box before closing it and showing him a yellowing piece of paper. "Granny was something else, Hoot." She thrust the note into his hand.

"Photos of family and friends and life," he read. "Dear Father, thank You for the blessings of those pictured here. May You meld my family into one heart, all in accord with Your plans. Lord, my prayer is that every one of these now with us will love You, worship You, and serve You, as You see fit."

"I'm finding these little notes all over the place," Willow took the paper from him and slipped it back into the box.

Quentin helped her to her feet. She held to a few pictures he'd not seen. "What are those?"

"They're amazing. Granny wrote on these—she didn't do that on many. This one is a picture of Scott, Agatha, Robert, Suzanne, and Ted standing by the lake. At Manna yesterday, Agatha mentioned in her catty way that she knew Suzanne. They must have been friends at one point."

Quentin nodded. Bear had alluded to that earlier.

The picture showed the two women in one-piece bathing suits, the guys wearing swimming trunks. Quentin whistled. "Look at Aggie. She *is* beautiful, and that hourglass figure. Who could imagine that today?"

Willow snatched the picture away. "You shouldn't be looking at them like that."

"Well, your mom …"

"Call her Suzanne, please."

"She's very pretty, but Aggie has the movie-star looks in that picture, not Suzanne."

"That's because in that picture Aggie's happy. She doesn't look like the pinch-faced prude of today. Suzanne looks unsettled, as if she's thinking ahead, not satisfied where she was at that moment."

If Willow wasn't careful, she'd end up looking like a pinched-face prude, but Quentin kept the thought to himself. "Suzanne's standing beside Ted, and not your dad—Scott."

"Uncle Ted looks a little put out, too, don't you think?

"A bit." Quentin narrowed his gaze on Ted's face then turned his attention back to Willow. "What else do you have?"

As if holding three cards from a deck, she fanned the school photos out, turning them in his direction. With her finger she pointed, "Scott … Ted … Robert."

In the picture, Scott Thomas looked like the all-American boy. Robert favored a bookworm. Maybe he was the Darrell of their generation, and Ted—the young man was impressive in stature and in the serious flint of his brown-eyed gaze.

"Something, huh?" Willow rubbed her moist eyes and placed the pictures on the dresser beside the old jar of buttons he despised so much. When all he'd wanted to do was run out and play, she'd get it in her mind that she wanted to mess with the buttons. Must have been a little-girl thing.

Quentin shook his head and turned his attention back to her. A single tear slid down her cheek, and he wiped it away. "Why so sad, Scrappy?"

"I don't know. Maybe it's because when I came along, these brothers were already separated by time and space. Maybe I miss what I never had or I feel sorry for Granny because she had this, and it went away." She sat hard on the edge of her bed. "Whatever it is, Hoot, it's something deep inside, and I can't put my finger on it."

He pushed her hair behind her shoulder then placed his hand against her cheek. "Those emotions are good to have, and letting them out is a good thing."

She peered up at him and released a sigh. "Thank you for taking care of the security around here."

"I'm still standing guard on the porch tonight."

She didn't argue, and for that Quentin was glad. "Keep the place locked up. I need to run one more errand and then go home and shower. I'll take you out to eat."

"I think I'll lay down for awhile, try to get rid of this headache. Lock me in, okay?" She pulled back the covers and lay upon the bed.

"Sure." He lifted the sheet and blanket and tucked her in.

Her dark hair fanned the pillow, and he reached to touch a strand of silkiness. His body flamed with desire, and he pulled back.

"Hoot, what did my dad tell you?" She reached for his hand.

The flames died at the mention of her father, and he forced the flinch from his features. "Your dad?"

"I could hear you on the phone earlier. You got pretty testy with him. Is he coming?" Something akin to hope peered at him through her chocolate-colored eyes.

Quentin put on his best smile. "I don't think so. I told him I'd take care of everything."

She turned on her side. "You may have to knock loud when you're ready to go to town. I'm pretty tired."

"Willow?"

She waited, head turned, her perfect lips slightly parted.

He moved close to her, sitting on the bed beside her.

She sat up, and he encircling her with his dirty arms, pulling her close, sure his sweat-soaked shirt would leave a stain on her top. He waited a long moment for any protest. When none came, he lowered his lips to hers. She returned the kiss, and he pulled her closer before releasing her. "Sweet dreams." He flashed a smile as she dropped back against her pillow. He swooped by the dresser, slipped a picture into the palm of his hand, and walked out the door.

"Hoot McPheron," she roared then her laughter rang out like the crisp sound of a fine wind chime. "Now I need to take a shower. You stink."

She hadn't noticed his little theft. He was happy for that, and what was even better yet, she wanted him. Her actions spoke louder than all her opposition from the night before—and that little kiss had taken the sadness from her eyes.

"Sorry, Granny," he muttered. "But I couldn't resist." Now, he understood why Granny had imposed her rules upon them.

LeBlanc clicked the photo, holding the camera where no one would notice.

The place was abuzz with the news. Some folks in the gathering crowd murmured the woman lying on the ground in a pool of blood didn't deserve such cruelty. Others shook their head and muttered their thoughts aloud, "It was only a matter of time."

"Back away. Back away folks." The law arrived. "Ambulance is on its way. Did anyone see what happened?" The burly sheriff scanned the crowd.

"Found her here, Daniel. Just like that," a man said.

A sneer lifted the corner of LeBlanc's lips. He'd seen that man before. Seen how he treated people—his son, Willow's boyfriend. He'd watched what he'd done—the liar.

The brick of a lawman—Sheriff Dixon—bent down, felt for a pulse, and pushed the button on the radio on his sleeve. "What's taking so long? Back alley, Manna from Heaven, now!"

Before the radio crackled a reply, pealing sirens split the air. Moments later the red vehicle clipped the corner, two EMTs jumping out before it came to a complete halt.

"Did you see anything, Cooper?" Sheriff Dixon asked Liar.

"No—no, Sheriff, nothing." Liar backed away from the scene and walked back across the street to the tire store.

A deputy started out after Liar.

"Let him go. I know where to find him." The sheriff lifted his hat, scratched his head, and looked about the scene.

LeBlanc stood his ground. He was just an innocent bystander in the crowd, after all.

CHAPTER NINE

Anger didn't begin to define Quentin's feelings for Scott Thomas. Quentin never suspected him of being as self-centered as his wife, but what would make a man stay with someone like Suzanne?

Love?

One side of anything built nothing. How could a man hold on to a woman who showed disdain for the things he loved? Was it fear of being found out? Was Scott only playing the role of father to keep the press from condemning Suzanne? Whatever he was doing, Scott's games hurt Willow, and Quentin was through with letting that happen.

Quentin remained a bachelor, aloof from other women, depending upon God to answer his prayer and bring Willow home. If Scott wouldn't help him protect her, Quentin would do it himself.

After his shower and a change of clothes, he walked around Willow's place checking the doors. Then he headed down the street to the dirt path leading to the cabin behind Willow's home.

Rounding the corner, he stopped at the bottom of the rutted driveway. Sunlight glinted on Robert Thomas's black Lexus. The front door of the cabin opened, as if Bear had been waiting for him. "Good way to get shot, boy." Bear motioned him inside. "Anything wrong?"

Quentin stomped up the old wooden steps, long worn by years of work boots and weather. "Can I talk to you?" he muttered as he stepped inside the older man's home.

"Hey, son." Robert Thomas stood from the chair at Bear's small kitchen table.

Quentin shook Robert's hand. "Good to see you, Mr. Thomas."

"So what brings you here while Willow's home alone?" Bear cracked his knuckles and glared at Quentin.

"I have a question or two, and we can include Mr. Thomas or not. It's your choice." Nice and even. Bear wouldn't have a clue speaking so bluntly had been hard for Quentin.

"Say what you've come to say."

Quentin fished in the back pocket of his jeans and pulled out the picture he'd stolen from Willow. Casting a weary glance at Robert, he tossed the photo onto Bear's table. "I think you're this guy."

Robert picked up the picture. "He's got you there, Teddy. No hiding it, even with your beard."

Bear shook his head. "He never could keep a secret." He chuckled. "Yeah, boy, that's me. Now, what do you plan to do with the information?"

Quentin straightened, raising his height to that of his opponent—the man he wanted to make his ally. "I'm not going to do a thing unless you tell me. I'm not out to hurt you, Bear, but Willow had a visitor today."

Bear gave an uneasy look toward Robert then turned his attention back to Quentin. "I kept a pretty steady lookout until I saw your vehicle come roaring by."

"I was in the back fixing locks and putting up motion-sensor lights."

"What's all this about?" Robert asked. "The press chasing our girl again? I'll get an injunction and have them run out of town."

"The press hasn't arrived yet," Quentin told him. "Thank you, though. There's a man, and he's frightening her, making some very obvious threats."

"And her visitor?" Bear asked.

"He brought a package. She opened the door to him."

"The mailman?" Robert asked with a laugh.

"Hear him out, Robert." Bear motioned for Quentin to sit.

Quentin chose to remain standing between the two men in the small cabin. "Earlier in the day, Willow discovered she'd lost a bracelet—the one Granny gave her before she died. I'd seen her with it since she arrived. I know she had it on at Appleton's earlier yesterday, but she didn't have it last night before we saw the guy on the dock."

"Guy? Dock? What are you two talking about?" Robert looked between them.

"Let him finish," Bear said.

"A man delivered an envelope with a label covering an old address. It contained Willow's bracelet and this ..." Quentin dug in his other pocket. When he pulled out the note, Bear didn't wait for Robert to react. He snatched it from Quentin's hand, read it, and thrust it at Robert.

"I touched you, and you didn't even know it. Watch out, Willow. I'm closer than you think," Robert read.

Why did it sound so ominous spoken aloud? When had this man gotten close enough to take Willow's bracelet? If he'd taken it between the bookstore and her car, it meant Quentin failed to protect her.

Bear stared at the note in Robert's hand for a long second before Robert handed it back to Quentin. "Yesterday, when I saw you two in town, she stumbled."

"She nearly passed out on me. The stalker left her a calling card."

"Maybe she lost the bracelet then." Bear stepped toward the door.

Quentin nodded. That scenario soothed some of his concern. If the creep had picked it up off the sidewalk after they'd left, he hadn't been too close to her. "The bracelet isn't what has me worried. Willow says that envelope is an older one delivered to her in New York—something she ordered. The reason she's here is because the man trashed her apartment. He must have taken the envelope then."

Quentin allowed a moment for the truth to sink in.

Bear turned. "Go on."

"He didn't mail it. He just knocked on her door, stepped into the house, handed the package to her, and walked right out," Quentin reasoned. "He's pretty calculating."

"If our girl's in danger, we need to call Scott." Robert paced in front of them.

Our girl. Robert used the phrase twice now. Quentin liked the tone of it, but the fact it didn't come from Bear bothered him. He pressed his lips into a straight line.

"You've called Scott?" Bear narrowed his eyes.

Quentin nodded. "He's too wrapped up in Suzanne right now to care about his daughter. Willow's frightened, and I'm not afraid to admit I'm more than a little concerned."

"Let me call him." Robert reached in his pants pocket for his phone. "He'll come if he hears it from me."

"Let him go, Bobby." Bear muttered, low but in command. "I guess if Willow's going to let me in, she'll have to know the truth."

"Do you think that's wise? You've worked so hard to stay anonymous." Robert studied his phone for a second. "Scott wouldn't stay in California if he knew his daughter's being threatened. Let me talk to him."

Quentin stared at Robert. How could the man be so naïve?

"Since when do the two of you do anything anyone wants you to do unless it's at the whim of a beautiful woman?" Bear baited.

Quentin coughed only to keep from releasing his caged anger. Suzanne might be an older picture of her daughter, but on the inside, her ugliness was as deep as a festering cesspool.

And no one could see past the anger and bitterness to the likeable, but far from beautiful face, of Agatha—but he'd seen the proof. Once upon a time …

Robert's cell phone rang. At the same time, Quentin's phone vibrated, and he had to dig in his pocket. He fumbled with it.

"Slow down, honey. Say it again." Robert spoke into his phone.

"Hoot!" Before Quentin got his phone to his ear, he heard Willow cry out.

He jerked the phone to his ear watching Robert. "Willow?"

"Laurel, where? How did it happen?" Robert fell back against the old wooden table. It moved under his weight, scraping the floor.

"Dead. She's dead." Willow screamed. "He sent me her picture. Agatha. She's lying in her own blood. Quentin, he killed Aunt Aggie."

"What is it?" Bear asked as Robert lowered his phone.

Quentin stared, waiting to hear the words from Agatha's husband.

"Quentin." The panic in Willow's voice grew.

"Teddy, Laurel says Agatha's on the way to the hospital. They found her behind Manna. Unconscious." Robert walked like a man who'd just been given a death sentence, his step slow and wobbly. "Aggie," he cried his wife's name.

"I'm going with you." Bear braced his younger brother. "Give me your keys."

"Where are you?" Willow cried. "Quentin, I'm afraid."

"I'm right around the corner. Don't hang up." Quentin ran for the door. Either Willow or Laurel had the story wrong, and he prayed to his Mighty God that it was Willow.

LeBlanc moseyed into the tire and auto store. Not that he thought the man who'd earlier scampered into the building would wait on him.

Meandering through the aisles, he breathed in the scent of rubber and leather. Some of the stores offerings could be useful. He'd take this special opportunity to stock up.

Only a coward would hit a woman from behind and leave her bleeding on the pavement.

He wouldn't even stoop that low. He looked all of them in their faces—when they shook with terror, when they struggled to free themselves from him, and even as their wide eyes lost the spark of life and went cold on him, still open, yet no longer seeing.

He lived for that moment when the life drained from them, leaving a hollow empty shell.

He reached for the rope on the shelf, fingering it. Polypropylene. That wouldn't tie as tightly as he needed, yet it would close around Willow's tender throat. He strolled along the aisle until he found the heavy-duty twine. Good for keeping his prey where he wanted her until he finished toying with her.

He waited another moment. Liar didn't come to the front of the store, so he tucked the rope and twine into his shirt and headed toward the door.

"Can I help you, sir?"

With a slight turn, LeBlanc met Liar's gaze. "Just wondering what kind of a thrill a man like you gets when his victim can't see him coming?"

"Excuse me?" Liar straightened.

"The law and the ambulance have gone. You might have gotten away with it, but maybe you didn't." He walked closer to Liar, leaning toward him. Liar backed away. "Liars often find themselves accused of things they didn't do." He clucked his tongue twice. "Thanks for the alibi, Mr. Goodyear."

LeBlanc took the rope and twine from the inside of his shirt and waltzed out.

Liar wasn't coming after him. Cowards seldom did.

CHAPTER TEN

Willow looked out the hospital window to the mountains beyond while Laurel and Robert fawned over a comatose Agatha. Quentin said his presence would crowd the room. Willow had clucked at him like a chicken in an attempt to taunt him to stay. While he'd protect her from a psychotic stalker, Willow suspected Agatha was just a bit too scary for him. He was waiting downstairs.

"Who would do this?" Laurel asked.

"Honey, are you kidding?" Robert said. "Who wouldn't?"

Willow cupped her hand over her lips. How ungodly would it be to laugh right now? And if she started laughing, she'd never be able to contain herself. God help her, but she was worried about Agatha despite the flaw in her own character that always caused her to laugh in tense situations.

"Daddy, that's awful," Laurel admonished, but amusement laced her words.

Willow lowered her head. Her stomach contracted, and the air pushed from her nose once, twice, three times. Her body convulsed in a silent show of amusement. God would definitely get her for this one. Could she get away with claiming nerves?

Uncle Robert came to stand beside her. "She's been rough on you, and I'm sorry." He slipped his arm around her. "The doctor said she'll be fine. Nothing to cry about."

Willow swallowed hard to purge the hilarity then looked up into her uncle's face. He winked at her, and his lips turned into a knowing smile.

She bit her lip, and his eyes twinkled.

"Uncle Robert, this is my fault." She managed to take control of her battling emotions.

"You don't know that." Laurel sat on the side of her mother's bed. "The sheriff said she probably didn't see her attacker. Whoever it was hit her from behind."

"Was it a robbery?" Willow could only hope.

"No. One of the bakers went outside to put some trash in the dumpster. He found her behind it."

"Who else would do this and send the picture to me?" Laughter forgotten, Willow paced away from her uncle. "I'm so sorry. I should have stayed in New York."

"Yes," the mumbled voice came from the bed. "You should have." Agatha raised her IVed hand to her head. "Wh—what happened?"

"You're okay, Momma," Laurel cooed.

"I am not okay," Agatha barked. "My head is throbbing."

Robert moved beside his wife. "Laurel meant you're going to live, and you should thank God for His goodness."

"You're on such good terms with him, Robert, why don't you just thank Him for me?"

Robert's intake of breath bore his impatience, but he exhaled fully before he spoke. "I thank Him for you every night."

"You still haven't answered my question. What happened?"

How hard did one's heart have to be not to notice the love flowing with Uncle Robert's statement?

"You were hit over the head. The doctor said a little harder and to the left, and you wouldn't be here now." Laurel straightened her mother's pillow.

"Who? Who did this to me?"

"We were hoping you could tell us. Were you arguing with anyone?" Laurel brushed her mother's bangs from her forehead.

Agatha pushed her touch aside.

Laurel stood back like an abused child afraid to make another move.

And to think Willow had longed for a family like this. For the first time in her life, sorrow for her cousin raged in Willow's heart.

"I didn't argue with anyone," Agatha declared.

"There's always a first time." Robert looked to the ceiling.

"Aunt Agatha, I think I owe you an apology ..."

"Uh, uh, uh," Robert muttered. "You're standing in the middle of the coliseum, and your words just opened the lion's cage."

Agatha glared at Robert for a full minute before turning her attention back to Willow. "You sure do, honey. You owe me an apology for everything. Your life has been the bane of mine."

"Agatha, there's no reason—" Robert started.

"You stayed here, Robert. You took care of both of them—Granny and the family orphan. Thinking she was Ted's little bundle of joy was bad enough. Then we learn she's actually Suzanne's little unwanted whelp. Your mother ups and dies because of the trauma, and to add insult to injury, she leaves everything to her." Agatha put both her hands to her head. "I can't take one more minute."

"That's enough," Robert slammed his hand down on the bed rail.

Agatha winced.

"My mother had the right to do whatever she wanted with her property. Willow is a precious part of our family—if only because Momma loved her. I'm tired of hearing the same old story, Aggie. You'd think I never provided for you or our daughter. I've done everything I could until I could do no more. Then I turned it over to God. Because, Aggie, only God can take the bitterness out of you."

Laurel left her mother's side and stood by her father.

"And there you are, both of you, siding with her while I'm the one who was attacked." Agatha moaned and leaned her head back against the pillow.

Willow lowered her head and started for the door. She only wanted to make sure Agatha had survived. She had, and so had her temperament.

"Ms. Thomas." Sheriff Daniel Dixon entered the room before Willow could get out the door.

"Yes," Agatha answered.

"I meant Willow. Sorry."

Willow blinked. Funny, when her own life was threatened, she never dared to call the authorities, but when she'd received the picture of what she assumed was a dead Agatha, she'd picked up the phone and dialed. The dispatch told her someone had called in the incident and insisted she forward the e-mail to the department.

"Let's talk in the hall." Sheriff Dixon stuck a copy of the photo in her face.

Willow took it and followed him into the corridor. "Is there something wrong?"

"There's something fishy about this picture."

Willow had known Sheriff Dixon all her life. He was a deputy for the unincorporated town when she was younger. Granny and his mother, Grace, were good friends. Now, Sheriff Dixon looked anything but friendly. She searched his face for a clue of what he meant. He offered none.

She studied the photo. "I don't understand."

He pointed to a pair of shiny shoes beside Agatha's prone body. "Those belong to a member of the department—to be exact, this member of the department. This picture was taken after the incident while I was at the scene but prior to the arrival of the ambulance."

"If my stalker did it, why would he wait for the police to arrive to take the photo?"

"Exactly. The person who e-mailed this to you uses a prepaid, untraceable phone. We're working on finding an e-mail address."

"Sheriff Dixon, there are two detectives in New York City working on a case that I'm sure has everything to do with what happened to Aunt Agatha. A man ruined my apartment. He phoned me at my office and told me to check my e-mail. He'd been sending me photographs taken of me during the day, but nothing so malevolent until that night. The paparazzi got news of my call to the precinct, and the detectives helped me get out of town unnoticed."

Sheriff Dixon slipped a pen from his shirt pocket. He clicked it, and turning the paper photo over, waited, posed to write. "What were their names?"

"Hominski, Bob Hominski. He called the other man Jim, but I don't recall his last name. Maybe they've learned something."

"Do you happen to recall the precinct?"

Willow shook her head.

"Did they give you a card?" the sheriff pressed.

"No, they didn't."

"I'll have to do some legwork to find your detectives, but if we're lucky, they may have dug up the information." He handed her the photograph. "Write your New York address on the back. I'll need it to locate the precinct, but whoever he is, he hasn't committed a crime in Amazing Grace. I suspect that in a long line of Agatha's enemies, this person isn't one of them. Taking a picture is not the same as aggravated assault."

They walked together toward the elevator. "But who else would really harm Agatha?"

Daniel Dixon punched the down button for the elevator. "Everyone I spoke with admitted they could be a suspect. I'm on the list as well."

"Sheriff, do you remember someone around the crime scene, someone who shouldn't have been there? A young man, maybe?"

"I spoke to one person—Cooper Goodyear—and if he saw the crime, he'd never say. There's no love lost between those two. My deputies interviewed other folks at the scene."

The elevator opened, and they stepped inside.

"Hold up." Laurel ran toward them.

Willow looked to Laurel as she joined them. "My family's in danger now. You'll contact the detectives?"

The sheriff nodded. "We'll let you know what we find out. You don't plan on leaving town anytime soon, do you?"

"Why?"

"You have the major piece of evidence, and along with about ninety-five percent of this town, you have a motive."

In Willow's heart, the motive might linger, but in reality, she had an alibi and a reason for staying in town: Quentin McPheron.

Willow wanted to see Quentin more than she'd ever wanted anything in her life. Her desire remained unfulfilled as she and Laurel exited the hospital's elevator.

"Let's grab something to drink?" Laurel pulled at Willow's arm.

Willow nodded and followed. In the cafeteria, she looked around the room filled with white-coat professionals and hospital staff wearing scrubs. Quentin, in his navy blue t-shirt and nice-fitting jeans, wasn't among them.

"How about a soda?" Laurel directed, not releasing her hold on Willow until they reached the soda fountain.

Willow chose a plastic cup and held it against the ice drop. Cubes plopped into the container. Standing back, she studied her option and decided upon root beer. The taste would sure beat her only source of hydration at home—tap water, with or without ice.

Drinks in hand, they sat at a small table in the corner. Willow continued to search for Quentin.

"Something wrong?" Laurel asked.

Willow tapped her fingernails on the side of her cup. "Looking for Hoot is all." She leaned back. "Can I ask you something?"

"Sure."

Willow braced for the answer before asking the question. "Am I really like your mother?"

Laurel sipped her drink then stared away for a moment. "We're all carrying around our past. Momma's had a little longer to pack it away." She looked at Willow. "I suppose your load is lighter, but the two of you are a lot alike."

Willow blinked. She'd asked for the truth. She'd expected it to sting but not this much.

"Like the nightgowns Granny gave us—"

"And the prom dresses." Willow smiled.

"No. I liked my dress," Laurel smiled. "But I wanted the color of yours. Just like I sometimes wished your life could have been mine."

Willow bit her tongue. A tirade about the ice queen in Hollywood wouldn't help her case.

"When we were younger, and we all thought your mother died in childbirth, and a brokenhearted Ted left you with Granny, I was jealous."

"Of a lie?"

"Your mother was supposedly dead. Mine is Agatha."

Willow laughed. "Well, you may have a point."

"No, Willow. I was wrong. My jealousy turned to bitterness, and I made your life miserable because of it. Then the news broke about Scott and Suzanne. When I saw the pain their abandonment caused you, I realized how wrong I'd been. You left so suddenly after Granny's death I didn't have a chance to apologize. Then Tabitha died." Laurel's lips trembled. "Did you hear how it happened?" She took a sip of soda.

Her cousin had waited ten years to make her apology. The thought humbled Willow. "No. Quentin probably wouldn't have said anything last night except I went all Agatha on him.

Laurel choked on her drink.

Willow patted her back. "Sorry. I know she's your mom."

"That's why I understand it so well." Laurel coughed.

"Quentin said only that she died." And in Willow's anger and bitterness, she hadn't cared how it affected Laurel.

"Willow, I put a lot of bitterness in Momma's heart. After you left, I got involved with Cooper Goodyear. I'm the reason he and Momma don't get along."

"Cooper was married when I left town. He had a little boy, didn't he?" Willow asked.

"Yes. Cooper threw a party at his house one night while his wife was away. A bunch of young college kids and this twenty-nine-year-old man. I thought I was so cool. Quentin and Darrell wouldn't have anything to do with it. They showed up at the party to convince Tabitha and me to leave, but by that time, we were pretty wasted. We refused. Quentin caused a scene. The black eye he's sporting today is nothing like the beating he got when Cooper had some of the kids kick him and Darrell off his property. Quentin's football buddies turned on him, and ..." Her words trailed. She looked off in the distance. "I never realized until now. Quentin's star player, his quarterback, is Cooper's son."

Willow straightened. "He never holds a grudge, does he?"

"Well, he does hold one against Cooper, and that's because of me, too."

"What did you do?" Willow sipped her root beer.

"I could blame it on the alcohol, but I wasn't in my right mind for a long while after Granny died."

"I know the feeling."

"I'd planned to stay a while with Cooper then go home later, not that I could drive. Tabitha didn't want to wait on me. I told her I'd call a cab. She got behind the wheel, crashed her car, and died on impact. News of my affair with Cooper got out. His wife left him. Tabitha's parents blamed me. Quentin and Darrell blamed each other, but Tabitha's death rests solely on me, and believe me, Momma never lets me forget it."

Willow leaned forward, still toying with her cup. "What helped you to get over the bitterness?"

"As cliché as it may sound, Jesus changed my life." Laurel fished in her overlarge purse. She pulled out a small notebook, the edges of the papers inside yellowed by time. "Since I ran into you at Manna, I've been carrying this with me waiting for the right time to hand it over. This morning didn't seem like the right time."

Willow took the notebook and opened it. Granny's familiar handwriting covered the pages. Prayers filled the book, much like the ones on the strips of paper Willow found in the house.

For Laurel Elizabeth and Willow Jade. From your grandmother, Elizabeth Jade Thomas.

Willow sat back hard. How had she forgotten the significance in their names?

"In case you're wondering, she gave it to me the day before she died—a sort of graduation present. She asked me to read through it thoughtfully then to give it to you."

Willow touched the bracelet on her arm. Granny hadn't asked her to share her gift, but would she?

As if reading her thoughts, Laurel placed her hand over the bracelet. "Granny left me something of my own, but she said you would have to find it in due time and give it to me. Read this, Willow. I think you'll understand why I've turned away from being like Momma."

Willow nodded.

"Jesus can change your life, too."

Willow rose, leaving the notebook on the table. She refreshed the root beer she'd barely finished and returned to where Laurel was sitting. Standing behind her chair, she cast a weary glance at her cousin.

Laurel stood and pushed in her chair. "I'm worried about you."

"I can't trust God again. Look at the life He's given me."

"Take the first step and trust Granny. Read her prayers thoughtfully, like she asked."

Trust Granny? She'd been the author of the fictional life Willow led until she'd turned eighteen. Willow took a deep breath and picked up the notebook. Granny had kept her safe, and warm, and loved. Maybe if she concentrated on those things the trust would return. She leafed through the pages. "To think, she left me a couple of notes and you an entire notebook."

Laurel opened her mouth to speak then closed it, shaking her head.

Willow scrunched up her nose. "What'd I do now?"

"You're jealous about a notebook she asked me to share with you?"

Willow closed her eyes. "Okay, I deserve the misunderstanding, but that's not what I meant. Granny was wise. She knew I'd never share this with you, not then anyway."

"If it makes you feel any better, when she first gave it to me, I had no intention of giving it to you"—she leaned forward, a wicked smile on her face—"ever."

"Fair enough."

Laurel pulled away and began to straighten her skirt, her top, her hair. She focused on something beyond Willow and waved.

Willow turned to see what gained her cousin's attention. She smiled but held tightly to the back of her chair. What would Quentin McPheron think if she ran into his arms?

He'd think she'd finally gone completely insane.

Laurel came beside Willow. "God has a purpose in our lives. I think one of yours is standing over there. I know mine is."

Willow blinked. After all her suffering, would God allow her to claim the love of the boy next door? Did she consider the prize worth the price?

Yes, she did. After all these years, her heart still yearned to gaze upon the original picture she'd drawn of Quentin. What if God meant for her to have the original in him? "Laurel, whatever happened to my picture of Hoot?"

Laurel widened her eyes. "You haven't seen it?"

"Would I ask you if I had?"

"Not telling." Laurel hugged her. "But I hope I get to see your face when you find it."

Stalking Willow

CHAPTER ELEVEN

Willow ducked under Quentin's arm as he held open the door to Appleton's. Laurel and Darrell scooted by on the other side of him.

As Quentin started past, he slipped his arm around Willow's waist, drawing her to him. She shivered at his touch. This was how it should have been in high school. She'd missed out on so much because of her bitterness.

"Cold?" His forehead creased. "I might have a jacket in the Jeep."

She couldn't say she didn't like his concern. "No, I'm fine."

Quentin drew out a chair, and when she started to sit, he bent as if he planned to take the seat. Then with a teasing smile, he motioned for her to take it. A more gallant Darrell pulled out the chair for Laurel and waited for her to sit.

"What can we get you two ladies?" Quentin asked.

"Sweet tea and a piece of apple pie." Laurel didn't hesitate.

Willow nodded. "Sounds great."

"We'll be right back." Darrell started away. He stopped. "You'll wait, right?"

Laurel wore a brilliant smile. "Right here, Darrell."

When Darrell made his way toward Quentin at the counter, Willow leaned forward. "He's so nervous."

"Adorably so." Laurel's eyes swam in unshed tears. "He's always been so respectful to me even after all the pain I caused."

"How are the Thomas girls this evening?" Henry Appleton's slow stride brought him alongside the table.

"We're doing well, Mr. Appleton." Laurel smiled. No red nose. No blotchy face.

If any kind of tear threatened to make an appearance, Willow would look like a train wreck. Just one more thing to hold against her cousin.

But she wouldn't. Not with Granny orchestrating things— as she'd always done.

"How about you, Willow Jade?"

"I'm fine, Henry. Where's Annie?"

"We hired a new boy." Henry motioned to the counter where Darrell and Quentin waited.

"He must have ducked in the back. A good worker. I sent Annie home. Thought she'd rest, but that crazy duck went home and threw together a card party for her and her cronies."

Willow laughed. "I bet you're glad you're here."

"Believe me, Hon, I am." He winked and moved on.

Quentin and Darrell sauntered over.

"Order placed." Quentin pulled out his chair. "Darrell and I wanted sandwiches, and he had to go to the back for the meat."

"Henry keeping cattle back there now?" Laurel batted her eyelashes Darrell's way.

"No. The meat's in the refrigerator," Darrell said without an indication he'd gotten Laurel's joke.

Willow grinned at Quentin and waited for Laurel to answer in typical Thomas fashion. When Laurel nodded her head and gave no indication of Darrell's misunderstanding, Willow shrugged. She'd never miss such an opportunity to goad Hoot.

Darrell closed his eyes and leaned back. "Of course, you were kidding. I'm sorry."

Quentin and Willow burst into laughter, but Laurel reached her hand out. "Let's get the awkwardness out of the way, here. Darrell. I love everything about you. I always have. There. Done."

Darrell's eyes widened. "You're that easy?"

Fire flashed in Laurel's eyes. "What?"

"Whoa!" Quentin stood.

Darrell looked to him and back to Laurel, then as if begging for a pardon, he cast a questioning gaze in Willow's direction. "What?"

"You," Quentin pointed at Darrell, "think about what you said. Laurel, he's nervous."

Tears might not make her a mess, but anger on Laurel made her look like Agatha. Vindication. But Willow didn't enjoy it as much as she thought she would.

Darrell faced Laurel. "After all this time of being afraid to ask you out, I'm surprised you're so open to the idea. That's all."

"But you said ..." Quentin moved his hand in a circle, palm toward his body, encouraging Darrell to remember.

Darrell waved him off. "Whatever I said, I meant it only in the best light."

Laurel closed her eyes. "Who knew words could hurt so much?"

"My words?" Darrell took her hands in his. "I would never purposely hurt you."

"I know." Laurel offered him a smile. "Momma's words have made me a little more vulnerable. That's all."

Willow fell back against her chair. If she could smack Agatha right now, she'd do it right against the gash on the prude's head, but Willow deserved the same punishment. She hadn't been too nice to her cousin either.

"Here you go, Coach. Four sweet teas, two apple pies, and two ham sandwiches."

Quentin took the tray.

Willow looked to Henry's new employee. She blinked, and looked closer.

"You!" She jumped to her feet, slamming into Quentin, pointing her finger at their server.

Quentin juggled the tray. Darrell reached to steady it.

Ice tea, four large cups, bounded off the tray and tumbled in the same direction—right toward Laurel.

"Willow!" Laurel screeched, attempting to swim through the brown, sugary liquid.

Did the boy actually smirk at Laurel's predicament? "You!" Willow repeated.

The boy backed away, hands up. "What did I do, Coach?"

"Coach? Quentin, this kid is my stalker. He's the one who delivered my bracelet."

"Willow, no. Denton is my quarterback," Quentin slapped a hand on the young man's shoulder. "A good kid."

Darrell ran to the counter for towels and attempted to mop up the tea that drenched Laurel.

"I did deliver a package to your house this afternoon on my break." The young man looked her in the eye. "This guy gave me twenty dollars."

Quentin whacked the kid in the head. "What were you thinking?"

Willow fell into the chair, taking deep breaths.

"I'm sorry, ma'am. He said you were an old friend. He wanted to surprise you with the gift before seeing you."

Willow looked from Quentin to the boy. He did seem remorseful until he cast his gaze upon Laurel. Then a quick smile turned his lips.

"Willow, meet Denton Goodyear. He's usually a bright kid, thinks things through, and I believe his story."

Goodyear. That explained the smirk. Willow nodded and turned her attention to Laurel. She burst into laughter. "This is how I always dreamed getting even would look like."

"What?" Laurel's eyes grew large. Tea dripped from her hair. A droplet slid along the bridge of her nose and plopped onto her skirt.

Willow leaned back in her chair, grabbing her sides to keep the ache at bay. "But I never knew we'd be friends."

Quentin laughed, stopped, leaned behind Denton then laughed again. The kid joined in. Darrell was Laurel's only stone-faced friend, but only for a second. Laurel giggled, and Darrell's laughter rang louder than all.

Willow wiped tears of glee from her face.

Quentin motioned Denton to the side, taking care of business. Too amused at her cousin's calamity, she allowed him to get the details.

Quentin cast an uneasy glance at the stoic woman sitting in his passenger's seat. Contentious. Willow had been that way with him since leaving the bookstore. They had fun, but as soon as they'd separated from Laurel and Darrell, she'd grown sullen.

"What did the Goodyear boy say he looked like?" Willow pressed for the third time now.

"Non-descript. What else can I say? Denton isn't keeping anything from us." Quentin turned to head down the other side of the mountain toward their homes. No matter how often he drove the road, even when he wasn't behind the wheel, the hairpin turn caused anxiety.

Willow placed her hand on the dashboard of the Jeep until he made it around the curve.

"He's going to keep an eye out for him, and he'll call. Sheriff Dixon was going to get the information from him."

Willow looked beyond him and to the lake below. The sun was sinking behind the trees, reminding Quentin of a charcoal drawing she'd done years before. Where had her artwork gone? Had she given up so totally on her dreams?

"I'm glad you and Laurel made nice." Maybe changing the conversation would bring the happy Willow back to him.

"Did you know we're both named after Granny?"

"No, or if I did, I don't remember it."

"Her middle name is Elizabeth, and mine is ..."

"I know your middle name." He cut her off, her bad mood rubbing off on him, or was he simply annoyed she'd never realized everything about her was engraved on his heart?

"What's wrong with you?" they both asked at the same time.

"Just the way you're acting, Willow, as if you blame me for something. What have I done?"

She crossed her arms over her chest and huffed once, settling down with a scowl on her face.

"Really, I'd like to know. Speak, Scrappy."

They were heading down the mountain road into the holler they both called home.

"I don't know what's wrong with me, *Hoot.*"

"And I'm supposed to take the brunt of your nasty disposition because you don't know how to handle an emotion?"

"Shut up." She frowned.

"So, what are you feeling right now? Let's get to the bottom of it." He turned his Jeep into her driveway.

She grabbed the door handle, and he pushed the button to lock it.

"Hoot, let me out."

"Not until you tell me why I'm under fire. Your entire attitude changed right after we left the store."

She reached across and pushed at him. "I'm afraid. Okay? I'm really afraid of the psycho playing games with me."

"And that means you can treat me like this?" Yet, who else would allow her anger to be taken out on him? He'd loved her forever. He would never stop.

She started to retort but clamped her mouth shut.

"Willow, I'm here. I'm doing my best to keep you safe."

"It's not your job."

"Well, I enlisted, and I will not abandon my post."

A smile slid across her lips and melted into nothingness. "I don't know why you would. I'm bitter and hard. Even now, I'm making you miserable."

"No." He touched her arm. "You're frustrating me. I'll take that over miserable anytime. To tell you the truth, the only time I was miserable was the ten or so years you were gone, but who's counting?"

Again, a smile peeked through.

He leaned toward her. "We had a good time tonight. Laurel got all sticky from four cups of sweet iced tea. That's a good evening for Willow Jade Thomas."

Willow stifled a giggle with her hands. "Yeah, I guess it was."

"So, let's go watch a movie or something and enjoy the evening before I take up residence on your front porch."

She leaned away from him. "Why do you insist on the front porch?"

He studied her face. Had her morals been so corrupted by a New York lifestyle that she didn't realize a compromising position? "Because I don't want anyone to talk about you, to give you an undeserved reputation."

"So gallant," she teased. "But when no one notices you, it's pretty hard to gain a reputation."

He touched the soft tendrils of her mahogany hair and pushed them aside. His hand brushed her cheek and lingered there. "I've noticed you."

She leaned into his touch. "You left me alone."

"Because someone told me lies, someone who wishes she hadn't. But that's in the past."

Willow closed her eyes, and a single tear ran along the edge of his hand to his wrist.

"Oh, baby, don't cry. Let's just start over here and now."

As if awaking from a dream, Willow pulled from his touch. "There's no starting over, Hoot."

He took a deep breath. Would her bitterness forever keep them separated? Robert Thomas's face crossed his mind. How did he live with Agatha day in and day out? Quentin nodded. "You know what? I think you're right. Until you can let the past go and realize I'm the future, there is no new beginning for us." He flicked the lock up and opened his door.

Before he could get to her side, she was halfway to her porch. He hurried after her, not wanting her to lock him out before he had a chance to check the place over.

Her scream pierced the air.

He ran in front of her, arms out to protect her from whatever she'd found. "Bear," he breathed. "You scared us."

"What are you doing here?" Willow demanded. "Get off my porch. Get away from me."

Bear cast Quentin a weary look.

"For all I know, you're the stalker. Maybe you're working in combination with someone. I don't know why—" Willow moved around Quentin.

"He's been here in Amazing Grace for over five years," Quentin said. "Come on. Give the guy a break."

"I'm not your stalker, Willow." Bear cocked his head to the side and smiled at her. "I'm your uncle."

Willow had started toward her front door to unlock it. Now, she spun toward him. "You're what?"

"Uncle Ted," Bear reinforced.

She stared him down. Quentin didn't know how the older man stood up under her scrutiny. When she straightened, Quentin remembered to breathe. She cast a glance to him and then to Bear. "Good night, gentlemen." She walked inside, closed the door, and turned the latch.

"Willow, I'd like to check the place over. Open up."

"She's fine." Bear nodded. "I've surveyed the perimeter. No one's gotten inside."

"I guess I better go get my rifle, sleeping bag, and pillow."

"Give me a minute, will you?" Bear stepped off the porch and into the yard with him. "I've been thinking about the attack on Agatha. Why would the stalker harm Aggie?"

"To get Willow's attention. To frighten her, which he's done."

"But anyone who saw those two together knows there's no love lost between Agatha and Willow. If he wanted to gain her attention like that, he'd go after you, boy."

"Maybe this guy sees himself as ridding Willow of her enemies."

Bear shook his head. "No. He's threatening Willow directly. The profile doesn't match."

"So now you're a profiler."

"I've studied people for a lot of years." Ted raised a brow. "I think this guy stumbled across a great opportunity to scare Willow. The photo Willow received wasn't immediately after the attack. The deputies were there."

And how did Bear know this? Willow told Quentin later at the bookstore. Did Bear have connections? Yeah, he probably did. Sheriff Dixon and Bear were good friends, had been since Bear's arrival—probably were friends most of their lives.

"Yeah, I know all about the case," Bear grumbled. "And don't you worry how I know. Anyone could be a suspect. Aggie has a lot of enemies."

And one of those enemies had threatened Agatha earlier in the day. That enemy had a trademark way of attack—cowardly and from behind.

Tomorrow, Quentin would confront that enemy, and he'd take a witness with him when he did. "Mind sitting here for a minute while I get my stuff?"

"I can hold watch tonight. You need some rest."

"Nothing doing. If you want a sleeping bag, I'll bring you one, but I'm staying here."

"Bring me one." Bear nodded.

CHAPTER TWELVE

Confronting Cooper Goodyear seemed like a good idea to Quentin until he pulled up in front of the man's business. Flags advertising different brands of tires blew in the soft April breeze. Inside, Goodyear stood behind the counter.

He'd like to think even Cooper wouldn't attack Agatha, but the woman could be a wildcat. Still, he'd known the man to be far less than a gentleman—a womanizer, an adulterer, a letch, a man who served alcohol to minors, and seduced young girls.

"What are we waiting for?" Darrell pulled on his tie. They'd come from church, both still in their suits.

Quentin had left Bear watching out for Willow so that he could teach his middle grade Sunday school class and attend worship.

"You wouldn't let me go home and change, and now you just sit here?"

Quentin couldn't argue. He needed the truth. If Goodyear had harmed Agatha, he could at least give Willow the good news her stalker had not attacked her aunt—unless Cooper had planned this entire setup to bring Willow home and complete some kind of revenge upon Agatha. The thought made him angry, but it didn't fit with the guy hiring Denton to take the package unless you added another layer of conspiracy. "Let's go."

He pulled the glass door open and walked inside. The smell of rubber assaulted his senses. Quentin rubbed his nose to keep from sneezing.

Cooper looked up, continued with some paperwork and then did a double take. He put down his pen. "Unless you're here to buy a set of tires, I have nothing to say to either one of you."

"Normally, I'd agree with you, but I want to know where you were when Agatha Thomas was attacked yesterday." Quentin leaned against the counter and watched Goodyear's face for even the slightest twitch. Darrell hung back. Quentin had only asked him to come to act as witness. Goodyear was surely capable of making up any kind of story.

"I don't see you wearing a badge on your scrawny little chest now, do I? So you can just get out of my store, or I'll call the police."

In Quentin's peripheral view, Darrell straightened. "That didn't answer Quentin's question."

"What do you know about Willow Thomas and a bracelet delivered to her yesterday?" Quentin asked.

Goodyear narrowed his eyes and shook his head. "That blow I gave you to your face knock your brains loose or something? I don't even know the girl. I remember something about her parents abandoning her to live the high life in Hollywood, but that's about all I know."

"And you didn't have someone give Denton a bracelet yesterday to deliver to Willow?"

"Get out of here," Goodyear looked back to his paperwork. "I only talk with paying customers. I don't need you losers taking up my time with conspiracy theories."

Quentin slammed his hand down on the papers. "Let's pretend you know nothing about Willow or the bracelet. Fine. Let's move on. Why did you attack Agatha?"

The man's beady eyes darted back and forth between Quentin and Darrell. "Get your hands off my stuff, and get out of my store before I call the police."

"That's the second time you've threatened us with that. Go ahead. I'll let them know about the argument and the threat I overheard yesterday." Quentin stuck his hands in his pants pockets.

Goodyear stomped from behind the counter to stand toe-to-toe with Quentin. "Get out of my store."

Whatcha gonna do if I don't. The words were so tempting, but Quentin stood his ground. "Tell me you didn't harm an innocent woman, and I'll get gone and stay gone."

Goodyear laughed. "Innocent? That woman? No one is stupid enough to believe Agatha Thomas didn't get what she deserves."

"No woman deserves to be treated the way you treat them, Cooper. You're a lousy little weasel. I suspect you saw her standing outside." Quentin pointed across the street. "Her back was to you, and in your usual fashion, you clobbered her from behind. Must make you feel like a big man doing that to a woman."

Goodyear's fist rounded toward Quentin, who ducked the blow. The force spun Cooper around. He looked stunned for a moment. Then turning back, he swung. Quentin moved away unscathed, but Goodyear stumbled backward against a display. Tires wobbled and fell, bouncing to the ground around Cooper, who fell clumsily into them.

Quentin watched the older man get to his feet before starting for the door. He motioned to his friend. "Let's go."

Darrell gave a solemn nod, and they turned.

The door opened. "Coach—Mr. Jacobs—I have great—" Denton's eyes widened. "Coach, watch out!"

Quentin spun around. Cooper stood with a shotgun leveled right at Quentin.

"You coward." Quentin lunged, taking the man off balance.

"I'll kill you!" Goodyear fought with Quentin. "Why do you have to get involved with everything I do, always lousing it up? My marriage? My kid? A little harmless ..."

Quentin wrestled the man, attempting to wretch the gun away, struggling to get Cooper's hands off the trigger. The gun went off. Quentin felt the power of the weapon against his hand. The explosion rocked him. He stumbled backward. His foot hit one of the tires that had fallen earlier. He found the rack. Putting his hands out, he braced himself and stayed on his feet.

"Lord, no." Darrell choked out. "No! No! No!" He fell to his knees near the door.

Goodyear dropped his gun.

Quentin's world turned in slow motion, and he could only follow Goodyear as the man scrambled to his son. Blood soaked Denton's shirt.

Police vehicles from the station only a block down pulled up in front of the store. Armed policemen ran inside, guns raised. Quentin held up his hands, though he didn't know how long he could stay on his feet.

Darrell swallowed and looked up to Quentin. His friend shook his head.

"What have I done? What have I done?" Goodyear released a guttural scream.

The paramedics arrived, and the officers fought to pull Goodyear away from Denton.

Quentin held his breath, waiting for a pronouncement. He expected them to give up, but instead, they began to work, shouting orders to one another. "I have a pulse. I have a pulse."

Darrell made his way to him. He grasped Quentin under his arm as Quentin's legs refused to support his weight.

Goodyear stood outside blubbering, trying to climb into the ambulance.

A deputy stopped him and brought him back into the store. "I want statements from all of you. Now."

Willow ran from Bear's truck into the emergency room. She stopped short when she saw Darrell, the front of his shirt and his hands covered in blood.

Darrell nodded to the opposite side of the room. Quentin sat, his head in his hands, rocking back and forth as he prayed. "Give him life. Give him long life. Dear God, please don't take that boy away from the people who love him."

Willow looked back to Darrell. "What happened?"

Darrell shook his head. "Quentin struggled to get a gun away from Cooper Goodyear. The gun went off. Denton was in the line of fire."

Willow trembled. "The boy—Quentin's quarterback? The one who works for Henry and Grace?" She pushed her hair from her face. "Why would that boy's father want to harm Hoot? Is this over the fight they had at the school?"

Darrell shook his head. "Goodyear is the one who put Agatha in the hospital. Quentin went there for the truth. He wanted to assure you the stalker hadn't attacked her."

Willow fell back against the wall close to Darrell. Hoot could have died—because he wanted her to feel safe. If he'd been killed, she'd never get to say she was sorry for treating him so badly the night before—for treating him so badly most of their lives.

Now Quentin would blame himself for what had happened. Coming back to Amazing Grace was a big mistake. Hoot was alive, but a young man could die because of her.

"Dear Lord, Your will be done in the life of this boy. Guard over his family. Hold his parents up during this time.

Show us mercy, God, as only Your perfect will can attest."
Bear's voice lifted in prayer from his seat beside Quentin.

Quentin continued to rock back and forth.

The emergency room doors opened, and Laurel ran inside.
Her gaze darted around the room. "Oh, thank You, God." She
came to stand beside Willow. "I went to Manna's for coffee.
They told me." She reached up and touched Darrell's face with
her hands then she took his hands in hers. "Are you hurt?"
Laurel showed none of the hysterics Willow would have
suspected.

Darrell shook his head. "I'm fine."

"You're not. You're shaking."

A woman entered through the glass doors and hurried to
the front desk. She slammed her hand on the bell several times.
"Nurse ... Nurse!"

Was it Willow's imagination or did Laurel slip behind
Darrell? The woman looked around the room, and her gaze fell
upon Laurel before she rang the bell again.

The attendant came from behind and opened the glass.
"I'm Denton Goodyear's mother. I want to see my son."

Quentin stood. "Mary?"

Denton's mother raised her hand. "I can't, Coach
McPheron. Not now."

Quentin nodded. He sank back into the seat. He
swallowed hard, his gaze lingering on the doorway the woman
had entered.

Willow sat beside him. His chair shook with his
trembling.

Bear reached across the back of Quentin's chair and
touched her.

Quentin buried his face in his hands. "Merciful God,
merciful God, merciful God." The two-word prayer spilled
from his lips. "The Lord hath heard my supplication; the Lord

will receive my prayer. Merciful God, merciful God. Let this boy live a long life."

If she wasn't so far from God herself, she might find a way to pray. Instead, she listened to Quentin.

"Hear me when I call, O God o my righteousness: thou hast relieved me when I was in distress; have mercy upon me, and hear my prayer."

Bear lowered his head again. "Amen."

What could she do? She had no comfort for him. She stood and looked out the window. In the reflection, Laurel urged Darrell to the men's room to wash the blood off his hands. Darrell nodded. Laurel kept her distance, staring into the window of the attendant's station.

Willow had no comfort for her either. A fish could breathe out of water better than she could offer words of solace to these people.

God help them. Give that boy life. Thank You for sparing Hoot.

From where had that come? Prayer was foreign to her now. The words were stale in her mind. Would God hear such a non-descript plea when Quentin offered so many eloquent words?

The doors from the trauma center opened, and Denton's mother walked out under the care of a nurse. "I'm sorry, Mrs. Goodyear. I'm very sorry."

Mary gave a slight nod.

Darrell came from the men's room, drying his hands on a paper towel. He stopped.

Quentin pushed up. He took an unsteady step forward. "I'm so sorry, Mary. I never meant for this to happen."

Mary shook her head and walked outside. The woman's face was white pale, but not a tear flowed. Most people would think it odd, but Willow remembered the day Granny had died. She'd stood above her grandmother's body while Quentin tried to breathe life back into Granny. She hadn't cried. Couldn't cry. The pain was too deep.

Willow followed the woman. "Ms. Goodyear."

The woman turned, a question forming in the downward turn of her brows.

"My name is Willow Thomas."

The woman's face softened.

"I'm sorry for your loss. I know you don't know me, but ..."

Mary reached and touched Willow's face. She turned and stared through the glass. "Go to him. He needs you. I know who you are." She wrapped Willow in an embrace. "And you gave me one of the greatest gifts in the world, one I'll treasure until my dying day."

Willow stared after her as the woman walked way.

Bear came from inside. "I'm going to drive her. One of you take my truck. I'll get a ride home." He tossed his keys. Willow caught them.

Bear rushed forward and collected the distraught woman in his arms. He held her for some time before walking with her to her vehicle.

Willow walked inside.

Quentin paced back and forth like a lion awaiting release from his cage to devour a victim. He stopped and slammed his foot against the chair. "Why?" he screamed. "Why, God? Why?"

"God forgive me for this," Laurel wailed. "I might as well have pulled the trigger."

"Shh, no, that's not true." Darrell pulled Laurel into his embrace. "I won't let you blame yourself."

Willow reached out to touch Quentin's arm, to offer him some kind of comfort. Quentin shrugged from her caress. "Hoot?" she whispered his name.

He turned away from her.

She waited for him to collect his emotions, but he never looked back at her. He sank to the chair once again, his hands grasping his hair.

So, nothing had changed. God still didn't answer her prayers. He didn't answer Hoot's either, no matter how sincere. An innocent young man had died. And for what?

Laurel stayed wrapped in Darrell's embrace. Quentin remained unmoving in his grief, and Willow slipped out the door.

Alone. What had happened to Willow's protectors? How had she slipped by them, and how could he take advantage of this time?

LeBlanc sat back against the seat of his car and peered through the binoculars. This little alcove kept him hidden from the big man he'd learned lived in the cabin behind her home. In fact, Willow and the big man had driven out together, and she was driving in alone—in the big man's truck. Both times, they'd failed to see him in his hiding spot.

Now, she slowed to take that sharp turn downward. He had her alone on the mountain. His fingers itched to put a little more fright into her, but how to do it? With each scare, his body yearned for more. Of course, this had started out as a job, a small incident to get the paparazzi involved.

Willow Thomas's fright didn't make her irrational the way it would most women. She was still scared though, and he got a thrill out of seeing her pale and fidgety, yet never fully caving in. He wanted more and more. The familiar itch would soon bring her demise—as it had ended the lives of so many others.

The thoughts of how he'd reveal himself to her tormented him. LeBlanc needed the chase, the thrill of knowing she feared him, even if she didn't know who he was. He'd almost given himself away, gone too far, ending the charade. But he'd pulled it off. So close he'd even touched her, smiled at her, met her eye to eye—comforted her.

His cell phone rang. He dug it out of his pocket, rolling his eyes at the name on his caller ID. "Yeah."

"Where are you?"

"I'm where you want me." He lowered the visor and stared at his image.

"I don't understand why you haven't done what I've paid you to do."

"Takes a little time. She's a bit stronger than you led me to believe, and she's surrounded by a lot of people."

"Trouble's on its way."

"Why? Are you coming to town?" He laughed.

"Someone far worse, and I'd advise you to stay hidden."

Willow pulled into her driveway.

"Gotta go." He hung up.

No one would tell him how this would end. He opened the car door and slid out. He'd make his own ending. Right here. Right now.

Quentin had been unable to leave the hospital. Any minute now he'd wake up from this nightmare or a doctor would come out, looking for Mary to tell her he'd been wrong. The boy was still alive.

"Quentin?" Laurel touched his arm. "Where's Willow?"

Quentin looked up, running the back of his hand across his eyes. "Willow?"

Laurel's eyes were moist with her own tears as she stooped to look up at him. "She was here. Didn't you realize?"

Quentin shook his head. He remembered Bear. He'd whispered something about leaving to take Mary home. Of course, Willow would have been with him. Bear wouldn't have left her at home alone. In his grief, he hadn't noticed.

Darrell came around the corner from the main lobby. "She's not here."

"No." Quentin jumped to his feet. "She left alone?"

"I assume so." Darrell shrugged.

"She can't be alone. Laurel, give Darrell a ride home." He ran from the hospital, looking for Bear's truck. "Willow," he breathed. What would make her do something this foolish?

Pulling out of the parking lot, he looked in his rearview mirror. Darrell was driving Laurel's car, and he was right on Quentin's tail.

Willow lay across the bed, where she'd fallen in a fit of tears. She'd meant to throw her belongings into her suitcase and leave, but she couldn't. She didn't want to go back to the loneliness of New York.

She rolled over and stared at the ceiling. Who would blame Hoot for pushing her away? Her bitterness had ripped at him like a jagged piece of glass. He was close to Denton Goodyear, and now the boy was dead. She hadn't left him much to hold on to, especially when she'd slammed the door on him last night.

The coffee she'd brought out in the morning said little to either Hoot or her uncle that she cared. Yet Uncle Ted didn't leave her alone when Hoot left for church.

She sniffed and pushed herself up. Standing in front of the mirror, she looked at her red nose and blotchy face. How long had it been since she cared enough for anyone or anything to cry like this? She reached for the heart shaped jewelry holder and held it in her hand before taking off the lid and lifting the opal necklace with the ring attached to the chain. Granny's prayer note crinkled under her touch and she opened it.

"Dear Lord, in time, I pray my granddaughters learn that, like this case and this necklace, they complement each other. Both are the finishing touches on the world you've given to me. One is no more important than the other, because without either, I'd be less than what I am."

Granny understood her better than she ever understood herself. Even in her childhood, before the truth broke, the roots of resentment had begun to grow. Shallow then, she'd fertilized them with her jealousy of Laurel and her family, of dreams of her father coming home to rescue her.

By the time the tabloid story broke, the roots had already dug deep, choking out the chance for her to see any goodness. They wrapped around her heart and pulled her from everything she'd known. New York had given the bitterness more fertile ground to grow. The big city also separated her from anyone who could show her how ugly the bitterness looked on her.

In the mirror's reflection Granny's prayer journal caught her eye. She put the jewelry back inside, set the heart on the dresser, turned, and snatched up the notebook. With the treasure in her hand, she sat on the bed. "So, Granny, what wisdom do you have for me today?" She flipped to a random page.

"Set me as a seal upon thine heart, as a seal upon thine arm: for love is strong as death; jealousy is cruel as the grave: the coals thereof are coals of fire, which hath a most vehement flame. Many waters cannot quench love, neither can the floods drown it: if a man would give all the substance of his house for love, it would utterly be contemned. Song of Solomon 8:6-7."

Willow took a steadying breath before reading her grandmother's prayer. "Willow, Lord, may she understand the truth of these verses. Someday, this child will have to live without me. I've fought so long to dispel the anger burning in her heart. She thinks, Lord, You are not in control. Her heart is flooded with jealousy. May those flames one day be doused by floods of love."

Willow turned the page.

"A gift is a precious stone in the eyes of him that hath it; whithersoever it turneth ... it prospereth. Proverbs 17:8."

Willow read the Bible passage twice before she looked to her grandmother's written prayer. "Someday, Lord, I will give Willow the bracelet, and I pray she'll learn the significance for her. I will leave my wedding ring to Laurel, but Willow will have to be the one to gift her with it. May my granddaughters see both gifts were equally precious to their giver.

"Yes, Lord, I want Willow to give Laurel my wedding ring, but only when both their hearts can see through the anger and the jealousy, only when Willow's response to this request can be done with a heart filled with love for Laurel. I also pray by then You will let Willow receive the precious gift You've kept before her all these years. When she receives her treasure, my prayer is for Willow to give Laurel an even more precious gift. Yet, I would never ask it of Willow unless the other gift first becomes hers."

Riddles. Now Willow was sure the ring belonged to her cousin, but what was the other gift Granny left for Laurel, and what was the treasure Granny mentioned? "I'm sure you know, Lord. I guess You'll have to be the one to tell me."

The look on Laurel's face when Willow handed her back Granny's portrait was a memory that grew more precious each time Willow thought of it. In giving the drawing to her cousin, Willow had prospered. Her heart had lightened just a bit. Her soul had risen above the jealousy, if only for a moment.

She left the journal on the bed and moved to the dresser. With a gentle hold, Willow lifted the lid on the ceramic heart and again pulled out the necklace and the ring. Grasping the jewelry in her hand, she stared at her reflection.

No, she wasn't ready to do this. Yet, the necklace belonged to Laurel, too. If she started there ... She opened the clasp and pulled the ring from the chain, placing the ring on the dresser. Then she held up the necklace, letting it drape across her fingers. In her other hand, she grasped the ceramic heart. Granny had found them equally precious to her.

A scrape sounded below. Glass shattered.

Willow's entire body quaked. She dropped the heart-shaped lid. It fell against the hardwood floor, breaking in half. Again she heard the breaking of glass followed by the crack of wood. She froze, her breath coming in shallow gulps.

She'd been so caught up in her emotions she'd left herself vulnerable.

"Willow, I'm here for you." A muffled voice rose eerily from below, far below—perhaps in the basement.

With shaky feet, she made it through her bedroom door. She held to the banister as her wobbly legs managed to get her down the stairs.

She stopped by the basement door and listened. Someone was rustling through years of her grandmother's accumulation. She grasped the doorknob of the basement door and leaned hard against it. Her hands trembled. She fought to turn the bolt lock above the knob. Her fingers failed to tighten around it.

"Please, God. Please," she whispered.

She clasped her hand around the knob, and tightened her hold on the tumbler. It fell into place. Then she ran to the kitchen and grabbed a knife.

With soft steps, she made her way back to the edge of the hallway and lifted the blade above her head. The chain of the opal necklace she held in her fingers, dinged against the stainless steel. Willow didn't move. If he broke through the door, she'd be ready.

Only problem, her body shook as if she were the epicenter of an earthquake, the chain and the opal swaying back and forth like a pendulum. Could she really use the knife to defend herself?

She listened, daring to move closer to the door. With her ear pressed against the wood, she fought to keep her breath low and steady.

No sound.

Nothing.

She breathed a sigh of relief and lowered the knife. But if the stalker had gotten into the basement, he could break any window in the house, gaining entrance despite all of Quentin's safeguards.

Her false sense of security gave way to terror. A clamor on the front porch, and a turn of the knob on her front door loosened her grip on the knife. It fell to the floor. She covered her eyes and screamed.

Strong arms wrapped around her waist from behind, and she fought against them.

"Willow." Quentin held fast. "Willow, it's me."

She lowered her hands and gulped for breath. In his hold, she stopped her struggle and turned to bury her face against his strong chest, his earthy scent comforting her. "He's in the basement."

He started to pull away, but she clung to him. "No. Hoot. I want you. I need you. Don't leave me. Please don't push me away again. I can't bear it. I realized when you didn't want me to touch you in the hospital—I—I love you. I've always loved you."

"Go," he said to someone, then his hand brushed her tear-moistened hair from her face. "If I pushed you away, I didn't do it consciously. Forgive me." With his index finger, he tilted her head so she could see into his eyes.

"I'm sorry, so sorry for not telling you before and for staying away." Willow peeked up into the evergreen hue of his eyes.

He kissed her forehead as he held her close to him. "Ah, a weeping Willow in my arms. My prayers have been answered."

She hiccupped against him, and he held her to him, not moving for a long moment.

"There's a broken window. The wood is gone and all. Broken from the outside. I don't think this guy was playing around. He didn't expect us, but I think he heard us coming." Darrell came from behind.

Willow allowed Quentin to release her, but she reached for his hand. He laced his fingers with hers.

"And footprints to and from the window." Laurel held to Darrell's hand in the same way.

Quentin growled low and turned to her. He held Willow's face in his hands. "Don't ever do this again."

If God would let her have this man in her life forever, she'd never argue with him again. "No. I won't."

"What's that in your hand?" Laurel asked her.

Willow looked down. Through it all, she'd clung to the necklace without realizing it. She held it up. "This isn't the gift Granny wanted you to have, but it does belong to you."

Laurel released her hold on Darrell's hand. She took the necklace and then wrapped Willow in an embrace. "I picked this out for her as a Christmas gift when I was little."

"We were ten," Willow told her. "She kept it in the ceramic heart I'd bought for her along with one of her notes and the other gift she mentioned in her journal." The ceramic heart with the broken lid.

Ironic that a broken ceramic heart laying on the floor of Granny's bedroom came with more healing to Willow's once shattered heart.

Laurel held the necklace up for Darrell. He took it from her and slipped it around her neck. Then he dropped his hands to her shoulders.

Laurel touched Willow's shoulder. "You don't ever have to give me the other."

"But I will—when I've met the requirements."

Laurel nodded. "I understand. Maybe someday it will be a most appropriate gift." She tilted her head to the tall fellow standing behind her. "If you know what I mean."

"What should we do, Quentin?" Darrell apparently missed the remark … or maybe he didn't. Darrell was a lot of things, but Willow knew he wasn't dumb. After all, he'd been the substitute for Quentin's lost friendship in high school—and he'd gotten her through calculus, patiently listening to her complaints that no one needed that much math.

"The stalker has to be hiding somewhere around the lake." Quentin slipped his arm around Willow's waist. She was sure the remark had sailed completely under his radar.

"Willow, where are you?" Bear ran into the house. "Is everything okay?"

"She's here." Quentin pulled her with him to the living room. "How'd you get home?"

"Daniel—Sheriff Dixon."

"We passed the area before Widow's Peak and a car pulled out of the woods. Daniel and I were torn between going after him, but I wanted to make ..." He took a deep breath and cast a weary glance in Laurel's direction. "He's long gone."

"Now we know where he was hiding," Darrell said. "Willow was home alone."

"Alone?" Bear narrowed his eyes in her direction.

"I—yes, I drove your truck home." She lowered her gaze. Was this what it was like to feel the chastisement of a father?

"He busted out a basement window. I think we scared him off," Darrell said.

"Thank goodness." Bear ran a hand through his graying hair.

"How's Mary?" Quentin's face bore the weight of the remembered passing of the young man.

Willow placed her hand against his cheek, and he leaned into her touch. Sadness lingered even with the soft upward turn of his lips. He took her hand in his and kissed her palm before turning his attention back to Bear.

"Her mother and father met us at her home. She's in rough shape. Losing your only child is a hard thing to endure." Bear looked away. His jaw rose with the clenching of his teeth. He cleared his throat and looked back to them. "She's going to have some long, grief-filled days. The pain never goes away."

Quentin sat hard on the couch. He closed his eyes and released a long sigh. "He was such a good kid. How will she go on?"

Willow had no words of wisdom for him. Her lessons in moving on had only started since her return home.

And she felt responsible for the lost life of the young man so important to Quentin.

She sat beside him and placed a gentle hand on his back. "I'm so sorry."

"So am I." He traced his finger down her chin. "But together, we can get through anything."

"Together," Bear mumbled. "Do you understand that, Willow? Together." He stormed toward the door.

Willow chased after him. "Bear!"

He stepped off the porch and turned.

Willow threw her arms around his neck. "Scott's not here. And I don't care. You're exactly the way I thought you would always be."

His arms tightened around her. "And you're more beautiful than I ever imagined. But, shh, Laurel doesn't know who I am. That's our secret. We don't want Aggie finding out, now do we?" He released her, and Willow stepped back. Bear put his hand on the top of her head, resting it there. "And don't give up on your dad just yet. I'm not through with him." He turned and walked toward the woods between their homes.

CHAPTER THIRTEEN

Quentin stood alone. The early morning dew caused recently cut grass clippings to cling to his best pair of shoes. A chill filled the air, but Quentin didn't know if a drop in temperature caused it or his bleeding heart.

The cemetery was a lonely place, and he'd come here to pray, to find peace with God. He reached and gripped the back of the old wooden folding chair sitting under the funeral tent. He lowered himself to the seat and bowed his head. "Denton, I already miss you, kid. I thought I'd feel this way when you graduated and went off to college. This is too permanent, Dent. I'm so sorry."

The funeral would begin in less than a half hour. Mary Goodyear would arrive, and he needed to know how to answer her, to comfort her. Yet, Quentin felt little comfort.

With eyes closed, he centered his thoughts upon God. When he needed peace he often found it in thanksgiving. So he began there, thanking God for his goodness toward him. He had so much abundance. Where would he begin?

"Thank you for Willow. Not yet all the desires of my heart, but Lord I'm trusting in you."

Over the past few days he'd seen Willow soften. They'd spent a lot of time with Laurel and Darrell. He'd helped her shop for a dress for the funeral. She'd even volunteered to join him here, but he'd needed this time alone. Instead, she planned to follow Bear down the mountain. Her uncle arrived at the house, suit and tie in hand. Bear planned to change while Willow dressed.

"Thank you for Darrell, my friend, who has gone through this with me, and for Laurel. Thank you ..." he choked. "For allowing me to know this boy, to have him touch my life, to have the memory of him."

The sobs began again. Every time he found himself alone, the sorrow devastated him. He'd allowed this to happen. "I'm sorry. So sorry, Lord, that I have failed You—failed Denton. Oh, Lord, how can I ever receive peace when I don't know where he is?"

Quentin rocked back and forth waiting for something, a verse, some sort of comfort.

O ye of little faith.

The small, still voice inside of him stopped his movement. "Yes, Lord. I have little faith," he said to the stillness. "But You said I can move mountains with a very small amount of faith."

Believe in Me.

But Denton was already gone. How could he ever know?

A soft hand touched his shoulder. He looked up to the woman who sat beside him. "This is not your fault," she said.

"If I'd let the police handle it. They'd have ..."

Mary Goodyear put her finger to her lips. "We can't go by what we should have done. If we're going to do that, I should have moved out of this town long ago when I divorced Cooper."

"Mary, He—Denton was a good kid. His biggest problem was thinking with his heart and not his head."

"Cooper tried for years to kill Denton's kind spirit. That's why Denton warred, choosing sometimes to fight for what he loved." She picked at a Kleenex she held in her had.

Denton's fight with Troy had been over his girlfriend. He thought he'd lost her to his teammate. He'd seen the boys since, laughing and cutting up, the fight forgotten. Thank God

Troy didn't have that on his conscious, not that he'd done anything wrong.

"Quentin, there's one person responsible for what happened to Denton, and that's his father."

"What's going to happen?"

She nodded. "Daniel said since he pulled the gun, they plan to arrest him for culpable negligence following the funeral today. I wanted to warn you he's itching for a fight. He's drinking to dull the truth of what he's done. Sheriff Dixon is sending officers in plain clothes. Daniel said you didn't want him charged with your attempted murder."

Quentin shook his head. "He's suffered enough. And I'm sorry you have to go through all of this."

She nodded again and looked at the casket. "My only son."

Behind them, mourners began to arrive. Car doors closed and the murmur of voices began to fill the morning air. Quentin stood. "If you need anything, you call me."

"I have something to give you." Mary looked up at him. "I'll bring it to you sometime later if you don't mind."

Quentin blinked. "Sure." He kissed her cheek. "Whenever you're ready."

She held to his hand for as long as she could before dropping it to let him leave. "He cared for you, Quentin. Very much."

Quentin turned. As if God had planned it that way, the first person he laid eyes upon was Willow. She walked toward him, her new black dress billowing around her shapely legs. Her dark hair hung in curls, and he smiled.

When he'd knocked on her door, she'd greeted him with curlers in her hair. As soon as he'd reached to touch them, she remembered. "Quentin," She'd squealed, running up the stairs while he'd let himself inside.

Beauty personified. That's what she was. She tilted her head with a knowing look before taking his hand in hers. Soft. That's the word that described her features. He could have chosen relaxed, but there was so much more to it than that. The hardness in her eyes and in the lines around her eyes and mouth had softened along with her heart.

She'd attended Wednesday night Bible study with him at the church, sitting between him and Laurel. Darrell had joined them there, too. At the end of the service, Willow had cried.

He'd left her alone, said nothing about it. When she was ready, she'd tell him—or she'd tell Laurel. They were all beginning to renew old acquaintances and to step beyond the boundaries of friendship. Darrell had teased him about how they had to be accountable to each other toward their relationships with those Thomas girls. He'd both cursed and blessed Darrell for that accountability over the last few days. Of course, he had the extra incentive of keeping on Bear's good side. Darrell could live in blissful ignorance, not realizing the danger so close to him in the form of Laurel's long-lost uncle.

"You look gorgeous." Quentin kissed Willow's cheek.

"Hoot, this is a funeral, not a date." She feigned aggravation. "But truth is you look pretty spiffy in your dark suit. I can't wait to see you in a tuxedo one day."

He stared at her for a long moment. Did she realize what she said? He cleared his throat. "You are the only one who will ever get me into a tuxedo."

"Hey," Laurel came beside her along with Robert.

"Saved by the relatives," he whispered into her ear.

Willow hugged Robert. Quentin didn't need to ask about Agatha. Still encased in her bitterness, the woman had declared Cooper Goodyear got what he'd deserved.

"And Denton?" Quentin's anger had flared.

"Well, Mr. McPheron, I assume that he's not too much unlike his father."

"That would be like saying Laurel is just like you, Agatha, and we all know that's not true."

Quentin wished he'd said it, but the words had come from her husband, and they had effectively shut down a very volatile argument. Needless to say, Agatha Thomas would not be giving her condolences to Mary Goodyear today or any day soon.

As Laurel walked past him, Quentin squeezed Willow's hand in his and said a silent prayer for Mary to render as much grace upon Laurel as she'd given to him. When Mary rose, she listened as Laurel spoke to her, then she nodded.

Emotion flamed within Quentin as Mary pulled Laurel to her and hugged her. Every eye seemed to fall upon the scene. A collective intake of breath released as Laurel kissed Mary's cheek and walked back toward them.

"I'm so proud of you." Darrell joined them. He placed his arm around Laurel's shoulder and stood tall. Why was it that alongside the adorable blonde, Darrell Jacobs lost his geek status?

"Coach. Mr. Jacobs." A group of boys encircled the four of them.

Darrell raised his brow, and Quentin shook his head.

"Mr. Goodyear just arrived. He's looking for trouble," Troy said. "We've got your backs."

Cooper Goodyear had arrived, and he made his presence known as he stumbled toward the coffin, falling upon it, his drunken cries making a mockery of the proceedings to come. Mary reached to pull him away, but he struck at her.

"Stay here." Quentin burst through the group. "Cooper, now isn't the time for this." Quentin kept his voice level and without the true animosity he felt.

"You!" Cooper swung at him, but Quentin stepped aside. The man fell on his face. "You—I wanted to kill you, not my son. Why didn't I kill you? Why did I have to kill my boy?"

"Please," Mary said. "Please, take him now. Let me have some peace."

Her summons brought forth two plain clothes detectives. They lifted Goodyear to his feet. He struggled until he realized they were walking him away, arresting him, giving him his Miranda rights. Then, he swung at the officers who took him down with no trouble.

"You okay?" Quentin asked Mary.

She looked at him with tear-filled eyes. "Thank you, Quentin. I'm fine."

The funeral director asked everyone to gather around, and a local pastor, one Quentin knew only by name, began to speak. Quentin found his way back to Willow.

Henry and Annie stood beside her now. They hugged him. Annie's trembling body held to him for some time. "Precious boy." She patted Quentin's face. "So fond of you, and he reminded me a lot of you."

The pastor began to eulogize Denton Goodyear, telling about his academic and athletic careers at Amazing Grace High School. "He loved being an Archangel. He looked up to his Coach, Quentin McPheron." The remarks went on and on, but Quentin heard nothing that offered him peace concerning Denton's soul.

Quentin's mind raced with the uncertainty of where Denton was spending eternity. "I don't understand, God. Tell me why? Why that boy?" he whispered the words, and Willow braced him as he sobbed aloud.

The murmured prayers around him jerked his attention from his own grief.

Several of the boys began to pray aloud, repeating the pastor's words. They prayed for God's love to fill them. They uttered prayers for Christ to make a difference in their lives.

The pastor asked those who'd just said the prayer to raise their hand. Quentin's team. *His entire team.* Quentin's eyes rested on the heavens above. God had moved mountains with Quentin's small faith, and he'd showed him undeniable reason. Until God saw fit to show Quentin without a doubt that Denton rested in God's presence, Quentin would believe.

"And Mary," the pastor said. "These are the ones who will someday soon come to your mind and remind you God has a purpose. So many lives changed by the lives of one young man."

As the service finished Quentin brushed Willow's hair from her face. "Go home with Bear. I want to talk to my boys. They've just made the greatest decision of their lives."

"I'll wait—right over there." She pointed to the old maple.

"Willow," Quentin stopped her. "I may not understand it completely, but God took the life of one to change the lives of so many."

She smiled. "Trust Him for the rest."

And in her words, there was testimony of God's goodness to him. Willow's heart was softening toward the Lord.

He stepped away from her, moving toward the circle of kids. Bear stepped beside him. "Think I can help?"

"Yeah, I'm sure you can." Quentin moved away from Bear as Troy Groverton came toward him. The boy's face was wet with tears, his nose was running, and he wiped his face with the back of his suit sleeve. "How can I be sure, Coach? How?"

Quentin moved with Troy over to a seat under the mourner's tent. "Did you say the prayer or did you mean the prayer?"

"I meant it," he coughed out the words. "I don't want to waste my life because it could end tomorrow. Denton didn't know he'd die."

Quentin wished he'd brought his Bible. He didn't think he'd need it. Instead, he'd lean upon God. He bowed his head, "Dear God, help me to make sense of this for this new child or Yours."

Quentin looked up and waited as Troy wiped his nose with his sleeve again. Quentin reached in his pocket for his handkerchief and handed it to the kid.

Troy took it, wiped his nose, and started to hand it back.

Quentin waved it off. "Troy, if you meant your prayer, God heard every word, and He answered your plea. God tells us He turns away no one seeking Him when we call out to Him believing that the death of His son paid for our sins."

"Did Denton believe?" Troy balled the handkerchief into a tight fist.

Quentin's gut felt like that wadded cloth. He swallowed hard. Troy's question would haunt him until God could provide an answer. He wasn't sure he'd ever know this side of heaven. "I'm not sure." He looked to the boys surrounding the preacher, Bear, Darrell, Henry, and a few other men. "But look how God used his death to bring so many others to Him—including you."

"But if Denton's death saved us, would God really let him go to hell?"

Quentin shuddered. The boy was chewing on meat, and at this moment, Quentin was prepared only to provide him a sip of milk. He took a deep breath and let it out slowly. "No matter what, God is good. He's in every detail of our lives. Denton's death seems senseless and tragic—and it is when we think of it in terms of our mortality. Yet God has a reason for everything that occurs. I can't tell you we'll ever know where Denton is spending eternity, but why don't we pray about it—see if God answers us here on earth? How many other lives could be changed with the truth—whatever it may be?"

"I'd hate to think he died without knowing how much I thought of him as a friend. He apologized to me first. I don't think I'd have ever let it go."

Quentin turned his gaze to the beauty standing and waiting for him. He'd hate for anything to happen to her before she understood the depths of his feelings for her. "Don't ever let pride stand between you and the ones you love."

Willow waited with her cousin and Annie Appleton. Laurel waved to Mary as she passed. Denton's mother looked between Laurel and Willow, and a sweet, peaceful smile lit the face of the grieving mother. How had Mary Goodyear so easily forgiven Laurel? Willow could understand her pain and how hard it would be to forget Laurel had ended her marriage—not that marriage to the man the police had hauled away could have been all that wonderful.

And Mary had said that Willow had given her a gift. How could that have ever happened? She'd never met Mary Goodyear before Sunday when Mary had lost her son.

Annie Appleton linked her arm with Laurel. "A funeral that offers new life and heals old wounds for those remaining isn't completely about loss." She smiled in the direction of Quentin, Bear, Darrell, and Henry, as the men talked with the boys.

Willow stepped away from the ladies, drawn to her grandmother's nearby grave. She bent and ran her hand along the etching, "Elizabeth Jade Thomas, wife, mother, and grandmother. Our life was made full because of her."

She'd not seen the stone before, and the wording shocked her. Over the past few nights, Willow had read her grandmother's prayer for her and for Laurel. The words on her stone were fitting.

Oh, to be missed like her grandmother.

First she had to live a life that would cause someone to miss her. If something happened to her now, would anyone know she'd once walked with God—when Granny was alive? Would they recall that she'd once been kind and trusting— again when Granny was with her? Would they even know she thanked God for those he'd placed in her life? Granny had wanted her. What did it matter that Scott or Suzanne didn't?

"I forgive you, Granny," she whispered, "and I love you so much."

"Willow?"

Willow sprang to her feet at the familiar voice. Think of him and he appeared. "Scott, what are you doing here?"

"That's not important. We should leave." He reached for her arm.

"I'm waiting on Quentin. How did you find me?"

"It's not so much that *I* found you. Just come with me. We need to get out of here."

She saw them then, the cars rolling to a stop, people running toward her, cameras in hand. The scavengers were on a hunt, and she was the main prize.

Willow cast a glance over at Quentin—to the young men who'd just begun a new life.

These bottom dwellers could stop something exciting—a miracle, the first glimmer of hope she'd seen in Quentin's eyes since the death of his young friend.

She rushed ahead of Scott, separating herself from him before they noticed who she was.

"There she is," the call rang out.

Cameras started clicking. Voices called out for her to stop.

She darted toward her car, pulling her keys from her purse.

A man stood up from behind the other side of her car. She knew him, had seen him somewhere. A tendril of fear sizzled down her spine. Had he known the car was hers, or was it only a coincidence?

The man smiled and held up a camera. The flash blinded her for a second.

Another one of the paparazzi.

She fumbled with her keys. When her frantic fingers missed the button, the man stepped back, a snide smile on his lips, his hands raised. Willow fought to get the key into her lock, scratching the paint on her car. Finally, she turned the key, opening only the driver's side.

She jumped into the seat, slipped the key into the ignition, and sped away. Only when she'd pulled away from the maniac did she click the seatbelt into place.

CHAPTER FOURTEEN

Willow pressed on the accelerator. If she could just get to the turnoff ahead of anyone else, she could make it up the mountain without being pursued.

She ran the yellow light on the north end of town. No one was behind her, but just in case, she took the long pass around town. If anyone knew where she lived, they'd miss her, and at her speed, she could beat them to the mountain road.

Why had her father chosen the funeral to make his appearance, and why did he bring the paparazzi with him? He'd visited Amazing Grace on numerous occasions. He came and left quietly with no one following him. So why was Scott Thomas here, and why did he want to put her in danger?

She came upon an old man driving a tractor and tapped the brake. The car slowed a bit, but not enough. She stomped the brake again and kept a safe distance, tapping a nervous beat on her steering wheel. The curvy road entered a straight stretch. Willow swung around the tractor and back into the lane.

She sped along, zipping through the outskirts of town. To head up the mountain, she only had to cross the main highway. With no oncoming traffic, she hit the dirt road and sped. Her tires slid in the dirt, and she fought to keep the vehicle under control.

The twists and turns kept her occupied, but as she neared the hairpin turn of Widow's Peak, she glanced in her rearview mirror. A car was speeding up the road behind her.

Still, at her speed, she'd never make the turn. She tapped her brakes to slow the vehicle and ready herself. The car slowed a bit but not as much as she'd expected.

She stomped on the brakes. The pedal thunked against the floorboard. She mashed it a second and a third time.

Nothing.

The peak loomed ahead. "Lord, what do I do?"

If she hit the edge and missed the curve by even an inch, her car would roll down the steep embankment, erupting in a fiery crash.

She had only a narrow chance of surviving.

Hoot.

She'd never see him again.

Her self-pity and bitterness had separated them.

He said he wanted her.

With as much weight as she could, she pressed her foot to the accelerator.

The choking sob scraped her throat as it burst forth into a primal scream.

Using one hand, she pressed the two front window buttons down, and with her other hand she held tight to the wheel. If she could only keep it straight, the lake was below—far below. With just enough speed, and God's will, she could clear the trees in the lower elevations. If she didn't clear them, she'd die from the impact—but the impact in the water could kill her, too.

"God, oh, God, help me."

She left the road, airborne. The car tilted to her right. The engine roared for a brief second and sputtered to quietness. Then the car tipped forward. If not for the strap holding her, she would have slammed into the windshield.

She covered her face with her hands.

The car hit the water, and something crashed into her body. She fought against it, opening her eyes. The air bag.

Something crawled along her feet.

Water. "No, no. Don't let me drown." She pushed again at the deflated air bag, struggling to get it out of her way. The water tickled her calf muscles now.

She untangled herself from the wafting air bag to reach the button of the seat belt. With a push of the button, she tugged at the strip of cloth pinning her in her seat. The clasp held tight. She yanked.

Jammed.

The cold water rose fast. Once the car sank deep enough, it would flood into the opened windows she'd counted on to escape the car.

"Help me!" she screamed. "Help me! Please, dear God, help me!"

She tugged again and struggled with the floating bag now devoid of air. Though no longer a problem, what did it matter if she couldn't free herself from the belt before the car went under?

And it did with a terrible swoosh. Water swirled through the open window, spinning the car. She pushed the button again, but the clasp would not budge. She held the cloth and pulled with all her might. Nothing gave way.

Water rose to her chin. "Quentin!" she cried out. "Oh God, don't take me away now. Help me."

The water continued to rise, and she closed her mouth and inhaled deeply through her nose. Maybe her last breath.

Completely submerged, she again fought with her inanimate captor. The deflated air bag slapped at her as it moved in the swirling waters.

Trying to squeeze out of the lap belt proved impossible. Her strength ebbed away as she fought to hold her breath.

Something fell across her hand. She screamed and choked. Then the taut fibers around her gave way.

Warmth pressed into her and pushed her toward the window, releasing her for a moment then surrounding her again. Up. She was floating upward.

She broke the surface and coughed out the water, gasping for air.

"You got her?"

Willow turned to her father, who shook the water from his hair. Then to the man holding her—Quentin.

She clung to Quentin as he propelled them both toward the shore. Her knee scraped against rock. Her feet touched ground, and she managed to pull herself up. Quentin moved with her until they fell together on the bank.

Scott crawled onto the shore, his heart pounding, his lungs sucking in the air. What had he been thinking? He'd done his daughter no good. Quentin McPheron had reacted, and his quick actions saved Willow's life. He'd jump out of the car on the downward slope from Widow's Peak and hurled himself over the mountainside as Willow's car careened toward the water.

Scott rolled over and lay back. He propped himself up on his elbows and tried to gain enough energy to even speak.

"Daddy," Willow wailed and threw herself against him.

Scott held her to him. How long had he waited to earn the respect that came with hearing her call him 'Daddy'? In the end, he really had not earned it after all.

Quentin McPheron pressed himself upward and stood over them. Scott locked eyes with his. Quentin turned his attention to the sobbing girl in Scott's arms.

Softness fell across the young man's gaze. Unconditional love.

"Someone loves you very much," Scott whispered into his daughter's ear.

"I love you, too." She held with an even tighter grip.

Scott smiled up at Quentin. "I'm so happy to hear you say that, but I meant someone else." He cleared his throat.

Willow released him by degrees before turning toward Quentin. Scott hated to let her go. He'd won her, and he lost her to the man he'd probably hand her over to at the end of a wedding aisle.

Willow struggled to her feet.

Blood covered Scott's shirt.

As his daughter stumbled toward Quentin, the man's face paled. "Get the car." Quentin commanded.

"Quentin, with all my heart, I do love you." Willow fell into his arms.

Quentin moved up the bank to the shortest possible walk up to the road. He held Willow close to him. He couldn't see a gash. The wound had to be somewhere close to her forehead. Blood covered the front of his shirt, and Willow was out cold.

He struggled up the embankment, one foot in front of the other. He dug in before taking the next step. One wrong move, and they'd both tumble down the hill again.

Scott slammed his car to a sudden stop. He jumped from the car and opened the door. Quentin climbed inside, holding Willow against him.

Scott drove like a madman. "We're going to have to deal with the press." He looked back at him.

Quentin searched Willow's scalp for the wound. She'd sliced it, just above the hairline. He pressed his hand against it to stop the blood flow. "She must've hit the doorframe or a broken piece of the windshield.

They approached the turn where Quentin had realized Willow would not have control of her car at the speed she traveled, that Willow might be on a suicidal mission.

He cradled Willow against him. "Why?" he whispered. "Why did you do this?"

CHAPTER FIFTEEN

Quentin sat in the chair beside the empty space where Willow's gurney had been. They'd taken her to X-ray or for an MRI or maybe a CT-Scan. He hadn't paid attention. Her face had paled, her breathing grew shallow, and he only wanted them to keep her alive.

He stared at his hands, pressed together as if in prayer. She'd called for him. In the depths of despair, she'd cried out for him—and she'd pleaded with God. But why had she cried out for God when she was so intent on ending her life?

Quentin, with all my heart, I do love you.

Then why did she try to take her life away from him? Didn't she trust him to protect her, to keep her safe?

What was Scott Thomas thinking? The man had pushed his daughter into a suicidal drive off a mountain.

When Willow dashed for her car, Scott ran after her. Quentin reached Scott's car before Scott had, and he didn't wait for the man to invite him to follow Willow. Quentin told Scott to drive.

Quentin wanted to strangle the man.

Where was he anyway? Wasn't he worried?

Quentin lifted his head, tilting it back and allowing his shoulders to knead the knots out of his neck and upper back. Standing, he twisted out the remaining knots and noticed for the first time the chill of the hospital's air conditioning against his wet clothing.

The curtain fell away, and Scott entered the room. "You okay?" he asked.

"No. I'm not. I'm sick to death of this hospital. I've been here three times this week, and I feel two out of three good results are a little too much to ask. I've already lost someone I cared for, Mr. Thomas. I don't want to lose Willow." Quentin stood and paced back and forth before stopping in front of Willow's father. "Where'd you go?"

"I had to make a call."

"A call?" Quentin grasped the nape of Scott's expensive polo shirt. "What call could be more important than your daughter? If she hadn't so plainly said she loved you, I'd take you out right now." Quentin raised his fist in the air.

"Patience, son." Bear entered the room.

"Bear, he brought them to town. He led them here like the pied piper, and for what reason? To push Willow over the edge?" He fought against the urge to slam his force into Scott's face. "Do you hate her so much? I swear if you've taken her away from me ..."

Bear placed a firm hand on Quentin's shoulder. "Down tiger. I don't believe Scott brought them with him. He's as much the victim here as Willow."

"Who are you, and what business do you have ...?" Scott wrenched from Quentin's hold and faced Bear. He stepped back. "Teddy? Brother, is that you?" Scott reached for Bear.

Bear stepped away, barring Scott's embrace with strong arms raised in defense. "Any man who chooses a woman like Suzanne over his daughter's welfare isn't any brother of mine. I wish to God she'd been my daughter or that I'd known the ruse you and mother put on. I'd have been here for her."

As if punched, Scott fell back against Quentin. "No." Scott shook his head. "I thank God she belongs to me."

Scott spun toward Quentin. "Don't you understand? Can't you see? I made a vow to Suzanne before I ever knew God would grace me with a daughter."

Bear rubbed a hand over his beard. "And that is one of the reasons God calls a man to lead his family. Then you have no failure of obligation."

"Suzanne wasn't willing—"

"And your daughter suffered for the selfishness of her mother. Do you think you've done your wife any favor by allowing her to lead you? Are wealth and fame worth it, Mr. Thomas?" Quentin stormed out of the room, leaving the estranged brothers to work out their differences.

In the waiting room, Darrell stood while Laurel raised a tear-filled gaze to him. "Nothing yet." He would not prolong their agony.

Laurel pushed herself up and wrapped her arms around his neck. "She'll be okay."

Quentin nodded and stepped from her hold. Still tense, he rubbed his left shoulder with his right hand. "Where's your dad?" he asked her.

"Enlisting Sheriff Dixon to keep those hideous gossipmongers away from the lake. He'll be here soon." She stepped toward him again. "Quentin, there's something you're not telling us."

He shook his head, thought better of it, then nodded. "Yes, but it's not about Willow. I've told you all I know."

"Then what?" Laurel pressed.

Quentin looked back in the direction he'd come. Were the brothers reconnecting with words or with fists? "Not my story to tell." He turned his gaze out the window where the world still revolved. He prayed the momentum wouldn't take Willow away from him for the rest of his life. "God, how I love her," he said then turned toward his friends. "What will I do without her?"

"Teddy?" Scott asked his silent brother for recognition. "Not a day goes by I haven't thought of you and wondered where you've been."

"I've been filling Willow's bank account you set up for the rent of the cabin."

"If I'd known—I thought you were a stranger. I'd never charge you rent to live on our place."

"Willow's place, and I'd never live there without paying her. Wouldn't be right."

"But couldn't you have told me—me or Bobby?" Scott snapped his fingers. "Bobby knows. He has known."

"I asked him not to tell you, so don't hold it against him. The boy, Willow, and Bobby are the only ones who know."

"The boy." Scott shook his head. "He's about to take my daughter from me before I even get a chance to claim her."

Ted grunted and looked at the empty space in the room. "What makes you think he'll be able to take her away? God may do that."

"Always the realist. You haven't changed." Anger reared in Scott, a sensation he hadn't expected. "It made you walk away from Agatha and away from Suzanne and eventually all of us."

"And because I saw both of those women for what they were, you blame me because you and Robert walked headlong into unrealizable dreams."

"At least we had the courage to dream. Where did your fears take you?" Who was Ted to tell him about Suzanne? He'd left her long ago. Ted never saw the vitality, the drive Suzanne possessed.

And Scott spent all his time trying to keep up with that life force.

Ted moved to the vinyl chair. He ran his hand along the edge of the ugly orange back. Then he held to it. "My fears took me to a tiny village in Thailand where I served God."

"Alone. All alone. You never let us know."

"Even if I had no one else, I had God, but I was not alone." Ted stared at his hands and Scott's gaze fell upon his tight grip there. "I had a wife and a child. A beautiful wife, a loving wife, who poured out her life for God."

Scott swallowed.

"And my three year old daughter died of pneumonia while I mourned the passing of her mother." Ted turned a glare as hard as steel upon Scott. "And if I'd known a young child waited for me to return to her here, I'd have come, and I would have pretended to be her father. I'd have pretended to compensate for the fact her father who, while he can write fiction, cannot live a life that is real." He picked up the chair and slammed it down upon the floor. "I told *that boy* I wouldn't, but deep down, I knew I'd have sacrificed everything for your daughter, Scott."

"Why?" Scott stepped toward him. "Why would you do that for me?"

Ted huffed and turned away from him. "You really don't know?"

"No. I don't. Tell me." Scott laid his hand on his brother's shoulder.

Ted lifted his gaze to the ceiling. "Because I love you, I'd protect her with all I have. If you had asked, I'd have fooled even her."

"Momma knew you would. She said so, and I laughed."

"So hard to believe, huh?" Ted muttered. "Maybe we should all thank God that our willingness to lie did not meet with His approval." He nodded toward the opening curtain. "I hate that she's had to suffer."

Scott turned as they wheeled the gurney inside. "All fixed up and awake." The nurse parked Willow's bed. As she moved, Willow brought her hand to her head.

"Are you hurting?" Scott asked her.

She nodded.

"The doctor will be in soon."

"Hey." Again the curtain opened.

Willow beamed and held out her hand.

As if bade by a queen, Quentin stepped to her, a lovesick grin crossing his face.

Scott smiled and looked to Ted. "Seems we've both lost our daughter's heart to *that boy*."

The doctor said she'd live. He'd written a prescription for pain medication and filled out the discharge papers. Now, in a borrowed robe sent into the room by Laurel, Willow awaited the arrival of the ceremonial wheelchair that marked the departure of every patient who entered within the walls of the Amazing Grace Hospital. But that didn't matter. Quentin was beside her, holding her hand in his. She'd never experienced a sense of belonging, not even with Granny's love, but Quentin, if possible, had taken possession of her. She had no desire to fight against him, even submitting to his demands to talk about what happened when they could be alone.

"Before we go outside, there's something you should know." Bear broke the silence.

"What?" Quentin straightened.

"Little brother didn't bring the paparazzi with him. Suzanne did."

Willow's head throbbed at the sound of her mother's name. "The ice queen is here?"

Quentin looked at her then back to Scott. "Robert's enlisted the sheriff's resources. We'll get her home."

"Suzanne isn't here," Scott protested. "I left her pouting in Malibu."

"Scott, has it ever occurred to you that you married a very fine actress?" Bear grumbled. "She didn't recognize me as she wailed to the press outside about how we weren't letting her see her precious daughter, how playing the part of a mother renewed her maternal instinct, and she yearned for her daughter's love and forgiveness."

Willow rubbed her hurting eyes. Quentin stood, and she reached for his hand. "Where are you going?"

"I'm going to ask Darrell and Laurel to get the prescription filled. You'll be able to take it when we get you home. And once we get there, we won't be able to leave the lake without being hounded."

He left her, and she sank back against the pillow. He'd been through so much today. They'd buried Denton, teenagers had come to know God, and they'd almost lost each other—again.

"Willow?" Her dad took Quentin's place beside her.

"I'll be okay." She winced as his tender touch caressed the bandage over her stitches. "Let me breathe, okay?

He pulled back as if burnt. Was that a look of vulnerability? Did Scott Thomas have a weakness, and was she it?

"I heard what you said when Quentin came into the room." She gave in to the tiny bit of remorse. "Thank you for being willing to share me with Uncle Bear, but you are very wrong if you think you'll lose me. Now that I know you want me, why would I let either of you go? I'm just glad *my two dads* are brothers."

"Wicked." Bear laughed aloud. "Just like your Granny."

A nurse's aide entered with the wheeled chariot of departure, and Scott helped Willow to her feet. She wobbled as the floor beneath her swayed. Holding her hand up, she made a silent plea for them to wait for her to gain her balance. Then, with her weight resting on Scott, she lowered herself into the seat.

The aide began to push her toward the curtain.

"Wait," she pleaded. "I'm going to be sick."

From somewhere, as if on cue, Bear produced a small trash can, and she vomited into it.

"Nice," Quentin said from somewhere outside the round plastic can.

"Shut up." A sense of belonging shouldn't come with such humility. She pushed the can away from her and felt the cool rag against her lips.

When she looked up, Quentin's smiling eyes met her gaze. "Now, I know you'll be okay. I like the old Willow a lot better than the demure, submissive one." He'd bent down to care for her, but now he stood. "Okay?" he asked her.

She nodded.

"Darrell and Laurel got away. They'll get the meds to you as soon as they can."

Again, she nodded as the nurse rolled her forward, out the doors to the waiting room where Uncle Robert waited. "You had us worried."

"I'll be okay," Willow assured him.

"The sheriff has a car outside. We're to follow the lead car, and a deputy will be behind us to make sure we get you home."

"Okay." Willow leaned her head and found Quentin's arm for a pillow. The complexities were too much for her. Uncle Robert had made all those plans just to get her home.

The aide pushed her out the door. With the bright sunlight, came sharp pain. "Oh," she cried out and covered her eyes with her hands.

"I have the bucket," Bear said, and Scott laughed.

The clicking of cameras began immediately upon the paparazzo's identification of Scott.

"What happened?" *Click.*

"Willow, did you try to kill yourself?" *Click.*

"How do you feel about your mother's return?" *Click.*

"Are you going to let Suzanne Scott into your life?" *Click.*

"What about it, Willow?" *Click.*

Willow tried to open her eyes against the brightness outside, but the pain would not let her. "Quentin?"

"We're almost to the—Mr. Thomas, get your wife out of here."

"Willow, oh, baby. Look at you. Does it hurt? Honey, are you okay?" Hands grabbed at her, and she pushed them away each time.

Click. Click.

"Willow, are you ready to die?"

At the question from the surrounding crowd, all movement around her seemed to stop. Willow again tried to open her eyes, but the pain kept them closed. Quentin's arm against her tensed. He'd heard it, too, and strangely enough, she knew the voice. Somewhere, sometime, she'd talked to that person.

"Get her in the car now," Quentin ordered. "Now. Now."

For a second she was weightless, carried to the car. Inside, she found herself shielded by Quentin's protective care. "That last idiot—he's the guy who called my cell phone. I'd know his voice anywhere."

With one hand, Scott drew Suzanne away from their daughter. He scanned the crowd for the person who threw out the question that momentarily silenced the crowd. He'd heard the voice before. Where? Probably amidst another crowd similar to this one, but the question sounded like a threat against his daughter.

"What are you doing?" He turned his attention to his wife.

"I'm worried about her. Poor dear, she's despondent over our lack of a relationship with her."

"She's not despondent. Willow has a concussion. She drove her car off a mountainside. Now is not the time for a publicity stunt."

Suzanne ran her fingers through her hair in a slow, even motion, as if she posed for a photographer. "So, you won't let me be with my daughter when she needs me."

Behind them the cameras continued to click and to flash.

"I have a room at the Amazing Grace Inn. Go there and wait for me. If Willow wants to see you, I'll call, and I'll send a police officer for you."

"I want to be with her now. You're the one who convinced me I could be a good mother to our child."

Scott grasped his wife's shoulder firmly. "Stop it now, Suzanne." He put his mouth against her ear. "If you ever really hope to have a relationship with your daughter, you'll do as I said. I'm not asking you. Do you understand?"

She jerked from his grip. "Do you think she really cares for you, *Daddy*? Look at the way she clings to Quentin McPheron. She's been with him since the day she arrived. You don't stand a chance in her life. She's got her a man, and she doesn't need you."

"Quentin McPheron ..." a murmur of voices repeated.

"And somehow the woman, who never cared about her daughter until she could use her for a publicity prank knows all about a man she's never met before. Tell me how, Suzanne?"

Her eyes widened. Then she blinked as if setting up for another Oscar-winning performance, her face void of emotion.

"What have you done?" he demanded.

Suzanne's blue eyes filled with darkness. She said nothing as she turned on her spiked heels and walked away from him.

Scott moved to Robert's car. Suzanne's antics had placed Willow, and now Quentin, in danger. He ducked into the car and spared a glance in his wife's direction. She stood on the curb, her ear bent toward a man holding a camera. Since when had she gotten so chummy with the rats with cameras? He'd find out soon enough.

The sheriff's car ahead of them moved away from the curve. Scott turned to check on Willow. His daughter was safe in the arms of Quentin McPheron. Before looking forward, he caught Teddy's attention. His brother sat on the other side of Willow. Ted gave Scott a brief nod. "You couldn't ask for a better future son-in-law."

The young couple hadn't heard a word. Quentin was whispering in her ear, and Willow was nodding. Scott would give anything to find out what that boy was saying to her.

Beside him, Robert laughed. "Look at the guy my daughter chose. Agatha will spit nails when she finds out Laurel's in love with a simple math teacher."

"I've talked to Darrell Jacobs," Bear said. "If that man continues to teach math in Amazing Grace rather than work in quantum physics, it will only be because Laurel asks him to stay here with her. There's nothing simple about him."

Scott settled back in his seat and pulled the seatbelt across him. He could almost believe all was right with the world. He used to believe Teddy could solve every problem.

Once upon a time, he had.

—

CHAPTER SIXTEEN

Finally. Quentin stepped away from the window as Darrell's car pulled into the driveway. "Meds are here," he told Willow.

Lying in the fetal position, she nodded. He left her. By the time he grabbed a cup of water—the only drinkable substance in Willow's home—Laurel handed him the bottle of pain killers.

"They should have given her something at the hospital," he mumbled.

"They probably wanted her to stay awake for a while," Laurel told him. "Tell her good night for me."

Quentin nodded and moved back upstairs. "Hey, what are you doing?" He made his way around the bed, sitting the water and the pills on the bed stand. "You can't get up on your own."

"I need to—I have to go ..." Her face reddened.

"Then I'll help you into the bathroom."

She held onto his arm as he escorted her there, leaving her alone until she opened the door again. Then, he led her back to the bed. She started to lie down.

"Wait," he said.

She stayed upright and held out her hand for the pill. He gave her one and handed her the water. She swallowed it. When she lay down again, he covered her with Granny's hand-stitched quilt. "Willow?"

Huh?" She opened her eyes.

"Why'd you drive your car off the mountain?"

She pushed up again. Silence stretched between them. She blinked and shook her head as if trying to clear her thoughts.

"That's what you think? You think I did it on purpose? I mean, I did do it on purpose, but not because I wanted to do it."

"You're talking in circles."

"Quentin, do you really think I'd plunge my car off the road like that just because my father arrived with cameras whizzing away. I did freak. I admit it, but those kids needed you, needed to hear what you had to say to them. My dad's arrival put that in jeopardy. I only wanted to get them away from you."

Railing against her would do no good, but he would have if her motive had been a selfish one. And what good would it do now to remind her that the stalker could have easily found her here alone again?

"My brakes malfunctioned. I had to think fast." She touched his hand. "When I was a little girl, Granny said something to me one day. That peak has always frightened me. When I was little, I'd always closed my eyes afraid we'd fall into the water. Granny laughed at me and said, 'Child, if this here car falls off of this here road, it'll burst into flames rolling down the hill. You don't need to worry about that water.' I didn't recall it when my brakes failed, but something inside of me said I'd only survive if I gunned the engine and shot over the treetops. Even then I wasn't sure."

Quentin sat hard beside her.

She winced.

He pretended not to notice. "Even way back then, God prepared you for today—saved you for me." He wrapped her in an embrace. Releasing her, he slipped to the floor, down upon his knees. "Marry me, Willow Jade Thomas. It's meant to be."

He *was* meant to be her protector. And if her brakes failed, he bet they hadn't failed by accident.

She smiled down at him before falling over against her pillow with another wince. "I will, Hoot, I promise. When my head doesn't hurt so much."

He sighed with relief. Of all the answers she could have given, this response was the perfect Willow Thomas response—one he'd remember forever.

A soft knock on the door brought him to his feet. He leaned over and kissed her cheek. "If you need me, I'll be near."

"I know you will." She smooched her lips. "And I love you for it."

Robert stood at the door. "The sheriff's downstairs. I told him Willow wasn't able to talk to him, but Scott wants you in on the conversation."

"What is it?" Quentin shut the door.

"Doesn't make any sense to us."

Quentin stopped the man at the top of the stairs. "The sheriff has jurisdiction up here. He needs to have Willow's car towed out of the waters. She says her brakes failed."

Robert nodded and followed him down the stairs in silence. "Sheriff." Quentin shook his hand. "What's going on?" He looked beyond the police officer to the other visitor in the room. "Agatha?"

His eyes searched the room. Scott stood near the kitchen, blocking Agatha's view of Bear. Laurel and Darrell came to stand beside Quentin.

Sheriff Dixon straightened his holster. The leather cracked under his tug. He held a notepad in his hand. "Quentin, Scott tells me you know about the case. I've been investigating the assault on Agatha, and I'm finding some discrepancies in Willow's report."

Quentin laughed. "What? You think Willow attacked Agatha? You know Goodyear did that. He confessed. His son died because of my meddling. I don't want to hear any harebrained scenario of Agatha's."

"You better listen to him, Quentin McPheron, before you get yourself involved with a psycho." Agatha sashayed around the sheriff and toward her husband.

"What discrepancies are you finding, Sheriff?" Robert asked.

"Well, Willow probably told you what we picked up on the photo she allegedly received from Agatha's possible attacker. We know they didn't come from Goodyear, and they were taken after my department's arrival at the scene."

"That only proves Willow's stalker was there with you and your men." Quentin ran his hand through his hair. Leave it up to Agatha to add worse to bad enough.

"Willow showed me the photos she claims were taken at her apartment. She asked me to check with two detectives in her precinct. She said they took the report, and they helped her get out of town when the paparazzi converged on her."

Quentin nodded. "The detective who showed her how to put tape on her door so she'd know if anyone came into her house when she left. She told me about him."

"She only gave me the full name of one and the first name of another. The precinct that would have responded to Willow's call doesn't have nor have they ever had a Detective Hominski. The two fellows on the force named Jim were never called to her apartment."

Agatha beamed beside Robert.

"Momma, that doesn't mean anything," Laurel protested.

"It means plenty, young lady. Willow is a liar and most probably a psychotic one, as well."

"Agatha," Robert warned. "Willow is family."

"Willow is also very sane, Sheriff." Bear stepped out of the kitchen. "I was here along with Quentin the night he received a phone call. I saw the man standing on the dock by the lake. I saw the fear in Willow's face. She's not an actress like her mother. Her fear wasn't contrived."

Agatha took a step backward, her gaze roaming from head to foot over Bear. Quentin said a prayer of gratitude that Bear's sudden appearance left Agatha speechless.

"And today, I heard a familiar voice in the crowd. He asked a question that sounded more like a threat," Scott added.

Quentin nodded. "The guy in the crowd is the one who called me. I'd stake my life on it."

"You just might be," Agatha harrumphed.

"We're looking into it." The sheriff looked down at his notes. "They do have a report of a call from Willow telling them of the break-in. I was told no report was filed, and that in itself is a little odd. Something should have been noted about the call, no matter how insignificant."

"Have you spoken with anyone in her office?" Scott asked. "She told me her boss drove her home after her apartment was ransacked."

The sheriff nodded. "A witness who met the two men would go a long way in proving Willow's allegations about the stalker."

Quentin looked around the room. The concerned faces of those who loved and trusted Willow stared back at him as if he had the answers. Only one face bore outright hatred. If Agatha wasn't careful, she'd lose everyone and everything she loved.

He opened the door and walked outside. He hadn't meant to leave the house, but he found himself starting across the lawn.

"Where are you going?" Darrell called to him from the porch.

Quentin turned to look at his friend. "I just need a minute. Agatha and the sheriff are accusing my fiancée of making up a stalker. A student of mine was killed by his father's anger toward me. Willow almost died today, and I believe it was attempted murder. Darrell, what am I supposed to do?"

"You pray."

"You believe Willow, right?"

Darrell nodded. "I don't have a doubt in my mind."

Quentin turned away and started toward his home again.

"Hey?"

"Yeah," Quentin called over his shoulder.

"Did you say fiancée? Does that mean you asked and Willow agreed to marry you?"

"Yes, sir, it does."

"Well, gee golly." Darrell gifted him with one of his best Gomer Pyle imitations ever.

CHAPTER SEVENTEEN

Quentin stomped up to his porch, pulled his keys out of his pocket, and opened the door. Inside, he turned on the foyer light and walked into the semi-dark living room. Looking above the fireplace, he smiled at the picture he loved so much—the reason he was convinced one day, the Lord willing, Willow Thomas would marry him.

Every line she'd etched on the drawing, the love she'd put into the picture of him sitting on Granny's dock, fishing pole in his hand, his once unruly curls sticking out all over the place. Yeah, she loved him back then all right. He never doubted it. Each line of that portrait kept his hope alive for years.

He pulled his gaze away and walked upstairs. In his room, he opened the drawer to his nightstand and pulled out the envelope he'd placed there more than eleven years before. He shouldn't have this heavy heart. Not today. Not when Willow had promised to marry him, not when he was close to finding the answer to the biggest secret in his life—what Granny had written in this envelope addressed to his fiancée.

His fiancée.

He trudged downstairs holding the envelope in his hands. He sat on the ottoman in front of the cold fireplace and bowed his head. He needed answers, but he didn't know how to begin to ask God for them. Since Willow's return, his life had been at once filled with joy and with fear, with love and with anger. Now, God had added Agatha's meddling to his growing list of bitterness. "Help me to see why? I don't understand why Cooper could even pull a gun when his son was in the store. I don't understand why someone would want to kill the woman I love. I don't understand why Agatha's heart is so hard, and even, Lord, why Willow's heart has softened. I don't understand why You have used such a tragedy to bring about the hearts of young souls. Dear God, please tell me."

Another knock. Annoyance filled him, and he thought about not answering, but it sounded again. He pushed off the ottoman and placed the envelope on the mantel. Maybe Willow needed him.

He pulled open the door. "Mrs. Goodyear."

"Mary, Quentin. Why be formal after all we've been through?"

He opened the door and motioned her inside.

"What a time I had getting up here. I heard about Laurel's cousin. I hope she'll be okay."

"She has a headache, but I suspect the painkillers have taken that away by now."

"Denton told me he saw you with her. He said she seemed to make you happy."

What could he say to that? Denton could have said so much more, and maybe he had. Did Mary choose not to remind him that Willow had accused Denton of being her stalker?

They stood in the foyer. "Come in. I just got home."

"I'll just stay for a moment." She followed him into the living room. When he turned to offer her a seat on his couch, he noticed for the first time she carried a notebook in her hand. She smoothed her skirt—the same one she'd worn to the funeral—and sat. "I don't think Laurel would find it amusing, but because of her, the night before Denton died, he and I shared a wonderful laugh at her expense. He explained how her cousin—"

"Willow."

"How Willow reacted to something, and how you'd accidentally dumped tea all over Laurel."

"I guess he had a reason to laugh at Laurel, and I think if you ever get to know her, you'll understand she wouldn't hold your amusement against you or him."

Mary looked at the book in her lap. "I've learned to forgive her, and now God has given me one more reason to write about being thankful to her—and to her cousin. When he was a baby, his little-boy laughter rang like a bell in my heart and filled it with real joy. When he laughed over Laurel's mishap, he sounded like that little baby I used to tickle and tease into laughter. I thank the Lord that Laurel was the instrument He used to allow me to hear that sweet melody at least one more time. The sound will never fade from my memory."

"Did you write it in your diary?" Quentin wiped the back of his hand over his eyes and looked to the book.

"No." She smiled. "I've always kept a journal, but I didn't know until after his death Denton had taken up the practice. I found this and some newer ones when I went to sit in his room after I left the hospital." She placed her hand over the green cover. "I used to complain about the sweaty smell of his room where he'd throw off his football uniform. If a mother only knew that one day the earthy smell of her child could be lost, she'd never utter a word of protest."

"Mary, I'm so sorry. If I'd walked away instead of struggling with Cooper for the gun. Maybe he wouldn't—"

"Oh, yes, he would have. Don't go through life wondering. Cooper never allowed anything to get in the way of his fury. So, no, you had nothing to do with Denton's death." She gave a definitive shake of her head. "We will never discuss this again. Cooper will have to face the law and God for what he's done to our boy. I do hope God can forgive him, because I don't think I ever will. But I didn't come for that." She opened the notebook to a page she'd obviously marked with a bend at the corner.

"I thought I'd be able to, but you'll understand why I can't part with even one page of this, but I wanted you to see the difference you made in Denton's life."

"I don't think ..."

"Read it, and then deny what Denton saw in you, and I'll stay quiet."

Quentin sat once again on the ottoman with his living room still bathed in the semi-darkness. He ran his hand along the clean script.

"If I'm right, that was his sophmore year. Junior varsity." Mary said.

Quentin nodded and began to read.

Coach McPheron got on to me today. He's tough, but I can take it. I messed up, and he told me so, and he told me why. Not one word about my being a screw up or that I'd never amount to anything. He called me out, and he called me over. The guys smirked, and I got embarrassed by it. I could almost see Coach counting down, probably from a hundred because it took him so long to speak.

"Goodyear," he said. "What's this about?" And you know, I think he really wanted to know the answer. Sure, he was mad at me. I'd have to be a dummy not to realize that, and, well, Coach reminded me I'm not a dummy. He actually said I'm a pretty smart guy. He even noticed I could remember the codes, and he realized how hard I'd worked to memorize the playbook. "Goodyear," he said again. "One day I suspect you'll get in the game. If you keep working at it, and giving me the effort, I can see you being my quarterback when Steve graduates." Imagine that. Me, the varsity quarterback, when my dad told me I didn't have what it takes to make the team.

I know Dad doesn't like Coach McPheron. I don't understand all of it, but I think it's all about Coach's friend, Ms. Thomas. Whatever it is, I suspect Dad's to blame, but I'd never say that to either of them.

So back to the first question. "What's this all about?" You know, I didn't have an answer for Coach McPheron. I told him I didn't. I said I guess I just wasn't thinking. Tell that to my dad, and I'd never hear the end of how stupid I am, or how I'll never be anything better than what I am today—a lousy, good-for-nothing kid. But Coach McPheron, he leaned back and looked at me. I thought he was counting down again, but then he smiled and patted me on the back. "Honesty, Denton ..." He actually called me by my first name that time. "Honesty, Denton, is a quality I can work with. Okay, so you weren't thinking. We know you have a thinker. Do you think you can use it?"

"I can use it, Coach. I promise." What a dumb thing to say, but I felt kind of proud to say it, and now that I've written it down, it doesn't seem dumb at all. It's actually a promise I plan to keep.

I wish I had a father like Coach McPheron because even though I know he doesn't like me, he still treats me fair when I've done something wrong, and he cheers me on when I've done something right. Everyone needs a dad like that.

Quentin pretended to keep reading even though he'd long since read the boy's praise of him.

When he looked at Mary, her eyes brimmed with tears. "I'll copy it for you, Quentin, if you'd like."

Quentin nodded. "He was wrong, you know."

"I believe one of Denton's best qualities was his ability to read others."

"Well, he was wrong because I did like him. In fact, as a student and a player I respected him. We were just beginning to understand each other, and forgive me for saying this about a student because I know in today's world they misconstrue words like this ..." Quentin fought to control his emotions. "I really did love your son. I've never been a father, and I hope to be one day. I hope I live up to Denton's praise."

Mary smiled and wiped away her tears. "When that day comes, I hope that you'll let your child call me Aunt Mary. Maybe I can teach him or her to laugh like my Denton."

Quentin nodded and looked to the floor, saying a quick prayer that Mary would one day have her wish.

She stood and moved around the room while he fought to find an emotional footing.

She looked above the mantel. "Interesting portrait."

"Willow drew it of me in high school."

Mary studied it closely. "You haven't changed much, Quentin McPheron."

"If there's anything I can do."

"I'd like to start a scholarship in Denton's name. I want you to be the one who recommends the best student— academically, athletically, and for morals and ethics." She walked toward the door. "After all, those are the three qualities you inspired in him."

"I know this might be a hard question to answer, but I have to ask."

Mary straightened. "Go ahead."

"Denton said you'd been attending church. Those kids today, Denton's life and his death changed their hearts and allowed God to work in them."

A bright smile spread across Mary's face. "One day—one day, I will see my son in the light of God's grace. God changed Denton's heart a couple of weeks before he died. I'm surprised he didn't tell you."

The memory of Denton's unfinished statement— interrupted by Cooper—flashed in Quentin's mind. "I think he tried. We were pulled away from the conversation, and I forgot to take it up with him again."

"Rest assured, Coach, if that loud Christian song Denton loved to play is true, and God does have a big, big yard, where we can play football, Denton's up there learning plays just for you."

"Somehow I believe Denton's too busy taking in the wonders of heaven to worry about me." Quentin gave a wan smile. Truth was, selfishly, he didn't want Denton in heaven. He wanted him here. "But I'm going to think of him in that big, big yard making me as proud of him as I was here on earth." Opening the door, he hugged her. "Mary, this was a special gift to me. Thank you for sharing."

"Oh, I'm sorry." Laurel stepped onto the porch. "I didn't mean to interrupt."

"No, it's okay. I was just getting ready to leave." Mary reached out and touched Laurel's cheek. "Next time we see each other, let's not act as if it's awkward for us. Let's tell everyone we've moved on. Cooper Goodyear didn't leave two bitter hearts in his wake."

Laurel took Mary's hand and held it in hers. "Thank you."

"Good night." Mary started down the steps.

"Willow okay?" Quentin asked Laurel.

"I'm hoping you have some clear soda. She woke up from a nightmare and threw up the pain pill."

"Wait here. I'll get my Ginger Ale. I didn't plan to be gone so long."

"Daddy left to take Momma home." She called into the house. "And Scott and Bear are fighting over the couch versus the guest room. I tried to tell them there are two guest rooms, but Bear insists someone needs to stay downstairs."

Quentin emerged from his house, a Ginger Ale bottle in his hand. He locked the door. "I'll sleep on the couch. Man, I can't believe I'm actually going to marry into your family. Is she worth it?"

"I'd answer that question if I didn't think you already know the answer." She linked her arm in his. "Unlike you, Darrell doesn't get leave from school until summer break on Friday. He needs to take me home and get some sleep. I'm off tomorrow, and I'll come take care of her."

"I appreciate that. I have someone I need to see."

"Well, Daddy convinced the sheriff to call Willow's boss. Scott said his name is Peterman."

"Maybe he does care. Those little things he remembers are signs he might."

"I can't believe Bear is my mysterious Uncle Teddy."

"So, he told you, huh?"

"Oh no. After you left, Momma set in on him. Daddy had to pull her off." Laurel reached the bottom of the steps. "I'm wondering if Darrell Jacobs has the same stamina you have that would make him want to marry into this family."

"Bear says he's capable of quantum physics. Maybe he could find a way to send the parents into parallel universes. He might be what your family needs."

She leaned away from him.

"What?"

"Willow's sarcastic wit is rubbing off on you—or maybe you were around Granny too much." She put her arm around his waist and walked with him to Willow's house.

Scott sat beside Willow on her bed. He pressed a cold compress to her forehead.

"Why, Daddy?" she asked, peering up at him from underneath the cloth.

This time the sound of his name and his title upon her lips fell bittersweet upon his ear. "I'm sorry. Why what?" He stalled for time.

"Why her and not me?

His mother had told him on the day he'd left his week-old daughter with her that Willow might one day learn the truth and ask this very question, Scott was unprepared, and despite his quick thinking, storytelling mind, he searched inside and found empty thoughts.

"You act as if you've always loved me, but you left me here, and you stayed with the woman who gave me up. I don't understand."

He touched the bracelet on her wrist. "Did your granny tell you I gave her this bracelet?"

Willow shook her head. "I always thought it was an heirloom."

"Well, it is. When I was in high school, I helped her run errands one day. On a whim, she went into Saved by Grace Antiques. I followed her inside. She went right to the jewelry display case and stared down at that bracelet as if it were the most precious thing in life.

"When Mrs. Dixon—the sheriff's mother—greeted us, Momma turned around quick, almost as if embarrassed by her desire. She spoke to Mrs. Dixon and shooed me out the door. She went into the shoe repair store, and I ran back to talk to Mrs. Dixon."

Willow lifted the cloth from over her face, but she remained silent.

Scott continued to turn the bracelet around on Willow's arm. "I wanted to know how much it cost."

"Granny said it was expensive, and I should always be careful not to lose it."

"Expensive. Back then I couldn't imagine ever having that much money."

"Then how ...?"

"I asked Mrs. Dixon if she'd put it away if I promised I'd buy it one day."

"I bet she laughed at you."

"Grace Dixon? No. Never. She took it right out of the case. Then she told me why it meant so much to your granny."

Willow sat up.

He had her interest now. Like his mother, he could spin a yarn, and this one was true. He hoped it would hold more impact than any fiction he'd ever put to paper.

"Granny's sister, Wilma, was an ornery old soul. If you think your Aunt Agatha has a corner on meanness, it's nothing compared to Wilma. Her face was permanently scrunched from frowning."

Willow laughed and held her head.

Was this what it was like to read your daughter a bedtime story—minus the head injury, of course?

"The bracelet originally belonged to your granny's mother. Your great grandfather brought it with him from Europe where he served in World War I."

"And Wilma sold it?"

"Who's telling this story?" Scott winked. "You or me?"

She smiled.

That was enough of a gift to make him continue. "Your great grandmother wasn't wealthy. Granny grew up in that small cabin where your Uncle Ted lives, but that woman managed to save two things of value for her daughters."

"Two?"

"That bracelet and a box full of notes your great grandfather mailed home during the war. They were prayers he'd written for his family—for his wife and his daughters."

"That's where Granny learned to do that. Her father did it for her."

Scott didn't understand, and he shook his head to tell her so.

"Open the drawer." Willow pointed to the desk.

Scott opened it and pulled out the yellowing piece of paper. "Lord, for my family, I pray you always find them busy, never idle, and always, Lord, looking to you," he read, studying his mother's handwriting. "I never knew she did this."

"I suspect we'll find quite a few when it's all said and done. Laurel and I are sharing Granny's book of prayers for us."

"I'm glad to see you and your cousin have found some common ground."

"How would you know any different?" Willow challenged.

"Despite what you think, kiddo, I kept close tabs on you. Always have."

"So tell me more of the story." Willow looked down at her bracelet. "Granny got the letters, didn't she, and Wilma got the bracelet."

Scott shook his head. "Granny got the bracelet. Wilma got the letters."

"Oh, good twist." Willow lay back down, her hand over her stomach, and Scott wondered if she'd be sick again. "Go on," she urged.

"Well angry, bitter old Aunt Wilma threatened to burn the letters in her trash. Nothing would keep her from doing otherwise until your granny offered to trade her the bracelet for her father's writings."

"And Wilma sold the bracelet after Granny gave it to her?"

He nodded.

Emotions flickered across Willow's face. He saw them there.

Anger.

Sorrow.

Grief.

"Daddy?"

Scott's lips trembled as she clasped her hand around the bracelet.

"How did you get it back for her?"

"Mrs. Dixon held that bracelet for five years. When I sold my first screenplay, I made a lot of money. More money than your mother and I'd ever seen. When I came home to visit you, I stopped at Saved by Grace, wrote the check for the payment I'd promised Mrs. Dixon, and gave the bracelet to your granny."

Willow stared at the heirloom for a long time before speaking. "I don't remember you ever visiting."

"You were young then. You wouldn't remember, and your granny thought it best for you to live the lie than to know ..." He swallowed hard against the truth.

"Know what?"

"To know how little we cared for you."

Willow closed her eyes tight, and he allowed his words to sink in for a moment. Dramatic effect. Bring the point home. Always the director—but this time, his entire relationship with his daughter rested upon what came next.

A soft knock sounded on the door, and at the same time, Willow turned away from him, pulling her legs into the fetal position.

Scott held up his hand to silence Quentin.

"Willow, I never realized the truth. I put not only your mother's selfish wants and desires before my little girl, but I placed mine in front of even those of Suzanne." He touched her shoulder. "I spent more love and devotion in giving that bracelet to your granny than I did in caring about you."

"Please, don't ..." she cried into her pillow.

Quentin stepped forward, jaw clenched and eyes narrowed. Scott motioned for him to remain quiet.

"But like Granny pining for that bracelet as it sat in the glass counter at the antique store, I want something I can never buy back—not for me or you."

Willow didn't move.

"Kiddo, if I went into that antique store today, and it contained every memory I missed, ever smile I didn't get to see...your first steps, your first birthday ... all your birthdays...I'd pay every cent I have and more. But I can't, and that's my fault, and it's something I'll live with for the rest of my life." He stood. "I'm asking you for something I don't deserve, and I hope you'll think about granting it to me."

Willow turned and stared up at him, her eyes moist, her face blotched from crying, pain screaming in her eyes. "What do you want?"

"A chance to share the rest of your life with you."

"But you never answered my question. Why? Why her and not me?"

Scott cut his gaze to the man standing in the doorway watching the drama play out. "Ask Quentin why he's waited ten years for you to come back here so he could see you one more time. Ask him why he carved, painted, and hung those beautiful shutters on the front of your home even when he didn't know if you'd ever see them, why he rebuilt the deck and kept up the house and yard. Ask him if he could place anyone but God above you. I loved Suzanne before you ever came along. I love her even now when I think she's done something terribly wrong. Trouble was, as your Uncle Teddy reminded me, I didn't love her enough to be the head of our family. I allowed her to dictate. That all ends today. I promise." He stood and walked away from her, placing a hand on Quentin's shoulder as he passed by. "I'm right, aren't I? You've waited all this time?"

Quentin nodded, but Scott didn't wait for an answer. He moved past and shut the door, and Quentin took his place on the bed. "I have some Ginger Ale. It may help to settle your stomach so we can get another pain pill inside of you."

"I don't want another one," she protested. "I had a bad dream."

He helped her to sit up and offered her the carbonated drink. "Sip," he commanded. "A little at a time."

She cut her eyes toward him, but she didn't complain.

When she'd taken a small drink, he put the glass on the bed stand. "What'd you dream?"

"You got me out of the car, but the water pulled us away from each other. Then someone else had me. He wanted to kill me."

"Not going to happen." He cradled her against him. At least not if he could help it. "Willow, I think you should know something."

"That doesn't sound good."

"The sheriff checked with the precinct in New York. They have no Detective Hominski on the force, and neither of the Jims said they were called to your place."

"That's not possible. They were helpful. I was frightened. Jim came up and told Hominski the press was outside. I had to talk Hominski into helping me keep it quiet and to help me get out of town. My apartment was a wreck."

"I just wanted you to know. Agatha's bent on proving you've made all this up."

Willow pressed her eyelids closed, wincing as if Agatha had thrown a punch. "And what do you think?"

"Well, I wasn't there. I don't know what to think."

"You do believe me?"

"In the words of the person I heard may be the world's smartest quantum physicist, 'without a doubt.'"

He reached for the glass and handed it to her again. "Another sip?"

She nodded and complied.

"And you don't want another pill?"

"No, maybe some aspirin."

"Okay. I have to go next door for it. Can you tell me why you haven't insisted *we* go grocery shopping?"

"Because until today I wasn't sure how long I'd be staying."

"And now ..."

"Did I dream you asked me to marry you?"

"Depends," he said.

"On what?"

He smiled. "On whether that would be considered a nightmare as well?"

"Quentin, did you ask me to marry you?"

With the use of his real name, he figured he had a fifty-fifty chance. "Yes, I did."

"And I said, yes, right?"

"Yes, you did." And if she'd said no, he'd have lied to her.

"Then I guess I'm staying pretty much forever."

He winked at her. "That's my girl. I'll be right back."

"Hoot. My address book is on Granny's desk. My boss is Peterman. He met the detectives. Will you call him?"

"Because you don't think I believe you?"

"No, because he can verify to you and the sheriff that I'm not making this up. I want to prove Aunt Aggie wrong."

"Scott gave the sheriff your boss's name."

Her lips trembled. "No. I want you to know. What I said happened—everything. It happened."

What insecurities led her to believe he would doubt her when he said he didn't?

"I want you to know," she pressed.

Quentin moved back to the desk and found the book. He picked it up. "We'll get to the bottom of this. I want you to rest." He moved to the door.

Willow peered up at him, her dark hair falling against her moist cheeks, a tentative smile on her face. "It's going to take all I have to learn to love Aggie."

"She's a challenge."

She nodded, her head moving against the fabric of the pillowcase. "But I understand her. She's holding on to some deep hurt, and until she can let go of it, Hoot, she's never going to be whole again. Believe me, I know."

Quentin smiled at her. "You amaze me Willow Jade Thomas."

She giggled and closed her eyes. "Keep that in mind the next time we have an argument, will you? I love being snarky with you, Hoot. It helps to keep my edge."

"I wouldn't have it any other way, Scrappy." He laughed and closed the door.

Quentin sat on his couch, Willow's address book open in his lap. It contained only three names, and one made him smile, as did the picture Willow had drawn on the inside cover. A miniature of the drawing above his mantel. Yeah, she loved him all right.

His name and address as well as the names and addresses of her dad and her boss were the only entries. He was sure she kept her business contacts on her computer, but the sparse personal entries screamed to him. Had her life kept her so afraid to trust?

But Willow had given him access to this, and it was a beginning. He pulled out his cell phone and dialed Peterman's cell phone.

"Jeff Peterman."

"Mr. Peterman, my name is Quentin McPheron. I'm a friend of your employee, Willow Thomas."

Peterman gave an audible inhale. "You're not calling me with bad news?"

"No. We had a scare today, but she's fine. She asked me to call you because she said you could add some insight into an incident that happened."

"How do I know you're who you say you are?"

Fair enough and protective.

"Mr. McPheron?"

"I'm here. I'm just thankful you feel that way toward her. Why don't I do this? Willow lives next door. I'll have her call you back to verify. She can't talk long because to tell you the truth, she suffered a concussion, and she's in a lot of pain."

"Concussion?"

"Her car went off a mountain road and into the lake here."

"You're kidding me? Was it an accident or a ..."

"We've asked the sheriff's department to pull her car out of the water. I think they'll do it tomorrow."

"Mr. McPheron, I don't guess I'd be giving any personal information. Willow's apartment was trashed. I had to make her call the police, and when she did, I drove her home. We were met there by two detectives who'd already gained entrance."

"Do you remember their names?"

"No, I don't think I heard them. I tried to wait and convince Willow to come home with me. I had an extra room, but she said something about rumors. Who cares about that in this town?"

"A woman whose mother is an actress and her father is a well-known director. Willow left Amazing Grace because of a tabloid story that broke. She was hiding in New York to get away from it."

"Ah, that explains it. I often wondered why a beautiful woman like Willow Thomas spent so much time alone. I guess now I know. Anyway, I left her with the officers. I told her to take a break. She earned it. Oh, she doesn't know the extent of this, and you might want to tell her. The account turned into a multi-million dollar campaign, and the artwork she left on her desk was hotter than the artwork she presented at the meeting with Angler Lures. The client loved it."

"I'll tell her." Quentin swallowed down the bitter pill of jealousy. Would Willow's success take her away from him? Would she refuse to marry him now that she'd brokered this deal? "One more thing, Mr. Peterman."

"Sure."

"Our sheriff plans to contact you. Seems the two detectives you met at her home don't exist, and Willow's character and her story are being called into question."

"You have him call me. I might not know their names, but I can send him a picture of their faces."

"You can what?"

"I took some shots on my phone. I don't know why. I guess the whole episode disturbed me. The detectives didn't notice, and I didn't say anything."

"God bless you, Mr. Peterman. Can you e-mail those to Willow? Do you have the address?"

"Yes, and will you tell her I'll be sending her the promo on her account within the next few days?"

"Definitely and thank you."

Not that he really wanted to tell her anything that might take her away from him again.

CHAPTER EIGHTEEN

A dull ache remained when Willow woke. She lay in bed for a long moment staring up at the ceiling, her hand pressed against the gauze headband and the larger bandage underneath. Then she raised her hand in the air, wiggling her ring finger. Soon, if she hadn't been dreaming off and on through the night, she'd have an engagement ring on her finger.

Why did she feel like such a girl? She'd never been one to fawn over wedding magazines or bridesmaid dresses. Nothing like that ever appealed to her, but Hoot would want a large wedding. How did she know?

A warmth settled across her. Despite all the years of separation, she remembered everything about him—his hopes, his dreams, his aspirations. They all settled here in the little lake cove and in the town of Amazing Grace.

A chill crept over her. She had a job. A new account she'd invested time to develop. Jeffrey—how could she leave the firm?

How could she not?

If Hoot's proposal was real and not a dream ...

If she survived this stalker.

To think Agatha tried to convince them Willow had fabricated the story. Now a red hot fire burned inside of her. Agatha. Suzanne. A stalker. All in the same town. What did she do to deserve this?

"Good afternoon."

Before Willow could protest to her cousin about knocking, Laurel entered, her hands full with a food tray hosting a bowl of soup and a cup filled with what looked like Ginger Ale.

Willow pushed herself up and folded down the quilt covering her. "Afternoon?"

"Two o'clock." Laurel sat the tray on Willow's lap and leaned over Willow, looking at her bandaged head. "We'll need to change the bandage later."

Willow looked into the bowl. "Where'd you get the fixings?"

"Annie Appleton came by this morning."

"She got by the press?"

"The sheriff's deputies let her through. They don't stop us when we're leaving, but they sure check us when we're heading up."

"So, you've been home?" She hoped Laurel hadn't spent the entire night here.

"Darrell drove me home last night after you went to sleep. I'm off today."

"Where do you work?"

Laurel's face reddened. "I work for Daddy. I'm his secretary."

"Hey, that's a great job. What a perk to have your father as your boss. You can get days off to tend to your hapless cousin." Willow swirled her spoon through the soup. "Why do I get the feeling you don't like working for Uncle Robert?"

"Oh, I like it." Laurel busied herself with straightening up the room, picking up two cups from the bed stand and bringing order to the desk. "But it does pale in comparison to an advertising executive."

Willow choked on her soup. "I work in advertising, but I'm not an executive." She wouldn't tell Laurel she was a junior executive. Her heart was telling her the title was temporary. She'd soon exchange it for Quentin's name.

"That's not what Quentin said last night. He said you'd won a multi-million dollar account. Your boss was proud of you, said your newest artwork was a hit."

When did Hoot learn anything about her job? She shook the cobwebs from her hurting head. That was right. She'd given him her address book, asked him to call Jeffrey.

"Well, I'm not an executive. I'm a junior executive. Where is Hoot?"

"He sat with you until about an hour ago. Said he had something to do." Laurel made her way to the door then looked back. "Your dad said you mentioned Granny's prayers for us, so you must be reading them. What do you think?"

Willow let the question settle over her. Just what did she think of this new relationship she had with an old enemy?

Standing in the doorway, Laurel looked tired and lonely. Willow was tired and lonely—and weary.

"Willow, you okay?"

An untamed, wild emotion washed over Willow. Her body trembled with it, and the tray shook. Laurel ran to take it from her and placed it on the desk. "Are you sick? Do I need to call an ambulance?"

Willow looked up to her. "Granny loved us, didn't she?"

Laurel smiled and sat beside her. "Yes, she did."

"Then why didn't we love each other?"

"I think we loved to bicker and fight with each other. That was our way of communicating when we were children. We became a little more sophisticated in our battles as teenagers. I used subterfuge. You just played hard to get at, and it worked." Laurel reached to the tray and pulled off a napkin. She wiped at Willow's teary eyes.

Willow took the napkin from her. "Truth is, I just didn't know how to fight like you. I stayed behind a silent wall of bitterness."

"Better a silent wall than a deep well spewing it out."

Understanding hit Willow like a sledgehammer. She placed her hand over her mouth. "Oh, no," she mumbled through closed fingers.

"What?"

"Despite the fact we had a much better example in front of us, we both turned into our mothers."

Laurel gave a half laugh that turned into a chortle that turned into a single sob.

Willow pushed her cousin's blonde locks over her shoulder. "You asked me to help you get your geek, now can I ask you to do something for me?"

Laurel tilted her head. "Depends. If you're going to ask me to off my mother ..."

"No, just the opposite. Will you teach me how to forgive?"

Quentin pushed open the police station door. The desk attendant, an old friend from high school, was on the phone. Quentin waited until he finished his call. "The sheriff in?"

"In a conference. He should be out soon."

Quentin pressed his lips together. He'd hoped he wouldn't have time for what God was pressing him to do.

"I'll let him know you're waiting as soon as I can, Quentin."

"Hand this to him when he comes out of the meeting." He held out five photographs he'd forwarded from Willow's computer to his for printing. "Any chance I can get in to see Goodyear?"

His old friend studied him. "Any particular reason?"

"Do I need any?"

"He did try to kill you."

"And you think I want revenge? Didn't the guy pay a hefty price already?"

"Yeah, I guess he did." He picked up the phone. "Go on over to the jail. You'll need to show some ID. I'll call and tell them to let you in."

"I appreciate it." Quentin walked outside and across the parking lot to the three-story building housing prisoners awaiting trial.

"Mr. McPheron?" A woman dressed in a guard's uniform looked at him through thick Plexiglas.

Quentin nodded and pulled out his wallet. He lifted the wallet so that she could make the ID.

She pressed a buzzer that allowed him to enter through a secure door. He waited on the other side, afraid of making the wrong move. He'd never been inside a jail in his life.

The female guard came toward him with a flat wand. "Hands up, turn around slowly."

If this was what it's like to enter as a visitor, he never wanted to find himself here as an inmate.

The wand buzzed, and he jumped.

"What's in your pockets?" She held out a basket.

He fished inside and dumped the contents out. The guard perused the items before running the wand over him again and motioning for him to turn.

Silence.

"Here's your wallet. I don't want to be responsible for it, but see me for your keys before you leave." She motioned for him to move forward.

"Yes, ma'am." He fought to keep from saluting her.

A heavy door opened in front of him, and another guard waited for him to enter. "You've got five minutes."

Did they have to treat everyone like a criminal? Maybe that's why they did their jobs so well. They trusted no one.

The room Quentin followed the man into was divided by a counter running its width, another solid piece of Plexiglas keeping him from the other side. A door beyond the Plexiglas opened, and Cooper Goodyear entered, looking somewhat puzzled. When his eyes fell on Quentin, he started to turn. The officer behind him blocked his way and pointed in Quentin's direction. A muffled argument ensued with the officer winning.

Quentin sat in a chair at the counter and picked up the phone there. Goodyear plopped into the chair opposite him and eyed the phone on that side.

One-two-three-four ...

Quentin started to stand. If Goodyear didn't want to talk, he'd done his best to follow God's lead.

Goodyear snatched up the phone. "What do you want?"

"I came to tell you how sorry I am about Denton's death."

"You've come to take the blame?" Goodyear leaned close to the glass.

Did the man think him that stupid? Was he actually trying to frame him for Denton's death? All jailhouse visits were recorded in Amazing Grace. Anyone who watched the local news was aware of that. "Cooper, I came to give you my condolences. That's all. No matter how Denton died, he was your son, and I can't imagine the pain you're going through."

Darkness formed behind dull eyes. A fire of anger lost its blaze.

"That's all I came to say."

"His death—it's on your hands. You walked into my store. You threatened me. I pulled out my gun for protection."

An ember had caught in the breeze of Quentin's apology, and the fire threatened to consume the man sitting on the other side of the glass. Quentin shook his head. "I was walking out. My weapon was the truth, and you wanted to protect yourself from it. Your volatile anger killed your only son."

"Because of you. Because of that beast, Agatha. Because her daughter didn't know how to control herself, flaunting her tight little body around me, taking me away from my family."

"I guess we're all a little to blame for your mistakes, aren't we?" Quentin asked. "Because at some point, we all chose to come across your path and destruction is your goal in life. You destroyed your marriage and left your ex-wife devastated by the loss of your son. You pushed your son away with angry, demeaning words, Cooper. You tore apart a young girl's youth. You even added another pound of bitterness to Agatha Thomas's pain." Quentin stood. "It ate at you, didn't it?"

"What?" Goodyear leaned back in his chair as if Quentin's words hadn't penetrated his soul, but pain flickered across his features. He'd been burned by his own fire. "What ate at me?"

"The fact that you couldn't destroy Denton's spirit. Even in death, he'll live on. He'll bring back the good name of your father—yeah, you even destroyed that, didn't you?" Quentin held to the phone wondering if he should say what the Lord has put upon his heart. He closed his eyes and let the Lord speak to him. When Quentin spoke, his voice was softer than before. "Cooper?"

"What now?"

"Before you hire a lawyer. Before you do anything, ask to see Denton's pastor, the one that led him to the Lord."

"Why should I?" Cooper smirked.

"Because I think Denton wanted you to step up and be his earthly father. He's with his heavenly Father now. Wouldn't it be nice to know someday you could see your son again without all the destruction between you?"

"You can take your pious—"

Quentin slammed the phone down, pushed the chair under the table and knocked on the door. The officer who'd shown him into the room opened the door and led him to the female guard. He retrieved his keys, thanked them both, and left. He never wanted to see the inside of that place again.

"There you are." Sheriff Dixon met him in the parking lot, the pictures Quentin had left for him in his hand. That had been a difficult thing to do. He'd sneaked into Willow's e-mail, forwarded Peterman's e-mail to himself, and copied the photos at home, but Willow was asleep, and he wanted her to rest. Surely, she'd understand, even though there was nothing for him to see. Her e-mail was as sparse as her address book.

"Sheriff." Quentin shook his hand.

The older man gave a brief look at the photos and looked up again. "I talked to Peterman today. Any way he could be involved in this with her?"

"Agatha clamping down hard, isn't she?"

"Wants Willow Thomas jailed by five o'clock." Dixon smirked.

"The guy is CEO of his company. I don't think Willow would have that much influence over him, and the pictures show two guys milling around her apartment looking official enough."

The sheriff studied the photographs this time before tossing a sharp look in Quentin's direction. He tapped the face of one of the men. "This fellow's in town. I saw him yesterday."

"Where?"

"Outside the hospital, talking with Willow's mother."

CHAPTER NINETEEN

Agatha looked up from her paperwork. A young employee stood in her office doorway. How long had she been there? "What do you need?"

"There's a—Suzanne Scott is here to see you."

Agatha rolled her eyes.

"Do you know her Mrs. Thomas?" The girl grew giddy enough she'd obviously forgotten to fear Agatha's legendary explosive temper.

With a deep inhale, Agatha nodded. "Make her wait five minutes. Then bring her back."

"This is so exciting." The blonde head covered by a hairnet bounced away before Agatha could scream.

Exciting? No. A nightmare. Yes. What did she have to say to Suzanne that hadn't been said years before? Oh, she had plenty to talk about.

"There you are." Suzanne sprang around the door. "The girl said you needed a few minutes, but I know you better. You just wanted me to wait. Suzanne Scott waits for no one."

Of all the nerve. Agatha stared up at her from her seat behind the desk. "What are you doing here after all these years?"

"I came to see my daughter."

Agatha snorted.

"Now, now, Aggie, just because you've grown to resemble a pig doesn't mean you have to sound like one."

Agatha ground her teeth together and said nothing.

"Still speechless in my presence, I see."

"Again, Suzanne, what are you doing here in my office?"

"I wanted to come by and see how small-town life treated you." Suzanne waved her hand. "Not good, I see."

Suzanne only gloated now because a very long time ago, Agatha had been the beauty. Yet, no one knew that today—because Suzanne had stolen the notoriety and the fame from her.

"Good enough," Agatha said. "I have a beautiful daughter, and a husband devoted to me." What did it hurt to lie to Suzanne Scott after the way her old friend had treated her?

"You've treated Robert good I noticed. His little round head and his large belly say a lot about your cooking skills, at least. Did he ever figure out you married him to spite Teddy?"

Fury at Suzanne ran deep. She had dangled Teddy in front of her like a carrot—a twenty-five carat diamond, brilliant in his physique and talent. And to think she had stayed in Amazing Grace rather than going on that casting call known in Hollywood history as the start of Suzanne Scott's career. On top of that, Teddy never really cared for her. He dated her once or twice to be nice, and who knew, maybe he dated her to spite Suzanne, not that the bimbo ever cared for Ted—not like Agatha had cared.

"Cat got your tongue?"

Agatha stood with as much nonchalance as she could muster. "Suzanne, I'm going to ask you not to talk about Robert the way you've just done. He may have thinning hair, and he may be a size or two larger than your husband ..." She walked toward the door. Suzanne turned and walked ahead of Agatha. As they passed the small cubbyhole beside the hot water heater for the kitchen appliances, she reached around and grasped the broom. "You see, while Robert may not be as fit and as trim as Scott or even Ted. Yes, Ted's in town. Have you heard?"

"No, I haven't." Suzanne swept into the open bakery and the table area like a princess invited to the ball.

"Well, like I said, while Robert hasn't written Hollywood blockbusters, and he doesn't have what little hair he has left on his head done in the finest of salons ..." Agatha brought the broom around and swatted Suzanne in the rear. "At least my husband stayed home and lived up to his obligations and raised our daughter to be a proper young lady, and when we had hard times, unlike your husband ..." She smacked her with the broom again.

"What are you doing? Stop that." Suzanne squealed trying to get through the crowd of stunned and unmoving onlookers.

"And when we had rough times, and our daughter was hurt, Robert didn't abandon us and run off to only God knows where. He stayed with us, and despite living with this pig of a wife, as you called me, he didn't give up on us." She pulled the broom over her head. "Now, get out of my business before I wop you upside your stringy hair. Whoever told you that you could pull off that look? If you're trying to look like your daughter, you failed. She's a hundred times more beautiful than you. Didn't the mirror-mirror on the wall tell you so?"

"Agatha ..." Suzanne ducked and ran out the door.

"And don't come back ..." Agatha chased her down the sidewalk as passersby stepped against store windows. "I never want to see your ugly face again as long as I live."

Out of breath Agatha stopped running and brought the broom down. She stood, leaning against it for a breath or two before turning. "Robert." She gasped.

A smile lit her husband's handsome face, and he brought his hands up to pinch both sides of her cheek. "I love you, too, Agatha Thomas, and I always knew you married me to spite my brother."

Agatha gulped air for a second.

Robert laughed and kissed her hard on the mouth. "But I also knew on the day Laurel Elizabeth was born, you fell in love with me, too."

And on that day, when she'd watched him hold their newborn daughter and touch Laurel's little hands and feet with his tender touch, counting each one, she had loved him, if only for that moment.

She grinned at him as he still continued to laugh. He brought his hand around and swatted her in the rear. "Aggie, you're the most beautiful woman in the world to me, especially when I see you smile."

She'd offered him so few smiles.

"I wish Laurel could have heard you say what you said."

Agatha clamped her mouth shut. Truth was she wished Laurel could understand how much she did love her. Someday. Maybe. And that troublesome little niece of hers. She'd never thought about it before, but Willow had never been anything like Suzanne. Both Laurel and Willow had gained much of their personality from spunky Granny Thomas. Neither of them deserved what they'd received from their mothers.

Well, that could change.

She kissed her husband's face.

Robert lifted a hand to his cheek, caressing the spot. "Oh, Aggie ..."

"I do love you, Robert. And I love our daughter." She gave a little shake of her head. "And, if you must know, I admire that little scamp your mother raised. I don't know what's going on with her now, but we'll find out, and we'll help her."

"I'm sure both would love to hear that from you."

Aggie shook her head. "I don't think saying anything to either one of them will mean a whole lot. I'll just have to learn to show them."

Down the sidewalk, Suzanne stuck her head out of doorway where she'd retreated, and Agatha raised her broom. Suzanne skittered away, and Agatha let loose the first real laugh she'd had in ages.

Scott toyed with his cell phone, turning it over and over in his hand. Strange. Suzanne hadn't tried to call him after the scene at the hospital. He imagined her feathers were ruffled a bit, but usually she at least tried to smooth things over with him when she'd been caught in some kind of debacle.

And yesterday's stunt at the hospital had been a fiasco. Either Suzanne didn't know or she didn't care she'd placed Willow in danger. Just who was the man Suzanne huddled with, actually standing within the circle of press and weasels?

"Call her already," Ted grunted.

Scott shook his head. "I think I'll give her a little more time to stew on this one. I'm trying to figure out her complete angle."

Ted said nothing.

"Look who's on her feet." Laurel had her arm around Willow as they came down the stairs together.

Scott was learning to read his daughter, and right now he'd say she wanted to pull from Laurel's motherly touch. Instead, she allowed her cousin to help her down the stairs.

Ted moved over and gave her space on the couch. "How's the head?"

"A little dull headache but nothing like last night."

"Well, don't stay upright for too long or that pain might come back," Ted warned.

"Daddy?"

Scott loved to hear her say that word. He'd never tire of it as long as he lived. "Yeah, kiddo."

"Where's Suzanne?"

"I asked her to stay in town at the inn. Why?"

"Have you seen her since yesterday?"

Testing him, he'd bet. "I haven't left here."

She yawned and blinked. "Don't you think you should make sure she's okay? I mean there's a stalker in town. If he's after me ..."

Ted straightened.

Scott shook his head. "That's part of what I'm trying to figure out," he spoke to his brother. They'd always had a way of communicating as kids. They hadn't missed a beat after the years of separation.

"Willow." He turned his attention to his daughter. "Don't worry about your mother. She's tough and savvy in this type of thing."

The cell phone in his hand rang. He looked at the screen and smiled. "Some lovesick young pup is calling to check on my daughter."

Willow smiled.

He answered. "She's fine and sitting with us here in the living room, Quentin."

"Mr. Thomas, I need to know where your wife is staying."

"Why?"

"Sheriff Dixon wants to talk to her about the man she was talking to in the crowd yesterday."

"Excuse me."

"Please don't alarm Willow. Is Ted with you?"

"Yes." Scott caught his brother's gaze and held it for a second. "Why?"

"Have him stay with Willow and Laurel, please. And call me back after you make an excuse to get out of the house. We'll need to know where to meet you."

"I guess you're right. I should go see what she's doing to spite me in my anger. She's probably ordered a dozen dresses from Rodeo Drive—on my credit card. The Amazing Grace Inn isn't far enough from California to keep her from doing that. Yes." He pulled the phone from his ear as if Quentin had spoken. "Your fiancé says to tell you he'll be home soon." He clicked off the phone. An amateur. The boy would never get over anything on Willow. Thankfully.

Scott stood and stretched. "Quentin said he saw your mother. She looks pretty upset."

"Go check on her." Laurel said. "Bear—Uncle Ted and I will stay with Willow."

"I appreciate that." He walked to Willow and bent to place a kiss on her bandaged forehead. Instead, she kissed his cheek. He pulled back, surprised.

"I'm so sorry for the ugly things I've said to you about the choices you've made."

Scott sat on the coffee table in front of her. "Honey, I never expected an apology for the truth."

"The truth is I missed out on a lot of good things because I always wanted what God didn't have for me. When I thought Uncle Ted was my father, I wanted him to come home for me. When I learned you were my father, I wanted you and Suzanne—Mother—to take me in your arms and love me and to have a family like Uncle Robert gave to Laurel. All that time of wanting and wishing for things made me lose out on what God had given to me—the perfect life, here on this lake, with Granny."

Laurel ran her hand down Willow's back. "And Quentin ... because of me and my plotting."

"And time with Laurel. I had a sister—a cousin-sister, and I allowed my anger and my wishes to stand in front of me like a cement wall I couldn't see over."

Scott held out his hand, and Willow clasped it in hers. He pulled her toward him. "Why all this? Why now?"

Willow turned questioning eyes to Laurel. Scott's niece ran up the stairs and returned with a journal in her hands. She handed it to Willow, and Willow presented it to him. "Granny." She wiped tears from her face. "Granny's book of prayers. All the years of prayers for both of us, and she never got to see them answered."

Ted drew closer to Willow. He reached around her and touched Laurel's arm, holding both girls in a loose embrace. "Laurel, Granny left that for you?"

Laurel nodded. "And in it she asked me to one day share it with Willow."

"Willow, your granny didn't expect to see her prayers answered on this side of heaven. I can guarantee you, being the woman of prayer your father and I always knew her to be, she had no doubts this day would come."

"But I've wasted so much time ..." Willow ran the back of her hand over her eyes.

"Well, you might have wasted it, but God sure didn't. Here you are today, apologizing to that rascal of a father of yours. In my opinion, he doesn't deserve it, but you're practicing—"

"Returning good for evil." Willow hiccupped. "Laurel just showed it to me in the Bible."

"Returning good for pure evil." Bear winked at Scott. "Don't you think you should check on Suzanne, maybe bring her for a visit?"

Scott stood. "I'll be back as soon as I can."

Willow nodded. "Be careful."

"You better believe I will," he said as he opened the door. "Our family has a lot of time to make up for, don't we?"

"We sure do." Robert, standing on the other side of the door, stopped Scott from moving forward. "Hey, look at you, Ms. Willow. Alive and on your feet."

"She shouldn't be up." Agatha pushed past Robert. "You need to be in bed. Laurel, help me get her back upstairs."

Scott looked back over his shoulder at a bewildered Ted and the two horrified young women. He wished he could stay to see what was up, but if he understood what Quentin was saying, Suzanne had a lot of explaining to do.

Willow clung to her cousin's arm as Agatha plodded up the stairs behind them. Were they both being led to the firing squad, and why wasn't Uncle Ted helping them? Instead, he ambled off into the kitchen, as if seeing Agatha loaded too large a burden upon his shoulders.

Silence dragged with them down the hall to her room, the quiet broken only by Agatha as they moved into the bedroom. "I see you've taken your grandmother's room."

"Momma ..." Laurel shushed her.

"What? I'm making small talk."

Dutifully, Willow made her way to the bed and climbed inside. Maybe Aunt Agatha would leave without making a scene.

Agatha stepped to the side of the bed and peered down at her as if Willow were a dead body in a coffin. If a corpse could see what was about to happen, would they fear the closing of the lid as much as Willow feared the actions of her aunt?

"Why are you looking at me like that?" Agatha demanded, touching the bandage over her gash.

Willow winced. "Like what?"

"I'm not going to kill you. Laurel will testify against me."

"Momma," Laurel laughed. "What's gotten into you?"

Agatha pulled the covers around Willow, tucking her in. "If you must know, I just had the best time I've had in years."

"Really?" Willow dared show curiosity.

"Really." Agatha went to the desk and looked out the window.

If Laurel wasn't about to ask, Willow sure was. "Do you want to tell us what you did?"

Agatha spun around, her arms crossed over her chest. "I chased a witch down the street with a broom."

Willow laughed now. Agatha could mean anyone.

"And I wanted to make sure you heard it from me before you heard it from anyone else."

Willow couldn't imagine.

"Your mother came into Manna. She said some terrible things about your Uncle Robert. I pulled out a broom and chased her down the road."

Willow pursed her lips. Agatha's face showed no sign of amusement, yet hadn't she said she'd had a good time doing it. Willow cut her gaze to Laurel who shrugged.

"So?" Agatha challenged.

"So, what?" Willow asked.

"What do you think of that?"

"Well, Aunt Aggie, if Suzanne said anything ugly about Uncle Robert, she deserved it."

"Willow." Laurel opened her eyes wide.

"Now, that's what I thought." Agatha smiled and then she leaned back and outright laughed.

The sound of it was like the thick ice of the lake breaking apart in early spring. Truly, Agatha could not have laughed in years.

"Oh, Momma." Laurel moved to her mother.

Agatha hugged her daughter, and Willow brought her hand to her face. Who would have thought that such a simple act of devilment could make Agatha seem nearly human? If it would have worked for Agatha to turn her mischievous spirit on her years ago, Willow would have allowed it simply to see the relief on Laurel's face.

"And so you know." Agatha held Laurel at arm's length. "I do love you. And I love your daddy." Agatha pulled Laurel back into her embrace. "I'm sorry if you ever thought I didn't."

Laurel's actions mirrored Willow. Her hand covered her mouth. Tears glistened on her cheeks as they fell down her face.

"And you." Agatha pointed. "I don't know what's going on with this stalker business. I haven't quite decided if you've made this up or if something else is going on, but I've suffered through this life with you all these years. Your leaving us now would be a shame. I lied when I said I wasn't happy you were back. I'm actually relieved."

Willow pulled the covers closer to her. "And if I told you I'm not making this up, would you believe me?"

"Not until I see the proof, but I'll wait to judge you until then. Get some more rest. Laurel and I will leave your two uncles with you. Robert said you have no food in the house. We'll fix dinner for everyone."

"Fair enough." Willow sunk down in the bed. How did Laurel ever do a willful act against such a formidable force?

And why was Willow craving Quentin's return so badly?

As the door shut behind them, Willow pictured her mother running from a broom-swinging Agatha. "Dear Lord, I hope they got some good pictures of that one."

With only one way to find out, she retrieved her computer from her desk. Watching the door to make sure Agatha didn't re-enter, she pushed the power button. But her computer wasn't off. Someone had already been on it.

Her Outlook popped up. E-mail from Jeffrey Peterman had been opened. Jeffrey had addressed the e-mail to Quentin. "These should prove what Willow's gone through. Let me know if I can help any further. Tell the million-dollar girl, we're proud of her. J.P."

Willow relaxed. Quentin. She had nothing to hide from him. He'd obviously arranged for Jeffrey to send the e-mail. She opened the attachments one by one. Hominski and Detective Jim inside her apartment.

And in the corner of her mind, something niggled there, like a memory just out of reach.

Another e-mail came through, the small notice to the right side of her screen. "Mommy Needs You."

The memory edged closer. The e-mail alert faded, but there had been another note. The package Denton Goodyear had delivered to her. The package had been in her apartment.

I touched you, and you didn't even know it. Watch out, Willow. I'm closer than you think.

That's what the note meant. The man had touched her. She had trusted him.

Willow, are you ready to die?

That voice.

Detective Hominski's voice.

She closed out Jeffrey's e-mail and opened the newest one. This one arrived with a receipt request. Willow clicked "yes" just to be rid of it. She gave a frantic tap on her computer mouse to open the attachment.

And her phone rang.

CHAPTER TWENTY

Scott scuffed his feet against the front mat of the Amazing Grace Inn and looked back at the patrol car parked in front of the old Antebellum home. Trouble loomed, and he was afraid to know what Suzanne had brought upon them.

He entered, and the inn's manager smiled at him from behind the desk. "Mr. Thomas, good to see you today."

"Thank you. I'm looking for my wife, Suzanne."

A door in the rear of the inn opened, and Sheriff Dixon and Quentin McPheron made their way down the lengthy hall from the solarium overlooking the backyard.

"Sorry," Dixon apologized. "We had to run off some scoundrels roosting here in the front room.

Quentin bent down and brushed some dirt from his jeans. "Run off, huh?"

"One of them gave the sheriff a hard time. He deputized me for a brief moment." Quentin offered a tense smile.

"Mrs. Thomas?" Scott turned back to the manager.

"Not here," Quentin answered.

"She left here about two hours ago." The woman's gaze moved to the other two men and back to him. "She wasn't alone when I saw her last."

"Why didn't you tell me that when I asked you?" Sheriff Dixon scolded.

"Because, Sheriff, it's none of your concern. She's Mr. Thomas's wife."

The sheriff shook his head. "Give me a minute." He pushed open the inn's door and walked out.

Scott moved to look outside. Daniel trekked to his car, opened the door, and leaned inside to retrieve something before making his way back inside. He laid several photographs on the counter. "Do you recognize either of these men?" he asked the manager.

She gave them her full attention. First one then the others. "This one. He's the one she went off with after Aggie Thomas chased her toward the inn with a broom in her hand."

"Aggie what?" Even Scott couldn't hide his amusement.

"Aggie even hit her a few times before your wife outran her. When she got back to the inn, that's when this man pulled up beside her, and she got inside the car."

"Did she look coerced?" Quentin asked.

"No. He spoke to her, and she climbed inside the car."

A weary loneliness seeped into Scott's heart. He looked around for a place to fall and found the oversized couch in the inn's front room. He wasn't some dull-witted boy from the hicks. Suzanne's actions meant one of two things to him. Either his wife had contrived to hurt their daughter, or she was being unfaithful to him.

Why would she hurt Willow, and why did he deserve her betrayal on any level?

"Mr. Thomas?" Quentin broke into his thoughts.

Scott blinked, looking up to the kid who loved his daughter. If he ever hurt Willow the way Suzanne's actions had cut him, he'd kill the boy.

But this boy had waited how long for Willow to return to him? Quentin McPheron was rock solid.

Willow was made of much better stuff than her mother. Granny made sure of that.

"Don't you think you should start calling me Scott or even get used to calling me Dad?"

Scott's cell phone rang, and he dug into his coat pocket. "Willow," he announced. He swallowed, pushing down the hurt and anger swirling upward from somewhere deep inside. "Hey, kiddo."

"Daddy?" Willow's voice whispered into the phone.

"What is it?" He stood.

"Tell her I'm on my way." Quentin sprinted for the door.

"Daddy, I just got a call. It's Suzanne ..."

Quentin threw open the front door. The two men sitting in the living room bounded to their feet. From somewhere, Bear pulled his rifle and aimed right at Quentin's heart. "Willow— where's Willow?" he screamed.

"She's sleeping." Robert moved with a cautious step and pushed the barrel of Ted's rifle down.

"I'm here." Willow made her way down the stairs, carrying her laptop in her hand.

Quentin ran to her, taking her face in his hands. "I thought you were hurt."

"No. I'm fine."

But she wasn't. She was even paler than when he'd pulled her from the waters. He pulled her to him. The hard case of the laptop pushed into his ribs before he released her.

The door opened, and again Ted lifted the barrel of his gun. "Knock!" he yelled. "Or lock the stinking door."

"What's wrong with your mother?" Scott ignored him, moving to his daughter.

Without speaking, Willow led them into the kitchen. She placed her laptop on the table, opened it, and brought up her e-mail.

Quentin put his arm around her and held her to him.

Scott cleared his throat. "What is it, kiddo?"

"Read it. I'm the only one who can help her."

Quentin shook his head. "No," he told her before turning his attention to the e-mail—a picture of Suzanne tied to a chair and a message he read aloud, "'Willow can save her mother. No police. No father. No uncles. No boyfriend. Come to me Willow, and come alone or your mother will die.'"

"No." Scott grasped Willow's shoulders and turned her toward him. "Listen to me. Quentin will verify this. The sheriff is on his way. He can tell you as well. Your mother set this up. It's a publicity stunt. She's trying to show the world the two of you have a relationship."

"But why?" Willow asked.

Scott glanced at Quentin. "I think I put the idea in her head."

"You what?" Quentin stepped around Willow. "You put your wife—"

"I didn't plan it. Suzanne's playing a secondary part in the movie. To get her to play the role, I told her a few times that this movie could redeem her in the eyes of the public who remembered she'd abandoned Willow. She's playing a mother." He lifted Willow's chin with his finger. "I didn't say it to exploit you, kiddo. I promise."

"But your wife is exploiting her," Quentin railed.

"No," Willow said. "Look at the fear in her face."

Bear peered over Willow's shoulder. "Willow, your mother's an actress. But she bores easily. Give it an hour or two, and she'll call Scott to tell him she's heading back home."

"Daddy?"

Scott paced back and forth.

"Daddy, I believe this. What about you? Would she go this far?"

Scott stopped on the opposite side of the room before facing her. Yet, his eyes met with Quentin's stare. "Yes, I believe she would."

Scott lied. Quentin saw it in the lines of his face. The man thought his wife was in danger, but he was protecting his daughter from the truth.

Willow turned to him. "I can't not help her. If she's behind this, and it's all been a prank, then I have nothing to fear. If this isn't a hoax—if he's got her somewhere—I know the man holding her."

"We've just figured that out. He was one of the detectives in your apartment."

"The lead detective, Hominski," Willow said.

"Sheriff Dixon is checking with some of the other scum invading the town to see if they can give him a real name. He'll be here soon."

"But she could be dead before then."

"Willow." Scott raised his voice. "The sheriff saw your mother with this man yesterday. I did, too. The manager at the inn saw her get into the car with him."

Willow leaned over and typed furiously.

"What are you doing?" Quentin tried to stop her.

She hit send before he could.

Quentin pushed her gently out of the way and went to her "sent" folder. He read her reply. "What are you doing?" Or, at least, what did she think she was doing?

"I'm asking him what he wants me to do."

Quentin raised his hands in the air and brought them down hard against the legs of his jeans. "Why?"

She searched his face, and he saw something he hadn't noticed—not even when she'd agreed to marry him. Suzanne had long ago caused Willow enough heartache to keep her from feeling much of anything. Now, Willow's heart was blossoming forward with buds of love and mercy.

And he had to walk a fine balance between shutting her heart down and letting her run head long into danger because of this newfound compassion.

"No," he demanded. "You will do no such thing."

"I have to, Quentin. Can't you see?"

"Why? For Suzanne Scott? She never cared for you." He hated this argument, this awful truth that could close her down again.

"Not for Suzanne." She held out her hand to her father. "For the man who loves her."

Someone did knock, and Ted opened the door for the sheriff.

"Willow, no. Not even for your dad. He doesn't expect it of you."

Willow eyed the computer screen then slammed it shut. She took a deep breath. "I don't know what I was thinking when I said I'd marry you. I was wrong. You haven't changed. I don't want anything to do with you. Never again. Leave me alone, Quentin." Her push sent him falling backward. He caught himself against the refrigerator, but she'd run up the stairs and slammed her bedroom door.

At least there, she wouldn't be on some foolish journey to help her mother. When she calmed down, he'd rethink the marriage proposal.

Scott slapped him on the shoulder. "How a young woman who never spent a moment with her mother could act just like her is beyond me. She's upset. Give her time to think this through."

Quentin nodded. He had a lot to ponder himself. He didn't think he could live a lifetime with a young Agatha. He didn't have Robert's stamina.

"Did you learn anything?" Ted asked Sheriff Dixon.

"Not good. Not good at all. If Ms. Scott is mixed up with this guy, he's been known to be a loose cannon."

"What do you mean?" Scott stepped forward.

"Seems he's stepped over the boundaries of proper etiquette a time or two. That says a lot coming from the crowd he's hanging with. He's stalked a few stars. They've filed suit against him. Gone to great lengths to hurt one or two. He's suspected in the death of at least one young starlet—last year. They found her body in the pool of the home she rented."

Scott nodded. "I met her once or twice. Nice girl."

"One of the pack of hounds said he saw him tailing her the night she died," the sheriff added.

"What's his name?" Scott asked.

"LeBlanc. Dennis LeBlanc."

Scott cleared his throat.

"You know him," Quentin accused. "How?"

"I don't know him," Scott argued. "I've heard his name. The lead in the movie we're wrapping, she mentioned she'd filed a restraining order. She had some uncomfortable moments with him. Last I heard he'd gone away. I thought the legal action had scared him away."

"And now, we know your wife is the reason he left. She put him on the trail of her daughter." Quentin stomped up the stairs.

Willow's bedroom door was closed, and he knocked. No answer.

"Willow?" He knocked again and tried the door. She'd locked him out.

"This is foolish, Willow. Let me in." Nothing.

"Willow!"

He'd had enough. Anger was one thing, childishness another. He leaned into the door. When it didn't budge, he used his shoulder. The frame splintered, and he expected her to trounce on him.

Instead, he found the room empty. Her gown and robe were on the bed. Her window was up. Her laptop was on. He hit a key and waited for her screen to come to life. When it did, he checked her e-mail. Nothing.

He started out but stopped. Going back to the laptop he checked her "deleted" files. Willow was smart, but time had kept her from outsmarting him completely. And he didn't like what he'd found.

With the swipe of his hand, her computer sailed across the room and hit the wall.

He flew down the stairs and out the front door, feeling in his pockets for the keys he'd shoved there. His pockets were empty. And his Jeep was gone.

Scott ran outside and stood beside him. "What is it?"

"Did you know your daughter's a masterful pickpocket? When she pushed me in the kitchen, she snatched my keys."

"I don't know what to say."

"I just hope she gets the chance to apologize to me." He ran toward his house and came back with his rifle in his hand. "Let's go."

CHAPTER TWENTY-ONE

Willow pushed open the door to Appleton's Tree of Knowledge.

"Hello, dear," Annie called from somewhere.

She needed to keep calm. Just keep moving. Say something. Nice and steady. Someone could be watching. "Hi, Annie."

"Can I help you with anything? I'm surprised you're up and around today."

Willow couldn't believe she got by the roadblock at the bottom of the mountain. But Laurel had said they checked everyone coming in. Going out wasn't a problem.

"I'm fine, thanks." She waved and moved to the east side of the store and meandered along the magazine rack. "Outdoor Life." She picked up the publication and fanned the pages. How ironic she'd come across an advertisement for Anglers' Lures. Would she live to see that multi-million dollar contract she'd only heard about through others?

There, between the page numbers the stalker had e-mailed to her, she found the information she sought. She read and memorized the simple instructions.

"Sweet thing, if Henry were here, he'd be teasing you about buying the magazine before reading it." Annie smiled at her.

Willow placed the magazine back on the rack, and having second thoughts picked up not one, but two of them, holding them tightly together. Without looking too obvious, she peered around the store. Empty.

Of course, Hominski wouldn't be inside—but he could be watching from the outside. He'd done that often enough.

She went to the checkout counter where Annie waited for her. Holding the magazines, she worked hard to keep them together while she fumbled inside her purse for her credit card.

Retrieving it, she laid the magazines and the card on the counter.

"Willow, honey, your head's bleeding through the bandage." Annie's eyes widened.

Willow lifted her hand and felt the moisture under her fingers. Pulling her hand away she found no stain on her fingers. When she'd swung from the porch roof to the ground, the pain had nearly made her cry out. She must have pulled a stitch.

She leaned forward. "Annie, I'll be fine. Please only ring up the top one, but don't pick it up, okay? The one underneath is the same magazine."

Annie narrowed her eyes but did as Willow asked.

She rang up the purchase and accepted Willow's card. Willow took the receipt and signed it, quickly writing the info Quentin would need on the top of her receipt.

Willow slid the magazine on the bottom in her direction and pushed the top copy toward Annie. Then she pointed to the page numbers she'd written on the top of the receipt along with Quentin's cell phone number. "Let me walk outside. Don't come after me. I'm probably being followed." She swallowed hard. "Annie, please tell Quentin if something happens to me, I didn't mean anything I said. I really thought my whole life was lived as it was so I could be with him forever." What a cruel joke it would be to find she'd been given life only to die trying to save the mother who never wanted her. *God's will be done.* Granny's voice played in her memory.

She pulled the door back and rushed outside before her emotions would keep her from moving any further.

"What are you doing, young lady?" Agatha moved down the sidewalk toward her. "Here we are buying all this food and getting other things for your house, and you're out and about."

"Aunt Aggie, I can't explain. I'm sorry. Laurel."

"I don't understand, Willow. You're bleeding. Why are you out here like this?"

Now, she'd lost even Laurel's newly earned trust.

"Agatha, come in here a minute. I have a bone to pick with you." Annie's angry voice boomed.

Willow jumped.

"I don't have time to deal with you," Agatha harrumphed. "I'm out shopping for a girl who doesn't deserve half the kindness."

"Get in here and get in here now, Agatha Thomas, or I'll tell the world about you."

Agatha took the bait. Willow cast a thank-you look over her shoulder.

"Willow?" Laurel rushed after her.

"Trust me. Please." Willow embraced Laurel, refusing to let her go. "There's something I have to do, and I have to do it alone. Please, Laurel. Call Darrell. Get him here. Quentin may need him." Willow pulled from her and ran toward Quentin's Jeep.

With tongue slithering across his lips, Dennis LeBlanc let the excitement run through his body. She'd gotten the instructions. For a moment, he expected her to be held back from her mission, but she'd managed to get away from the quarrelsome fat woman and that beautiful blonde cousin of hers.

LeBlanc waited for the Jeep to pull away. He'd followed her from the highway outside the mountain road leading from the lake. Clever how she'd taken her boyfriend's Jeep. How had she gotten away from him?

That girl had spirit. He'd seen it in her from the start. He never toyed with one of them this long, allowing the itch to keep him awake at night, dreaming of the fear he'd see on her face, and the pain he'd inflict upon her, just before he took the life out of her.

Suzanne's sudden arrival had almost taken this time from him. He'd acted spontaneously, slicing Willow's brakes to get the job done. He had to talk himself into it. Told himself he'd stare at her body in her coffin and get the satisfaction he needed.

That wasn't the satisfaction he wanted.

His body tingled the way it always did when he closed in for the kill. This time there would be double the pleasure. He'd let Suzanne watch. After all, she'd hired him. Of course, she didn't understand when he took a job, he was in it for keeps, so to speak. Suzanne had both set him upon and taken him from another adventure, but he'd get back to that pretty, young starlet who'd snubbed him soon enough.

Willow turned the corner, heading far enough out of town they'd be days, even months finding her body.

LeBlanc pulled away from the curb, looking in his rearview mirror. Thomas's black BMW pulled up outside the bookstore, and Willow's young stud jumped from the passenger side.

So, Willow thought she could go against his orders. He'd make her pay double for her mistake. Besides, they wouldn't know where to find her. Even Willow wasn't smart enough to get the information to Boyfriend.

Quentin sprinted from the car and into the store, leaving Scott behind the wheel. Agatha's arm braced a trembling Annie. "She just left." Agatha told him.

Laurel held up the subscription card for a magazine. "That guy—the stalker—LeBlanc, he'd told Willow to look into this magazine."

Quentin snatched it from her hand.

"How'd you get here so quickly?" Annie placed a hand over her chest, and Agatha helped her into a chair.

"I found something that told me Willow would be here." Annie looked ashen.

"Where's Henry, Annie?" Laurel asked.

"He went home for a bit to rest."

"Can you stay with her?" Quentin asked Laurel.

"Go," Agatha shooed. "We'll wait."

He blinked at Agatha's change of heart but said nothing.

"Darrell," Laurel breathed. "Quentin, Darrell's on his way from the school."

Quentin grabbed a pen from the counter and wrote the instructions on his hand then he thrust the paper into Laurel's hands. "Tell him to be careful. We don't know if this is a ruse or not." He held up his hand in good-bye.

"Quentin," Annie's voice grew stronger. "That little girl said she loves you. I want you to help her out of this."

Quentin nodded.

"Give me your cell phone, Laurel," Agatha said, but he didn't wait to hear what call she planned to make—probably to Henry.

He ran back to the car. "Take a left at the light. We're going up toward Shepherd's Rock."

Scott pulled away from the curb. "I guess he really didn't think we'd be on to him. We'd never find her there."

"Annie said she left the information for me," Quentin said more to himself.

"Smart girl, I never raised, huh?" Scott's attempt at humor fell flat.

"She expected I'd follow her." He clenched his fist. "She played me."

"And that makes you mad?" Scott turned the corner on two wheels.

"No, actually, it makes me kind of proud of her. In our lifetimes, I've played her a few times as well."

"Like ..."

"Not telling her I knew she was hiding behind the old willow tree drawing my picture while I sat fishing on Granny's dock."

"You ever going to tell her the truth?"

Small talk. That's all it was. Something to keep their minds off the possibility of losing the most wonderful girl in the world.

"I already did. Her first day back," Quentin told him. "I wanted to establish I had the upper hand in this relationship. I'd enjoyed the shock on her face when I acted so bowled over by the portrait. Even though I learned recently she mistook my excitement for disgust."

"Maybe she played you on that one."

Quentin thought on that for a long moment before speaking, "No." He held to the dash as Scott took another turn.

"How can you be so sure?"

"She left me out on her porch with a psychopath on the loose."

Scott took his eyes off the road for a split second.

"Here. Here. Turn here."

Scott's tires hit the dirt road and spun in a complete three-sixty. They slammed to a stop, one wheel of the car inside a ditch.

"Smooth," Quentin barked.

Scott breathed deeply for several seconds then slammed on the accelerator. The car lurched but didn't budge from the wide moat holding it captive.

Quentin threw open the car's door and stepped out. Looking, he appraised the situation in a second. "Might as well get out. We're going to have to run up that mountain—at least until Darrell can pick us up." He leaned in and picked up his rifle.

Scott climbed out of the car and looked up the steep mountain road. "I'll stay with you as long as I can, but I'm not in as good of shape as you."

Scott wasn't even in as good a shape as his older brother. He looked better on the outside, but Bear was fit and lean. Why hadn't he gotten Bear to help him?

He started to run, looking over at the man who fought to keep up with him. He'd chosen Scott because it was his job to protect his daughter.

They ran for a mile. Scott slowly fell behind him, but Quentin pushed forward. Turning, he ran backward for a few steps. Scott was doing his best to keep up.

"Go," the older man waved him on.

Quentin's legs ached from the exertion. He'd challenged his football squad, and he beat many of them, but Denton always passed him, making him feel like an old man. So, Quentin understood a little of what Scott experienced. Mortality.

That thought spurred him on. He didn't want the man to face the death of his daughter any more than he wanted to face losing her.

"Willow," he puffed out her name as he stumbled forward, fighting to stay on his feet.

Tires on the dirt road rumbled below him. They stopped for a moment, but Quentin continued to run. In a matter of minutes, Darrell pulled up alongside him.

Quentin jumped into Darrell's car, holding tight to the rifle in his hands. They'd lost precious minutes. He'd kill the pervert if he laid a hand on Willow.

"Thanks, buddy." He gulped for breath. "Do me a favor. Move slow. The sound of the car on the road will tell him we're coming."

Darrell nodded. "We can pull left at the fork and cut through the woods."

Quentin stared at his friend. "How?" He fought to gain his breath.

"My grandmother used to own a house up here."

"I—I never knew."

"She didn't like you." Darrell kept his eyes on the road.

Quentin looked in the backseat where Scott had chosen to sit. The man's face was beet red. Sweat poured off him. Quentin doubted he looked any better.

"There's a truck coming up fast behind us." Darrell nodded toward his rearview mirror.

Quentin again cranked his neck. He closed his eyes and thanked God for Bear Thomas.

CHAPTER TWENTY-TWO

Willow halted at the bottom of the drive. Cabin three would take her into a well-contained area. She threw the Jeep into first and moved it up beyond the drive. Then she got out. Without a gun. Without any kind of weapon. Without a plan.

Not very smart.

But she'd done okay so far, working off the top of her head—which at this very moment throbbed and threatened to make her vomit from the very depth of her stomach.

She walked with a quick pace up the meandering path until the cabin came into view. The drive in front of the place was empty. Heaven help Suzanne if the paparazzi jumped out and started clicking pictures of a forced reunion.

She stayed out of the view of anyone in the front of the cabin, heading toward the north side. Peering into the first window, she saw it was a two-room summer rental used by hikers and nature lovers. She also saw Suzanne tied to a chair, working frantically to free herself.

This was no ruse. Her mother was in trouble.

Willow worked her way around the cabin and eased open the back door. Her mother's captor really hadn't expected her to get loose. Willow rushed inside.

Suzanne's muffled squeal convinced Willow even further that danger lurked for both of them.

Suzanne slammed back in her chair as if the sight of Willow repulsed her. Once, another lifetime ago, Willow had been playing with Quentin when a beautiful cardinal flitted before them on the stem of a hibiscus bush in the woods outside of Granny's house. When the cardinal hopped around to face them, his little dark beaded eyes peered into hers and his bright red wings flapped as he missed the branch. "You're so ugly you scared him," Quentin laughed with glee.

Suzanne had the same look as that bird. Was Willow so hideous to her own mother the sight of her in rescue mode frightened her so much?

Despite the convincing nature of her mother's predicament, Willow leaned closer to her. "Is this a hoax, Suzanne?"

Suzanne shook her head, her long strands of dyed hair falling in her face. She looked old and tired with her makeup smeared across her face. She'd been crying.

All those years of seeing on the widescreen the beautiful woman who'd birthed her, and when she finally looked upon Suzanne, Willow got to see a real-life mess rather than a Hollywood fraud.

Still, it couldn't be this easy.

Willow leaned down to untie Suzanne. Her mother fidgeted, mouthing for Willow to hurry. Then, she stopped.

And the cabin's front door banged closed.

"Good to see you again, Willow. Now, let's see if you're really willing to make the choice. Your mother's life for yours."

Quentin climbed from Darrell's car, rifle gripped tight in his hand. Scott climbed out of the backseat, and they both waited beside the car for Darrell to return from flagging down Bear's vehicle.

Bear's truck skidded to a stop behind Darrell's car. Willow's uncle reached for his gun rack and brought his hunting rifle out. The sheriff got out of the passenger seat. His weapon of choice was a little more sophisticated than the other two. He pointed it upward and pumped the barrel. "Couldn't bring the patrol car. Didn't want to alert the maggots at the bottom of the hill." Daniel Dixon didn't look in the mood for taking prisoners today. "How far?"

"Not far. If we stay along the tree line here, we'll come out at the back of cabin three. We can get around the front without being seen," Darrell said.

"I hope you're right," Quentin muttered.

"Trust me." Darrell walked ahead of Quentin. The geek was turning into a knight. Maybe Laurel had seen something valiant in him after all.

Quentin frowned. At least Laurel was safe in Amazing Grace. His princess was running headlong on a stubborn streak toward the dragon.

Scott and Bear flanked him. "She'll be all right," Bear said.

"Scott, are you okay?" Quentin asked the man.

"I'll be fine as soon as I see that my daughter and my wife are safe."

Quentin wasn't sure he ever liked Scott Thomas very much, but he bowed his head. *Dear God give Mr. Thomas—and me—the desire of our hearts. Keep the woman I love—and her mother—safe from harm.*

"Are *you* okay?" Darrell asked.

Quentin nodded and peered straight ahead. He'd save Willow, or he'd die trying.

LeBlanc let the cabin door close behind him. He stepped toward Willow. Fright showed in her eyes. He'd seen that look before, and he captured it in his memory to replay like he did with all the others he'd terrorized.

Girls like Willow Thomas laughed at him. Called him names. Never had the time for him. He almost bought into her victim act in her apartment that night. He might have allowed Willow to live, take her mother instead, but she'd batted her eyes and sweet talked him into helping her leave New York, proving to him that she was just like all of the others.

Who was he kidding? He'd waited to see this look in her eyes, to watch her move away from him, thinking she could flee from him.

"Hominski," Willow held up her hand as if she could stop him with the gesture, "you don't want to do this."

"How could you ever know what I want to do to you, Willow?"

She stopped only when her back was against the wall. "What have I ever done to you?"

"What have any of *you* ever done *for* me?"

The girl blinked, as if she didn't know the power she had over men. Look at the way Boyfriend fell at her feet as soon as she arrived home. He hated the power beautiful women wielded. In high school, the lies of one girl had brought his world tumbling down around him. She'd accused his father of sexual assault. And the life in Malibu, the endless streams of money, the life of ease—they all ended with his parents' divorce and his father's ruin. He and dad had learned very quickly that Mom was in the marriage—playing both wife and mother—because of what it brought to her. And Dad had been unable to live with her abandonment. Despite the pleas of his son, his father had put the gun to his head and pulled the trigger.

Women like Suzanne Scott and Willow Thomas didn't deserve to live.

After his father's untimely death, he went from being the life of the party to nothing more than pond scum. Girls shunned him, taunted him, made him feel less of a man.

He hated women. Wanted nothing to do with them unless he could frighten them until he took their lives away.

"You were very nice to me in New York. I would have never known this side of you, Detective..."

He shook his head. "Don't try to cajole me, Willow. It won't work this time."

"Detective, please. We won't say a thing."

He moved in closer. "You've got that right. Dead women tell no secrets." He latched onto her wrist, pulled her toward him.

Willow's hand connected with his face, a nail digging deep into his cheek. He released her for a second and brought his forearm across his body, slamming into the area of her head covered by a bandage.

Willow cried out and fell to the floor.

She didn't move.

LeBlanc turned to Suzanne. The has-been actress stared at her daughter, who was crumbled at his feet then lifted her gaze to him.

"Who dies first, Suzanne? You or Willow?"

Suzanne lowered her gaze to Willow and up to him twice.

There'd be no real pleasure in killing a woman without a thread of a soul. He liked to watch them until their hearts stilled. Suzanne Scott had no heart beating within her.

CHAPTER TWENTY-THREE

The wooden edge of the cabin's old bed cut into Willow's leg as she lay sideways, and the pain in her head beat time with her heart. *Thu-dump, Thu-dump*. Blood slipped down the side of her head.

Hominski held her face in his hands, his grip tight, demanding she look at her mother. Willow remained motionless, unwilling to give him the satisfaction of knowing every bone in her body screamed out for her to run. Bound in the chair, Suzanne stared wide-eyed. Her childlike whimpers split Willow's frayed nerves like a sharp pair of scissors running down birthday wrappings.

The frightened woman was the reason Willow had experienced the birthdays of her past. That same person who'd never looked her in the eyes until today would most likely be the reason she never experienced another birthday.

She hated Suzanne Scott.

Not rendering evil for evil...

Hominski forced Willow to look at him. He turned his gaze upon Suzanne, staring at her for a long moment. Then, he screwed up his face and spit on her. "Compared to your daughter's beauty, you're a worn old hag."

Did Hominski think he was a beauty, the fat ugly beast?

Or railing for railing ...

Why in the world would these words bounce into her bruised, bleeding, and hurting brain?

But contrariwise blessing ...

And what blessing could she bestow on this madman who expected to take everything from her? This verse Laurel had helped her to memorize this morning—those words were to help her forgive.

Forgive Agatha.

Forgive Suzanne.

Willow shook her head free from Hominski to see her mother's face. The pain thundering across her skull made her wince—hard.

Hominski brushed her hair from her face, and Willow could see Suzanne more clearly.

Knowing that ye are thereunto called, that ye should inherit a blessing.

Laid bare of the trappings of Hollywood and the mystique of a powerful presence, Suzanne was nothing more than ... nothing more than her mother.

For he that will love life, and see good days, let him refrain his tongue from evil, and his lips that they speak no guile. Let him eschew evil, and do good; let him seek peace, and ensue it. For the eyes of the Lord are over the righteous, and his ears are open unto their prayers: but the face of the Lord is against them that do evil.

Willow closed her eyes against the sight of her enemies.

Dear God, is it true? I want to put away the evil of bitterness in my life. I forgive my mother. I forgive this man. I want your peace whether it comes in life or in death. Lord, if Your ears are open, set Your face against this man, and save my mother. Save her, Lord, if for no other reason than she allowed me to live.

Willow opened her eyes and took a steady breath. "I don't understand something, Detective Hominski."

He touched her hair, her cheek, her chin, her neck—the touch not sensual. He wanted to frighten her. Instead, the bile rose in her stomach, and her head continued to throb.

"My name's not Hominski, Willow. I'm surprised it took someone as smart as you this long to figure that out."

"I called the police that night. You're not an officer. How did you do it?"

He stilled then his lips turned upward into a grotesque smile. His eyes flared with something above insanity—tortured madness. "Jim helped me trash the place. We were there when the cops arrived. Didn't take much to convince them we'd been in the general area, would take care of it. The cops were a little skeptical. After all, they should have known us, but they didn't. Still, they took a look at the mess I'd made, and a little mention of the paperwork I'd taken on just answering the call, had them hightailing it right out of there." The smile widened. "I loved watching you. Fear in another person is a powerful drug. I crave it. From you, I hungered for it more than any before you."

She turned away.

"You can't hide it, Willow. I smell fear. I'm good at seeing even the slightest tinge. I terrify you." He snatched her chin once again and this time held his mouth close to her ears. "The name is Dennis LeBlanc. Your mommy knows me well. Ten years ago, she hired me to start a nasty little rumor about her and a daughter she'd left behind in some small rural town in North Carolina. Back then, I was starving for the work, and I took it."

"So that was you?" She jerked away from him. "You sure did a good job. I hope my mother paid you well."

"She paid me well to ruin your life so she could get the attention she wanted from the tabloids. You see, Mommy and Daddy call us bottom feeders when they want their privacy, but we're the ones who keep them on top of the world, lording above us. Any kind of publicity is good publicity when a movie is being launched, huh, Suzanne?" With the flat of his hand, he pushed Willow's head in the direction of her mother. "Answer her!" With his other hand, he yanked Suzanne's hair close to her scalp. Suzanne gave her a tearful nod.

"So ..." Her head ached and vomit threatened to spew. Willow swallowed hard to push it down. If LeBlanc wasn't careful, she'd end up with it all over him. "You think what happened ten years before ruined my life? Is that how you see it?"

"Didn't it?" He stepped back from them, staring from one to the other. "Mommy pushed you out of your comfort zone and left you alone in the big bad city to fight your battles on your own."

"Mommy did me a favor." Get him off guard, out of his own comfort zone.

He shook his head. "Some favor, Willow. I watched you off and on. You wandered the streets like a little homeless vagabond, seeking love but afraid to reach out for it. That boss of yours, Peterman, he has a thing for you. And there you were with his perfect little offer to stay with him, and you turned him down."

"But don't you see. God had me right where he wanted me. Just like God has my mother right where he wants her now—and you—right where He wants you."

The man gave a hollow laugh. "Yeah, Willow. If you want to believe some big God is out there pulling strings, that's okay. But just so you know, I'm going to kill you. Is that what you're saying your God wants?"

Lord, I hope that's not it. But whatever I must endure, please save Suzanne.

"That's a sick way of looking at life. Don't you think?" he asked.

"Yeah, but I'm not the sick one here. You are. First of all, for hire, you get pleasure out of destroying others."

"I've killed others for the joy of it, just like I'm getting ready to take your life—at the end of all of this—when I'm good and ready."

Willow forced her gaze to stay steady and straight, peering into the darkness of his soul. "God has you right where you are for a reason. I wouldn't think it was to give you a blessing, not if what you say is true."

"It's very true." He pushed away from her. "I'm done toying with you. I've waited long enough for this pleasure, and I won't let you take it from me." He made his way around Suzanne, kicking her hard as he passed. In the kitchen, he pulled something from a drawer and turned back, walking slowly, his gaze steady upon her.

Willow gasped at the noose dangling from the short end of a rope, his meaning all too clear. He was going to torture her, take her breath slowly.

In a second, he was upon her, pushing the rope over her head. Against her struggles, he slipped it down around her throat.

"No!" Strength welled up in her, born of years of suffering alone through lies, and heartache, and bitterness. In one moment, the swell rose through her like the waves on the ocean rolling upward, upward, until she spewed it out in physical force.

LeBlanc fell backwards, wobbling like a cartoon character pulled off balance by a rug yanked from beneath him. His head hit the edge of the fireplace. A curse fell from his lips. Willow pushed herself upward. The wood that had pushed into her legs seemed to rip her skin even beneath the heavy jean fabric. Her legs tingled with inactivity, and she looked downward to assure she'd found the wood flooring beneath her.

She fought to get the rope from around her.

LeBlanc rammed into her full force, knocking her onto the bed and to the floor on the other side. "Who do you think you are?" he demanded.

His fingers laced into her hair, pulling at the stitches in her forehead. She clawed at him, her nails sinking into thick flesh.

Blood fell into her face. Hers or his she didn't know, but the rich iron smell of it brought with it heaves of nausea. Before he could grasp the end of the rope, she vomited on his shoe.

"Get up! Get up!" He found the rope, yanked it hard.

But she was up. Or was she on the floor? The world tilted off its axis.

She managed to get one hand up and between her skin and the rope. With her other, she grasped the musty smelling bedspread of orange and green. The colors blended together. Hoisting herself to her knees, she leaned against the bed. If she passed out, he'd have to wait to see her terror. Would he kill her anyway?

Her eyes pained in the glint of something through the side window. "God's will be done." Her throat hurt, and she fought against his tightening hold to get the words out.

He released his hold a bit. "What? Are you praying for God to save your life now? If you're right where God wants you to be then why are you trying to get away from me? Let me have my fun, Willow."

"God's will be done," she repeated.

He yanked the rope

"God's ... will ... be ... done."

Granny's spoken prayers throughout the years—each one ended asking no matter what she prayed that His will be done. Laurel reminded her today all prayers are to be in God's will. So whether she was to live or to die, *God's will be done. God's will be done.*

The rope tightened against her hand, and she fought to pull it away.

He pushed her up on the bed, rolled her over, and stood over her.

"God's will be done."

"It will be in my time." The grotesque smile returned.

Boom!

She shook from the force. Glass and something moist fell over her—LeBlanc's blood and—and things she didn't want to think about. Did she scream?

Boom!

She drew her legs up and held herself in the fetal position. "God's will be done. God's will be done."

Warm arms went around her. She breathed in the familiar scene of Quentin's sweat soaked body. "Hoot." The scream pealed from her. She reached for him, clinging to him.

"Get an ambulance," he bellowed. "Now!" Quentin slipped the noose and tugged the rope from around her.

"He's dead." Bear's muffled voice came to her from somewhere. "Nice, clean shots, Quentin. Good job. I think you need to hire this boy, Sheriff."

"For Willow, Bear."

Willow winced at his fearful, loud voice.

"She's injured. Call an ambulance now."

"Willow?" A worried voice reached into the safe hold of the man she loved.

She tried to pull herself away from Hoot. "No." He held her tighter. "I don't want you to see."

Willow managed to turn her head. Her father's plastered smile met her. "You're going to be okay." The assuredness failed to fall in line with his tone.

A stomping began, a chair being lifted and thrown down. Willow wished it would stop. She pressed her hand hard against her temple.

"Shut her up," Hoot commanded none too quietly.

Scott turned away from them. Willow watched across Hoot's protective arm as Scott untied her mother.

With her hands untied, Suzanne pulled out the rag stuffed into her mouth. "I can't believe you left me tied up there."

"You're fine," Scott said.

"You left me here while you—while you ..."

"While I did what, Suzanne? While I rushed to the side of your daughter who saved your life?"

"He'd have tired of the game if she hadn't have made such an issue of playing the heroine."

"Issue?" Hoot turned with Willow in his arms. "An issue? Who made this all happen? Who caused that man to do this?"

"Hoot, it doesn't matter." Willow pulled at his collar. She shivered. "I'm cold. Hold me."

"Willow?" he choked, shifting her up into his arms.

"God's will be done." She kissed the nape of his neck. "I'm leaving you."

"Get the ambulance!"

"They're on their way. Five minutes." From outside, Darrell Jacob's reported.

"Shock, Quentin. Lie her down. Wrap the blanket around her," Bear directed.

"No." She fought to hold him close. "Don't let go."

"I won't let you go," he promised. "Don't leave me alone. Not after all of this." Something moist fell onto her face.

Hoot's tears.

Willow tried to reach up to wipe them away, but her hand refused to move. "I'm sorry, Hoot. So sorry."

CHAPTER TWENTY-FOUR

The emergency room waiting area—again. The entire family waiting to see if God would show mercy upon him a second time and allow him to take Willow home—alive.

He hated the helplessness that came from being here. And Suzanne Scott had not stopped complaining since they'd arrived. She needed this, or she needed that. Why were they waiting? The hospital would call when they had news about Willow.

He looked beyond Suzanne to her husband who'd distanced himself from the fray. Scott was on the phone, probably trying to keep the press from finding out about his wife.

If Quentin were Scott Thomas, he'd feed the aging actress to the media the same way she'd cut up pieces of Willow's heart to feed to them when it suited her needs.

The edge of his sanity reached, Quentin spun on the harping woman. "Get out of here or so help me—"

"Don't finish that statement, Quentin," Sheriff Dixon entered.

Quentin stormed toward Willow's father. "Take her out of here before I throw her out."

"You won't have to do that." Sheriff Dixon held up a pair of handcuffs.

Suzanne's mouth opened and then closed. Her gaze latched onto the cuffs.

"Suzanne Scott, you are under arrest for conspiracy and engaging in a contract for hire to murder Willow Thomas."

"Scott," her whiny voice pealed. "Are you going to let them do this to me?"

Scott clicked off his call and pushed off the wall. He raised his hands. "It's out of my hands. No matter your intent, Suzanne, your carelessness nearly caused the death of our daughter."

"Get me a lawyer," she demanded.

"He's meeting you at the jail." Scott turned away as if he couldn't bear to see his wife get what she deserved.

"Ms. Scott, turn around and put your hands behind your back." The Miranda rights rolled off the sheriff's tongue.

Agatha slipped her hand into Robert's. Willow's youngest uncle clasped his fingers around his wife's oversized hand. Did Agatha, at long last, realize the gift she'd been given in her long-suffering husband?

Darrell and Laurel shared a look with one another as Sheriff Dixon led Suzanne past them. From outside, shouts and the click of a multitude of cameras sounded then died down as the hordes followed Suzanne off to jail.

He thought Suzanne's constant complaints would push him over the top, but the growing silence after her departure, brought the madness in Quentin to the surface. He kicked the leg of the small table beside him. "Why won't they tell us anything?"

"Come with me." A strong hand settled on Quentin's back.

He ducked from Bear's touch "I'm not leaving."

"Let's just walk down the hall." Bear again reached for him.

"No." He shrugged from the older man.

"I'm not asking. Let's go."

Quentin dared to shoot a look at Bear. The man wasn't kidding, and Quentin felt it in the press of the man's grip on his forearm. Still, he yanked away and placed an arm's length between them as they made their way down the corridor. "I'm sick to death of this place."

"I know you must be." Bear stopped. "But what of the others?"

"I don't care about them." Quentin walked beyond him and then back.

"They're all here for both of you. Can't you see that?"

"I said I don't care." Quentin choked out the sob.

"Let me tell you a story about another man who didn't care. Let me tell you what he lost."

"Why should I care about Scott Thomas?" He didn't want to hear Bear spell out an excuse for Willow's father. The man was just as guilty as his wife.

"Do you care about Ted Thomas? After the last few days, boy, I hope you'd grown to like me."

Quentin stayed silent, waiting. He'd grown to love the man and his quiet strength and loyalty to Willow. And to him.

"When I left here, I wandered for a brief bit before going into seminary. I thought I was called to be a preacher. Then one day I stood in the back of a church at a mission's conference, and I saw the twenty-one year old daughter of a Thailand national. That young girl's father had almost sold her into slavery."

"I don't know what this has to do with Willow—or me."

"Maybe nothing. Maybe everything. Listen."

Quentin shrugged, aware that the scared little boy he'd tried to keep hidden was rising to the surface.

"That girl's father was plucked from the bondage of sin in time to keep him from sending his daughter into a lifestyle of childhood prostitution and slavery. He didn't know when he did it, and I didn't know when I fell in love with her, but on that day some years before, he'd saved that girl's life to save mine.

"I'd have never made it as a local pastor here or anywhere else. The call I'd felt, that was just God getting my attention for another of His purposes. I didn't speak to the girl that night, and I never expected to see her again. If I had, I'd have always wondered if God had called me to the field or if my heart had pulled me into it.

"And one day, two years after I began working in Thailand as a single pastor, I was called by my mission board and asked if I could help an ailing minister while he recovered from a broken pelvis. I already had a national pastor in place, so I was ready to take on a new project. With the Lord's guidance, I went off to this remote village where this pastor lived and worked."

Quentin longed for the waiting room and word on Willow. His gaze moved in that direction.

"I'm over here," Bear's terse voice cut into Quentin's inattentiveness.

"The village I visited, my beauty lived there. The pastor was her father. I worked alongside him for two more years before he agreed to let me court his daughter. Then, with much trepidation, he allowed me to marry her. Can you imagine, this man who'd once been willing to sell her for money, protecting her with such fierce determination?"

"Where is she, Bear?" Quentin wanted the story to end.

"That's what I'm trying to tell you. Where we were, there was no hospital. When my wife became sick, her heart weakening day by day, I had to carry her out of the remote village and to a hospital." He pushed Quentin against a wall. "You're half listening to me, boy, and I'm getting angry with you."

"Can't you see? All I want is to know Willow is okay."

"And I'm trying to tell you Willow could have died. She was hurt pretty badly before this incident. She lost a lot of blood. She already had a head injury. What if my niece has brain damage? What will you do?"

"I'll tend to her. I'll spoon feed her if I have to."

"And I did. My wife grew weaker as I watched her waste away day by day knowing in America there was hope. But her father, he loved her, and he couldn't see that allowing me to leave with her—with her and our two-year-old daughter—was for the best."

"Why didn't you take her, come here, let the doctor's care for her, and take her back to her father?"

"Because she didn't want to dishonor her father, so she wasted away day by day. When she died, I was left with her grieving father and a small child to tend. She trusted me with the lives she loved, and I got so wrapped up in my mourning, I lost track of them. Her father died of a broken heart. My child died of pneumonia."

Quentin straightened, giving the man his full attention. "Bear, I'm sorry."

"I don't want your condolences. They're empty words. Show me what you're made of. Willow's family and your friend, Darrell, they're hurting now. Whether Willow lives or dies, they still want to be a part of what you're going through, and you're pushing them away."

Quentin lowered his head. "When you put it like that—"

"Just shut up, and do what I'm telling you." Bear pointed.

Quentin started away.

"Hey," Bear said.

Quentin turned.

"Start with me." The gruff older man threw his arms open.

Quentin walked into them like a son to a father. "Thank you."

"Now go do me proud."

Quentin sprinted down the hallway, coming up short when he entered the waiting room. All eyes turned expectantly in his direction.

"Scott?"

The man gave Quentin his attention. "I'm sorry this has happened. I apologize for taking it out on you and on Suzanne."

"Are you kidding?" Agatha cackled. "She deserved everything she got."

"Uh-uh," Robert warned.

Scott nodded and looked to the floor.

"I'm asking you to allow me to marry your daughter. Would you grant me the honor of being your son-in-law, of calling you Dad?"

Scott closed his eyes and looked off to the side before opening them. "Why don't we wait and see her through this?"

"That's why I'm asking you now. I want you to know I love her enough to care for her—always."

"Why?"

"Isn't that what you've always done for Suzanne?"

"That's a different painting of a different landscape."

"Emotionally challenged, mentally challenged, or physically challenged, I don't care. Give me your blessing."

Scott straightened and looked beyond him. A smile brightened his face. "You got it." He nodded toward the opening doors.

Quentin turned. Willow sat in a wheelchair. Bear pushed her forward.

"Oh, thank you, God. Thank you." Quentin lifted his eyes to heaven.

"Do they ever keep you in the hospital when you come in through the emergency room? I'm worse off than Aunt Aggie, and they're sending me home." Willow touched her head.

"They only kept Agatha because I begged them to do it." Robert laughed.

Quentin fell down in front of her. "What did they say? Why didn't they come out and let us know."

"Bear was with me most of the time. He said you were resting, said Daddy was taking care of some things."

"You ..." Quentin stood. "... old goat." He pressed his face as close to Bear's as he dared.

"I may be an old goat, but I'm a crafty one." Bear reared back in laughter.

"What was all that in the hallway?"

"The truth."

"But if you knew, why'd you place the thought of never seeing her again in my mind?"

"To see how much of a vested interest you had in my niece and our family."

"I'll say it again. You old goat."

"I want to go home," Willow moaned.

"I'll take you." Darrell pushed by Quentin.

"You will not." Quentin grasped the wheelchair handles. "Everyone, let's get Willow back to the lake."

"Laurel and I have supper in the crock pot," Agatha announced.

"Well that was done with a lot of faith," Robert teased.

"Faith in the fact Willow will never leave me in peace. Now I have two daughters to marry off instead of one." She ba-boomed past Quentin and elbowed Darrell. "You better get to that proposal real soon, Mr. Jacobs."

"Momma." Laurel covered her face with her hands.

Willow lifted her eyes to Quentin. "I may learn to love that woman after all."

"Make a promise to me, please."

"Whatever you want."

Quentin pushed her forward. "Don't let me see the inside of this hospital until you give birth to our first child, and if you'll have the baby at home, that would be even better."

"God's will be done, Quentin." She reached back and placed her hand over his.

CHAPTER TWENTY-FIVE

Home again, and Willow's head throbbed, but she didn't want to leave the makeshift party of good food, family, and friends. Outside the sun was setting behind the mountains. She pushed up from the table and sat back down with a thump.

"Do you want to go upstairs?" Quentin leaned over.

"No. I want to sit on the porch and enjoy the first of many more sunsets with my family. I used to take them both for granted."

"That's a good idea." Scott grabbed his coffee cup, leading the charge. "Men, carry your own chairs. The women can have the ones out there."

Forced jubilance, again for her benefit. Having voiced the desire, she and Quentin were the last ones outside. He pulled her toward the swing, but she pulled back. "We used to sit there." She pointed to the steps. "I wish I felt good enough to get a glass jar and run through the yard with you catching fireflies."

"Tomorrow night." He helped her to sit on the step and sat beside her. "Laurel and Darrell will join us."

Willow leaned toward him and whispered in his ear.

He nodded and ran back inside, coming out with what she'd requested he retrieve from her bedroom. "Don't do a thing until I get back." He pressed the treasure into her hand and ran past her to his house.

"Hmm," Bear said from his seat behind them. "Brown does deliver everywhere."

"What are you talking about?" Agatha craned to look from her seat near the front door.

"There's a U.P.S. truck making the hairpin turn."

In the twilight, Willow watched the orange sky setting behind the trees, again reminding her of that charcoal drawing she'd made long ago.

The truck pulled into her driveway, the driver blasting his horn. On his way back from his house, Quentin met him and signed for a package. He shook hands with the driver and came back to stand at the base of the steps. "I can't let you have this," he said to her.

"I don't understand."

"Not unless you tell me I'm worth more to you than a multi-million dollar contract."

"You know you are."

Quentin held out the delivered package and another small white envelope. She reached for the smaller one. "What's this?" She touched her bandaged head. The pain would intensify if she needed to process any new information.

"Granny gave this to me a few days before we graduated from high school—before she died. She asked me to hold on to it until today."

"Oh, goodness. What that woman didn't have up her sleeve," Agatha chided. "She told you to give it to Willow on this date?"

"No, Agatha." Quentin sat beside Willow. "I should have given it to her last night when I asked her to marry me, and she said yes, but she was in no shape for it."

"Well, pray tell," Agatha pressed.

"Granny and I were working in her garden one afternoon. She pulled this envelope out of her pocket." Quentin brushed Willow's hair from her face. "She said, 'Young 'un, if you ever get up the gumption to ask my pretty little granddaughter to marry you, and if she tells you yes, and I mean only if she tells you yes, you're to give her this here note from her Granny, and don't you ever open it otherwise.'"

Willow used her fingernail to slice the flap, her eyes never leaving Quentin's face.

"We're dying with anticipation here," Uncle Robert said.

Willow nodded and looked down at the paper. As she read it, tears pooled in her eyes.

"What?" Quentin begged for an answer. "What did she say?"

"Help me up, please?" She raised her hand to him. He lifted her to her feet. She held to Quentin's strength as she moved toward the porch swing where her cousin and the geek Laurel loved sat. She lifted her hand toward Darrell.

"What?" he reached out palm upward.

Willow placed her treasure into Darrell's hold and kept his hand clasped in hers. "Do you love my cousin with all your heart?"

Darrell's face reddened.

Laurel looked away. "Willow, don't do this."

"Darrell, Laurel loves you. She loved you enough to come to me and ask for my help. She didn't need me. I know the answer to my question. I've always known it. You've been in love with Laurel forever. Tell her. Granny left what I placed in your hand for her, but it isn't for me to give to her. It's for you."

"Willow." Laurel's eyes brimmed with tears.

Willow stood back, thankful Quentin was behind her. She needed him. Her physical and emotional strength were waning as her spiritual strength grew.

Darrell opened his hand. He held up the wedding band. "I can't believe this," he said.

Laurel lowered her head. "I'm sorry. This family, we push. You're not ready for this."

"No, that's not it at all." He stood and dug in to his pants pocket. He pulled out a ring. "I was waiting. Quentin said he'd asked Willow to marry him, and I wanted to wait for our special moment. I—I've had this dream of you for so long. When I bought this, I knew I was being irrational, but I figured why not be crazy for once in my life." He bowed to his knee in front of Laurel, lifting both rings. "Laurel, will you marry me? They're a perfect match. Like us."

Laurel wrapped her arms around him. "So long as you know, Darrell Jacobs, I love you, and if I say yes, you'll never get out of it."

"I considered all the variables." He laughed. "And I decided this family needs me, especially if Quentin's coming aboard."

The family erupted in merriment. With Quentin bracing her, Willow could feel the laughter in his chest.

A hand touched Willow's, and she laced it in hers before looking down. Aunt Agatha smiled at her. "Thank you."

Willow smiled. "There's something else." She took a deep breath. "Quentin and I would like to be the first ones to give you a wedding present." She looked at the note in her hand. "You need a place to call home."

"I don't understand." Laurel stood.

Willow touched the softness of her cousin's blonde hair. They were so different but so loved. "Granny wanted you to have her home." She managed to get the words between her lips then let out a rush of breath. "This place, it belongs to you, Laurel. Granny only wanted me to know I always had a home to come back to. This place was a physical home. Quentin was my heart's home, and now that my heart has returned, I belong next door where I'll be with the man I love, while you'll be here, living with your husband. Our children will play together. They'll wear a path between the houses the way we did with Quentin."

"No." Laurel shook her head. "I can't take this from you."

"You're not taking anything away from me." Willow's heart filled. "When you brought that picture of Granny back to me, and I was able to gift it to you, I learned how good it is to give. So, I'm asking you to give something to me."

"What?" Laurel shook her head.

"Your friendship and your love. That's all I want. We had it once as little girls, even with all the bickering we did. I want my best friend to live beside me on the lake we both loved in the shadow of a grandmother who adored us."

"You are my friend, and I love you very much." Laurel hugged Willow then turned her gaze to Darrell. "I have to ask my man."

Darrell nodded. "Like Willow said. Your heart is my home."

Quentin slipped the note from Willow's hand. He read it and closed it, slipping it back into the envelope without a word.

"You aren't going to tell us what it says?" Agatha asked.

"No, ma'am," Quentin answered for her. "Too personal. For both of us."

Willow smiled, and Quentin slipped the other package into her hands. "Since you've given away your physical home, I think I'm safe in handing this to you now."

Willow open the padded envelope, and pulled the paperwork out. "Oh, no." She brought her hand up, hit it hard on her sore head, and winced at the pain it brought.

"What?" The collective question echoed in the mountain air.

"Hoot?"

"Yes, dear?"

"How much do you think your image is worth?" She held the papers against her chest with a heavy hand.

"My image? Do you mean my reputation?"

"No." She flipped the papers over for him to see. "Your image."

"Anglers' Lures. What's my picture doing on their advertising?"

"Nothing—if they're not willing to pay for it."

"Let us see," Laurel asked.

Quentin took the drawing from her and held it up. Now their collective laughs sent a gaggle of geese squawking in protest, taking flight over the lake.

"Care to explain?" Quentin lifted a brow.

"The night LeBlanc ransacked my apartment I'd known he'd been following me. He'd e-mailed me several times already. I was afraid to go home, and when I need to think, I always try to duplicate the picture I lost so long ago. I must have left a likeness on my desk." She offered a sheepish smile. "I can see why Jeffrey thought your portrait was for a client named Anglers' Lures."

"Let Peterman have it as a consolation prize." Quentin backed away, pulling her with him. "Excuse us." He nodded to the family as he led her with care down the porch steps.

"Where are you going?" Scott demanded.

"Let them go," Laurel said. "Quentin has a surprise for Willow."

Willow's heart pounded as Quentin slipped his arm around her waist and led her next door.

"You never lost that portrait." He kissed her cheek, opened his door, and led her inside. "It's been waiting for you to claim it."

"What do you mean?"

He pointed above his mantel. "It's been hanging here since I purchased the place from my parents, had it framed, and placed it there. You can have it back, but it comes with me."

Willow moved forward, propelled by the pure joy of seeing the vision so firmly planted in her heart. "I love you, Quentin McPheron. How could I have been so stupid to never realize I was always where God wanted me?"

"Maybe this love we have now needed to be strengthened by what we've gone through." He slipped his arms around her holding her against him. "Now, tell me why, exactly, you up and gave your grandmother's house away when that's not what the note said at all?"

"You didn't hear a word I said, did you?" She turned in his arms.

"I heard every word. My heart is your home."

"And Granny's note said if I was reading the note, you'd done what she'd always prayed you'd do. You asked me to marry you, and I'd done what she'd always prayed I'd do. I'd accepted."

"And?" He stared down at her.

"She said I needed to give Laurel what was most precious to me. And in her journal, she hinted at what that treasure was."

"I think she meant something else, like say, your stony heart on a platter."

She smirked. "That old hard-hearted thing? I threw it away when I asked God to renew His acquaintance with me."

"Glad to hear it." He kissed her bandaged head.

"And, well, I couldn't do it."

"Do what?" He pulled back, studying her face.

"I couldn't give Laurel what was most precious to me. She wouldn't want that old thing anyway. So I gave her the next most precious thing: Granny's home."

"I'm afraid to ask what she didn't get." He laughed.

"Don't you know?" She touched his face, tears in her eyes. "Oh, Hoot, don't you realize?"

His face lost its smile. "What?"

"You," she whispered. "You are my most precious possession." She turned to gaze upon the portrait. "Even back then when I stepped off the path and headed away from God and from you, my heart still clung to both of you, waiting for forever."

He held her close, and the blanket of safety she'd felt from time to time since her return to Amazing Grace, settled over her.

He kissed her bandaged forehead. "I'm so glad we can finally continue walking that path together."

About the Author

Fay Lamb offers services as a freelance editor, and is an author of Christian romance and romantic suspense. Her emotionally charged stories remind the reader that God is always in the details.

Fay has served as secretary for American Christian Fiction Writer's operating board and as a moderator for ACFW's critique group, Scribes. For her volunteer efforts for ACFW, she received the Service Members Award in 2010.

Fay and her husband, Marc, reside in Titusville, Florida, where multi-generations of their families have lived. The legacy continues with their two married sons and five grandchildren.

Visit Fay on the Web:
www.FayLamb.com

**Watch for more books by Fay Lamb
releasing later this year!**

Look for other books

published by

www.WriteIntegrity.com

and

Pix-N-Pens Publishing

www.PixNPens.com